Fast Forward

Juliet Madison

To Nan, I hope to grow old as gracefully as you did.

Chapter 1
Birthday Girl

"Old age comes on suddenly, and not gradually as is thought." –
Emily Dickinson

I CAN'T HELP that I'm beautiful. There – I've said it.

I'm not saying I'm God's Gift or anything, I'm just being honest. I won big in the genetic lottery, so of course I'd try to make a career out of it. Why should I apologise to my sister for my success? Just because I scored a modelling contract with the city's most prestigious agency, an apartment overlooking the park and the most gorgeous boyfriend in the world, does not make me a –

"... selfish, conceited cow!" as she put it, storming out of The Lava Bar during my pre-birthday speech about how good my life was turning out. I didn't even get to finish!

Growing up as a teenager, all Kasey wanted was to fit in with my friends and be one of the gang, despite being two years younger and having more in common with the seven-year-old bug-collecting boy from next door. You wouldn't know by looking at us that we're sisters. I was tall, slim, with glossy black hair and a well-proportioned face, whereas she was vertically challenged, had an unruly mop on her head from an unfortunate perm and was... how could I say it? A little... pudgy... to put it nicely. I loved my sister of course, but sometimes her jealous outbursts drove me mad!

As Kasey stomped heavily out the door, I went to dash after her but a hand grasped my forearm.

"Forget it, Kelli, there's no use going after her, it'll only end in a huge fight as always," said Selena, a fellow model with The Goldberg Agency, face of Mystique Cosmetics and my best friend for the past three years.

"She's right. Just leave her be." My boyfriend and highly sought-after photographer, Grant Mills, tucked an escaped strand of hair back behind my ear.

I sat on a chair and fiddled with the straw in my empty glass. "Okay, I'll talk to her when she's calmed down. Although, I wouldn't be surprised if she boycotts my birthday party tomorrow night."

"Are you kidding?" A wide-eyed Selena plonked her almost empty margarita down on the table and a drop of liquid splashed on my hand. "I doubt she'd miss a chance to rub shoulders with Max Sheldon. She'll be there, you wait and see."

She was probably right. Kasey had been at me for weeks about Max, asking if he had a girlfriend and whether he liked going snorkelling or bird-watching in his spare time. I could be wrong, but something told me the Max I knew – the most popular underwear model in the country, who held no modesty about his blessed DNA – was more likely to be found working on his tan than going snorkelling, and watching different kinds of birds behind his two-thousand-dollar sunglasses.

Grant's warm hand squeezed my shoulder. "Anyway, don't let your sister ruin your birthday celebrations, how about another round of drinks? Champagne all round, I say." Without waiting for our agreement, he walked up to the bar.

Selena leaned forward over the table and curled her finger in a 'come here' gesture. "I'm so glad I can finally speak to you alone," she said.

"What is it?"

I leaned closer and she whispered in my ear. "I saw Grant go into DSJ yesterday."

"DSJ, seriously?" They're only the most expensive jewellers in the city, specialists in diamond rings.

"Uh-huh." Selena nodded with a twinkle in her eye. "I couldn't see what he was doing, but he did come out of the store with a small gold bag."

My hand flew to my mouth and then rested on my friend's arm. "Do you think it means..."

"That he's going to propose – yes!" Selena bounced in her chair. "I bet he does it at your party!"

"Oh wow! I can't believe it. I mean, of course I'll say *yes* and..."

Selena leaned back in her chair as Grant returned, carrying a tray of champagne flutes with their bubbling gold liquid and I forced myself to act naturally, smiling as he handed me a drink. "Thanks, honey."

"So, have you decided whether to go to your school reunion on Saturday?" Selena asked.

"No, didn't I tell you? Grant's taking me for a weekend away as a birthday present. Besides, I'd rather leave those old school days behind." Grant draped his arm around me and I nestled myself into his side, revelling in the warm leathery scent and hint of citrus in his aftershave, Fahrenheit by Dior, which I bought him last Christmas.

"A weekend away is more enticing than a school reunion." Selena winked. "Especially as it'll be a good way to celebrate the…" she paused as my eyes warned her not to let the cat out of the bag. Her mouth was known to be as big as her paycheck. "…milestone of your twenty-fifth birthday!" She nodded briefly and downed a gulp of champagne.

After the third round of drinks and another hour of chatting and dancing, we called it a night. It wasn't worth having a shocking hangover the day of the real party.

"Don't forget this, babe." Grant handed over my silk scarf that I'd taken off to fling around during an episode of enthusiastic dancing.

"Thanks, honey." I hooked the scarf around his neck and pulled him in close, planting a hungry kiss on his lips.

We walked out of the bar and into the balmy night air, stained with the stench of inner city pollution. Car exhausts spat out their fumes and passers-by puffed cigarette smoke from their lungs. The eyes of a homeless woman pleaded with mine as we walked past her on the sidewalk, her petite frame encumbered by a worn-out men's jacket from the seventies, her nipples visible through a thin fraying singlet. I diverted my eyes from her uncomfortable gaze but then glanced back. I took a few loose coins from my purse and walked over, placing them in her hands. As though unable to speak, she nodded her thanks and squeezed my hand.

"Why'd you do that?" Grant asked when I returned to his side. "She's likely to just spend it on booze or drugs."

I shrugged. "Maybe she's hungry and she could sure do with a change of clothes." And her eyes reminded me of my mother's. I recognised that desperate stare too well.

"Here." Grant withdrew something from his wallet. "You don't know where her hands have been."

He held out a sanitisation wipe and I flicked my hand. "Oh, I don't think it's necessary. There are probably worse germs in the bar we've just been to." But at my boyfriend's insistence I took the wipe and slid it over my hands before tossing it in a nearby bin. It was nice that he wanted to protect me, despite an invisible and possibly non-existent threat.

"Quick, there's a taxi letting people out over the road, let's catch it," Grant urged, tugging on my hand and stepping out onto the road.

An engine revved and the screech of car tires stung my ears as a black Holden spun around the corner. "Grant, watch out!" I yanked his arm, just as the car sped past. He toppled backwards onto me and I lay panting on the sidewalk, my hands clutching his body.

"Whoa, that was close." Grant remained still, his expression stunned.

"Oh my God! That idiot driver! He could have killed you!" I clung tighter to Grant as we stood back up, moving as one body.

"But he didn't. I'm okay, don't worry," Grant said, and he resumed walking while I remained stuck to the spot. "Kel, you coming?"

Visions of Grant sprawled on the road, thick dark blood oozing from his broken body flashed in my mind. I shook my head at the disturbing visual and at the thought of my dream man suddenly vanishing from my life.

"Are you all right, babe?"

"It's just... you could have died," I replied. "And I just wondered... what would I do without you?"

"Well, unless the universe has something against me, you won't ever have to find out." He smiled as he slid an arm around my waist and we walked over to a taxi pulled up on our side of the road.

My eyes strained to open and my body struggled to move the next morning, but the need to use the bathroom won out. Eyes half-closed, I stumbled out of bed and headed for the en suite. It seemed further away than usual, but eventually I got there. My body ached with an unfamiliar heaviness, but I'd only had three drinks. It didn't make sense. Maybe at twenty-five the human body suddenly becomes less capable of holding its liquor or something.

A shower. That's what I needed to wake me up. I lifted off my nightgown and went to turn on the shower, but it wasn't where it should be. It was in a different corner. Weird. Inching my eyes open a little further I noticed that everything was different.

This wasn't my bathroom!

Had I slept at someone else's house last night? No, I distinctly remembered crawling into my bed at eleven forty-five, after washing my face and applying Age-Proof Smoothing Serum. So where the hell was I?

My eyes darted around the strange bathroom and the even stranger contraption on the wall of the shower. There was also a device against the far wall that resembled a giant hand-dryer, large enough to fit a person. I looked in the mirror and saw the scariest thing I'd ever seen in my entire life staring back at me. Wrinkles... a ton of them.

Crow's feet, laughter lines, forehead furrows and... Oh. My. God. Were there wrinkles on... my lips? I squinted and leaned closer to the mirror. If that wasn't bad enough, I even had a few rogue hairs on my chin and a neck that looked like a turkey's. Plus, no longer did my hair resemble a silky black cascading waterfall, but instead a burnt-out forest with pathetic little branches of smoky-grey hairs poking out from my scalp. This had to be a nightmare! Yes, that must be it. I'd had one drink too many last night and now I was paying the price.

But it feels so real! Maybe someone spiked my drink. I didn't know how, but it was possible. I bet it was that creepy dude hiding behind his phone at the table nearby. Probably filmed me too, the jerk. I bet I'm being viewed on YouTube as we speak. And maybe it's going viral and I'd be in tomorrow's newspaper:

Exposed! Aspiring Supermodel Kelli Crawford Is An Alcoholic!

My hands cautiously touched the face that *was* me but *wasn't*. I took a step back and then another, edging away from the nightmarish vision in the mirror. Until the cold edge of the bathtub collided with my legs. I fell backwards, knocking over some bottles. A glass vase fell to the floor with a high-pitched, splintering smash. Glass shards launched themselves up into the air like rockets, puncturing the skin on my left arm and dark red blobs of blood bulged out. "Ouch!" I winced, grasping my arm.

And then I saw something even scarier. In terror, I struggled to lift myself from the bath, flailing around naked like a fish out of water, falling back in twice – until I finally stood again at the mirror, my mouth gaping. I lowered my hands to my abdomen, lifting and prodding clumps of loose skin that felt like a bag of jelly.

What in the name of Dior happened to my flat stomach? Not only did I have a freaking jelly belly, my breasts drooped so far south they were practically residents of Antarctica!

There is no God.

Nope, this wasn't a nightmare and I'm positive no one could have spiked my drink. This was real. I could feel it. Not to mention see it. Here I was; still me, but... old. And if the hideous vision before me was anything to go by, there was no way in hell I was turning around to look at my arse.

"What was that noise, did something break?" A man barged into the bathroom.

"Arghh!!" I instinctively covered myself as much as possible with my hands, cowering in the corner near the toilet, my eyes searching frantically for a towel. Why were there no towels in this bathroom? My nightgown, oh thank God! I picked it up and held it in front of me. "Get out of here!" I shooed him backwards like an annoying insect, but he kept coming towards me.

"What's the matter, honey?" He glanced at the vase remnants on the floor and then at my arm, blood dripping from the wound. "Are you all right?" The brown-haired man eyed me with genuine concern. His skin oozed the spicy scent of an aftershave I didn't recognise.

"I'm fine, go away!" He appeared perplexed at the continued shooing movements I made with my hands.

"Okay, okay. I just wanted to make sure you were all right. And wish my wife a happy birthday, of course." He leaned in for a kiss but I pushed him off, horror overtaking me.

Wife? I wasn't his wife and this old guy certainly wasn't my husband! Grant was supposed to be my husband. Well, after tonight's inevitable proposal. Oh God, tonight! My birthday party. I couldn't go looking like this!

A high-pitched jingling sound interrupted my thoughts and the man made a strange movement; pinching his watch with his thumb and forefinger and appearing to pull some invisible strand to his ear.

What was he doing?

"William speaking," he said, as he walked out. Finally.

William? Who the heck was he and why was he saying I was his wife? This was all too weird. Dizzy, I held on to the wall as I racked my brain for an answer, a solution, anything to make sense of this... situation. William... his eyes looked kind of familiar and the way he walked out of the room, that bouncy stride. I'd seen him before... somewhere.

I know! I clicked my fingers. William McSnelly from my school days. Could it really be chubby-no-friends William McSnelly who never seemed to notice the multiple *Kick Me* Post-its stuck to his back? Wow, he'd actually turned out all right. Okay so he's ancient, but for an old guy he's not bad.

Wait... if I was married to William McSnelly, then that would make me... Oh God, no!

Kelli McSnelly. *Shoot me now.* I didn't end up with McDreamy or McSexy, uh-uh. I ended up with McSnelly, or *McSmelly* as the kids at school used to call him. Me included... and now I was Mrs McSmelly.

Like a wilting plant my body softened, my hand slid down the wall and the nightgown escaped my grip. Instead of landing on the floor, my butt landed sharply on the cold toilet seat, the shock of it interrupting my Oscar-worthy fainting episode and causing me to stand up suddenly. I could hear William talking outside the door and when he said goodbye to whoever he was speaking to, I quickly picked my nightgown up off the floor and fed my head and arms through it.

"Kel, what's going on?" William re-entered the bathroom that was beginning to feel like a prison. A cruel, although seemingly sanitary prison with no towels and weird mirrors that made me look old.

All I could do was shake my head in disbelief, my body soon following suit. My hands trembled and my breath came in short gasps. "Where am I? Why do I look so old?" William touched his hand to my shoulder and I flinched, although his touch seemed strangely comforting. "I don't understand. Yesterday I was young and happy and now I'm an old shuddering mess!"

"C'mon, honey, you look great for your age. And you're only

fifty, don't be so hard on yourself," William said, rubbing my shoulder.

"Fifty?" I blurted, almost choking as the word launched from the slingshot of my voice box. "I'm not fifty! I'm supposed to be twenty-five!" I shook his hand away from my shoulder and he dropped it to his side. "Why aren't I twenty-five?"

"Honey, it's natural to feel emotional on a day like today. I mean who wouldn't love to be twenty-five again?" William smiled. "But you're still beautiful and today's going to be great, especially tonight's party. Come seven o'clock our house will fill with all the important people in your life. You must be looking forward to that?" He lifted my chin with his finger and I reluctantly met his gaze.

Looking forward? I wanted to go backward! Back to my real life and my real self, where I was only twenty-five and my stomach didn't resemble my father's beer belly. Soon they'd be calling me Kelli Jelly Belly McSmelly. Oh, how on earth did this happen? What the hell was going on? *I can't take this anymore!*

"Where's Grant? I need Grant!" I said, shoving his hand away.

"Grant? Who's... oh, surely you don't mean Grant, your ex?"

"Yes. No! I mean, he's not my ex!"

"Honey, you haven't had anything to do with him since we started dating twenty-five years ago." William's expression changed to a frown. "Or, have you?"

"Twenty-five years ago? But Grant and I... we... he was supposed to propose to me on my birthday."

"Kelli, you broke off your relationship with him, remember?"

"I did?" It's quite possible I'd gone mad.

William nodded. "But I proposed and you said yes. And

here we are, still happily married after almost a quarter of a century."

Okay, Kelli, just breathe. In... and... out. There had to be some explanation for all of this. *Think!* Maybe I'd had a bump to the head and have amnesia. That could be it. I'd simply lost all memories from the last twenty-five years. Yes, I could have fallen in the bathroom and sustained a head injury. I did remember falling, although that was after I noticed I'd become old. Maybe it happened yesterday, as in my forty-nine-year-old yesterday and now I'd lost my memory. But my head didn't hurt or anything.

I walked over to the dreaded mirror again, but failed to see any suspicious bruise or lump. It must have happened before. Maybe I woke up as my normal twenty-five-year-old self on my birthday and had some sort of accident then. And maybe William was the paramedic or doctor who treated me, and I fell in love with him because he looked after me. But Grant would have looked after me, wouldn't he? Time I pulled myself together and asked some questions.

"Um, William?"

"Yes?"

"Have I ever had any sort of accident, perhaps a head injury of some kind?" I asked feebly.

"No," he replied, confusion and concern meshed together on his face. "Why, do you feel sick or something? Are you having a bad headache, is that it?"

"No, my head's fine, I just..." Geez, I felt like Drew Barrymore's character in *Fifty First Dates* and William was Adam Sandler, humouring me in my unfortunate condition so I didn't lose the plot. Hmm, a bit too late for that... but anyway. "I just feel like time has caught up with me, that's all. Life seems to have gone by so fast." If I played along and kept it together, maybe this terrible morning would somehow go away and I'd be transported back to my normal life.

I needed a shower. I'd close my eyes and focus on the water and my fifty-year-old self would wash away and when I opened my eyes I'd be twenty-five again. Worth a shot.

Except the shower had no faucets and I didn't have any idea how to turn the bloody thing on. "I think I'll feel better after a shower. William, er... honey, can you take a look at the shower thingy? I think it needs fixing."

This seemed to please William, as he rolled up his sleeves and walked over to the contraption on the wall. "Let's have a look." He pressed a few buttons and waved his hand under the diamond-shaped showerhead, and the second time he did so, water streamed from the tiny holes. "Works fine," he said.

"Could you try turning it off for me too, just to test it?"

He pressed a button on the top side of the contraption and the water flow came to an abrupt halt. "That works fine too." He smiled and turned towards the door. "See you in the kitchen for breakfast."

"Wait!" I lunged at him. "Could you turn it on again, you know, to save you having to come back in, just in case it plays up again?"

"Anything for the birthday girl." William repeated his earlier process and this time I watched him like a hawk. He pressed one button on each of the three rows and a red button in the middle, then waved his hand twice under the showerhead.

Got it. I think. Well, hopefully I'd be out of here soon and wouldn't have to use this thing again.

When William closed the bathroom door behind him, I took my rather confused nightgown off again and stepped under the stream of water. The pressure and warmth soothed my skin and for a while I felt like my old self. I mean my young self. I imagined being in my own shower in my own apartment, looking forward to my twenty-fifth birthday party at the hippest restaurant in the city, followed by a beautiful speech from Grant and culminating in his proposal by which I'd look completely surprised, and accept the DSJ engagement ring with a resounding *yes!*

Pleased with my visualisation attempt, I opened my eyes and prepared to say a silent thank you to the universe upon seeing my familiar bathroom and youthful face in the mirror. Instead, I said a few not-so-silent profanities upon seeing the same unfamiliar bathroom that was fast becoming my least favourite place in the world.

I thumped my fist on the button on top of the shower contraption, stopping the water flow, and stepped out of the shower. Clamping my lips tightly together to stop from screaming, I crept towards the mirror, knowing all too well what would greet me.

The same crow's feet I'd seen before that framed my eyes like a broken fence around a dilapidated old house. Damn!

The same laughter lines formed an arc around my mouth, looking more like remnants of inconsolable sobbing. Bugger!

Lip wrinkles, a saggy neck and forehead furrows that have turned my face into a landscape rivalling The Andes mountain ranges. Crap!

And of course, the *piece de resistance*; Kelli's jelly belly. Yep, despite my impressive visualisation, I'm still fifty!

Damn. Bugger. Crap. Multiplied by ten.

Desperate to dry off and cover my hideous body, I automatically reached for a non-existent towel. Having run out of expletives, I simply said, "Brilliant. Just brilliant."

Standing with my hands on my hips, I examined the giant hand-dryer thingamajig and tilted my head to the side, furrowing my already furrowed brows. It must be used in place of towels, there's no other possible explanation. I prodded and poked the machine tentatively but nothing happened, so I inched myself between the two parts of the machine, hoping it wasn't some kind of vice that would squish my body into oblivion. Although, on second thoughts...

"How do I turn it on?" I asked myself out aloud and at that moment, jets of warm air pushed against my front and back. Reflexively I shut my eyes and mouth. After a few seconds it stopped, my body completely dry. Maybe this bathroom wasn't so bad after all.

Anxious to finally get some clothes on, I opened the door a fraction, checking to see if the coast was clear. I tiptoed into the unfamiliar bedroom and pulled back a sliding door. The good news was an array of clothing hung from a rack, so I'd be able to put a long overdue end to my nakedness. The bad news was I wouldn't be caught dead in most of the outfits. Who would wear such things? Well, me obviously. But surely my fifty-year-old taste couldn't be that bad? I was a fashion model for Christ's sake! I knew what's hot and what's not, and this stuff wasn't even lukewarm.

So I had three choices:

1. Remain naked.
2. Put my nightgown back on.
3. Suck it up and wear one of the outfits.

As my stomach grumbled for food and my nose detected a faint smell of something good cooking, I stepped into a coral-coloured starched skirt in which the hem ended halfway down my calves before turning upwards into a revolting curved abomination and looking like a baby catch-all bib. The matching top was just as bad, its hem curving upwards too, but if the need arose at least I'd have a place to store snacks. Or Valium.

Now desperately hungry and looking like a middle-aged Oompa-Loompa, I followed the smell out of the bedroom, down a hallway and into a kitchen, where William sat at the bench sipping from a mug. If he was there, then who was cooking?

I looked towards the source of the delicious aroma and nearly threw up into my curved hems. A young man stood there in a pink apron. He was tall, with various pieces of metal jewellery adorning his pierced skin and his hair was jet black despite one hot pink streak falling loose from his mullet/Mohawk/ponytail thingy.

"Happy birthday, Mum!" he said, and for the second time that day I wilted to the floor.

Chapter 2
Breakfast at McSnelly's

"Inside every older person is a younger person wondering what happened." – Jennifer Yane

"Mum! Are you all right?"

Warm hands patted my cheeks as I opened my eyes to the concerned faces of two men hovering above me, one apparently my husband, the other apparently my...

No way! I had a son?

"No, I'm not all right! Yesterday I was young, unmarried and... firm, and now I'm old, married and... saggy," I said with a quivering lip, as the men each hooked an arm under my armpits and lifted me up, leading me towards a chair at the dining table.

"Your mother's just having a few issues around turning fifty, Ryan," William said to his son in hushed tones, before looking at me with a hopeful smile. "But you'll be right, won't you, honey? Once you've had breakfast you'll feel better and then you can get started on the birthday of your dreams!"

Birthday of my dreams? Not in this body.

My stomach grumbled as I buried my face in my hands and the young man, Ryan – my son – placed a plate of food next to me on the table. A warm, buttery aroma wafted into my nostrils and I lifted my head from my hands. Ryan quickly shoved the plate in front of me.

"Eat up, Mum."

Two boiled eggs, shiny curls of smoked salmon, toast and grilled tomatoes. My stomach grumbled again at the sight and without thinking I slid a curl of salmon into my mouth. Yum. Maybe I was just experiencing a severe bout of low blood sugar. It wouldn't be the first time. Once, a swimwear photo shoot had taken three hours longer than planned, due to unforeseen weather changes and faulty equipment, and I'd collapsed on the beach not having eaten anything since the bowl of blueberries I'd had for breakfast. The last thing you wanted when you're modelling swimwear was a bloated stomach from a hearty breakfast.

But could my low blood sugar really be severe enough to cause a realistic hallucination like this? Unless I'd collapsed and was in a coma, having some sort of coma-dream. That might be what's going on. Soon I'd begin hearing the caring voices of hospital staff around me as I slowly woke up and Grant would be there holding my hand.

"Buuurrrrp!"

My fork dropped to the table with a clang as the loud, revolting sound escaped Ryan's mouth.

"Ryan!" William scolded.

"Sorry, those eggs do it to me every time," he said, sitting down opposite me and scooping the rest of the boiled egg into his mouth, swallowing it in one gulp.

"If you took smaller bites and chewed more thoroughly, they might not give you any problems," William suggested.

Ryan shrugged, tipping his head back and dropping a sliver

of smoked salmon down his throat, before releasing an encore performance of even greater intensity.

"Sorry, Mum. I really can't help it."

Strangely, it didn't bother me. I was preoccupied with my breakfast and couldn't believe how hungry I was. I picked up a slice of toast but then hesitated. Normally I'd never eat this much, maybe I should go easy on the carbs. Then again, this wasn't really my body and if it was just a dream then I'm sure calories didn't count in dreams, right? I tore off a corner with my teeth and chewed the crusty bread till it disappeared down my throat. I then tapped the side of the egg and peeled off the shell, before digging my spoon into the smooth white flesh. Hopefully the burping problem wasn't hereditary. I dug the spoon in a second time and then paused, my eyebrows drawing together.

"There's no yolk in my egg," I remarked.

"So?"

"So? Eggs have yolks. Why doesn't this one?"

"You always prefer to have the yolkless eggs, Mum," Ryan said.

Yolkless eggs? If I wasn't so confused and distraught at my predicament I'd jump for joy at the brilliance of it. "Oh, um, of course. I just thought with it being my birthday and all…"

"Oh, you wanted a treat. I should have thought, sorry," Ryan said.

I shuddered at the mention of the word… Mum. I wasn't a mum. I'd never been pregnant, or been through childbirth and yet here I was having breakfast in the McSnelly residence with the young man who was apparently my son.

I wolfed down the rest of my breakfast, hoping somehow the rising blood sugar would reach a magical point and turn me back into my normal self. I clenched my eyes shut and opened them several times, hoping for the best, but without any luck. Swallowing hard to quench a developing burp (yep, hereditary!),

I pushed my chair back with a grating screech and stood, glancing around the open-plan house. Coffee-coloured walls merged with coffee-coloured carpet on the living room floor, on which sat a semi-circular couch of muted aubergine. An odd-shaped lamp stood in the corner and multiple tiny light fittings hung like stars from the ceiling. A variety of ornaments, vases and candles decorated the room, and a bulky multi-coloured blanket hung heavily on the couch. The room was subtly stylish in one way and irritatingly homely in another. I couldn't decide if I liked it or not, but either way, it wasn't the sort of decor I'd choose.

"Dad, while you're up, do you mind making me another egg?" Ryan asked, as William took his mug and put it into some sort of chute on the kitchen bench. A moment later it popped out of another chute and William put it away in a cupboard.

"You've got to be kidding, right?" he replied.

"I'm still hungry. You wouldn't deny your growing twenty-one-year-old son adequate sustenance, would you?" He raised his eyebrows.

William sighed and put an egg into a large machine, pressed a couple of buttons, and held an egg cup against an opening from which the now boiled egg emerged. He placed it on the table in front of Ryan, who began peeling off the shell.

"We really should upgrade the Kitchen Assistant," Ryan said. "That one's ancient. The new version not only boils the egg in five seconds but peels the eggshell for you too."

There was no doubt about it; I was definitely in the future. Twenty-five years into the future. Genetically modified yolkless eggs and Kitchen Assistant machines that boiled them in five seconds. Maybe there were flying cars as well. Curious, I walked over to the window and peered outside. The street was quiet, except for a dog that appeared to be walking its owner and a little girl walking... *rolling* down the street with her mother. She must have those shoes with the inbuilt wheels. Nothing new, I'd seen them before. No one was on hoverboards and no cars were airborne, although the few vehicles parked nearby certainly looked different. More square-shaped – and taller – and not at all what I'd imagined cars to look like in the future.

"What are you looking at, Kel?" William asked, as I peered up, down, around and around, trying to spot anything outside that looked different.

"Um, nothing." I said, stepping back and smoothing out my clothes with my hands, a gesture I always did whenever I felt uncomfortable. Which wasn't often. Until today.

"Do you feel better now, having eaten?" he asked, slipping his arms into a suit jacket and shrugging it into place.

Translation: 'Do you now accept that you're really fifty and not twenty-five and have you finished with your mid-life-crisis freak-out episode?'

No.

"Yes, of course." I reassured him. He was obviously anxious to get going somewhere. Some husband – rushing out the door on my birthday and leaving me alone with my egg-addicted, burping punk son.

"Good." He leaned into me with lips puckered and I turned my face sideways so his kiss landed on my cheek. "I have to go, but I'll see you at the office this afternoon for the meeting."

"Ah... meeting?" I asked. "But it's my birthday. I think I'd better, um... cancel the meeting."

William laughed. "I don't think so, honey. After waiting over a year for this opportunity we're not going to let it go. Mr Turrow's heading back to the UK tonight, remember? Today's the only chance we'll get and there's more likelihood of success if we meet face to face than via e-pad."

What was he talking about? What opportunity? Who was

Mr Turrow? And what in the name of Dior was an e-pad? And I couldn't work in an office, it just wasn't possible. What happened to my modelling career? Unanswered questions swung from one side of my brain to the other like a trapeze, picking up others on the way and throwing them all over the place.

"Oh, and I'll give you your birthday presents later on," William added.

"Presents? There's more than one?" Okay maybe he wasn't such a bad husband after all.

"Yep, there's two. And you'll love them," he said with a confident smile, before leaning in close to me again and whispering into my ear. "Actually, make that three. I'll give you the third one tonight after our guests have gone home." His cheeky wink sent a jolt of dread through my veins.

Does he mean what I think he means? Oh hell, how am I going to get out of that?

William disappeared through a door and moments later an engine revved, building to a crescendo before abating in the distance. I rushed to the window to watch, but the car didn't fly. What a disappointment. If the universe was going to hold me captive in the future, you'd think it'd have the decency to provide technology that was more fun to experience than an egg boiling wonder machine.

The arrival of a tall white vehicle with fake flowers protruding from its top had me glued to the window, as a man walked up the pathway to our front door, a bunch of colourful flowers in his hand. Ryan removed his apron and opened the door at the exact moment a bell sounded and he took the flowers from the man's hands, thanking him.

"Special delivery from Her Royal Highness," he said in a posh voice, handing me the flowers.

"Who?" I asked, turning the card over to read the greeting.

Wishing you love and luxury on your birthday ~
Selena xx

Selena! I had to speak to her. She'd help me make sense of what's going on, she'd believe me when I tell her what happened. "Where's my phone?" I asked Ryan, plonking the flowers on the kitchen bench.

He looked at me like I'd asked him where my feet were. "Your phone?"

"Yeah, I need to call Selena, right now!"

"Then you better get your e-pad from its charger, Mum."

There's that e-pad word again. I turned side to side, not knowing what on earth I was supposed to be looking for. Ryan came up to me and placed his hands on my shoulders. "It's okay, Mum. I'll get it. You just sit down and relax, okay?" He led me to the chair and then disappeared into my bedroom, before emerging with what looked like a wristwatch. Just like the one William had used that morning. "Here you go." He strapped it to my wrist. As soon as the clasp locked it made a subtle beep sound. He pinched the tiny screen and flicked his fingers in front of me, and I jumped in shock as a holographic menu appeared before my eyes.

"Selena, Selena..." he said, scrolling through the screen with his finger. "Here she is, although I bet you won't be able to reach her as usual."

Why the hell not? We spoke to each other pretty much every day. I pressed her name and the holographic screen disappeared. "Where'd it go?"

Ryan scoffed at my technological incompetence and pinched the e-pad, drawing an imaginary line to my ear, just like William had done himself when his e-pad rang. "When you call someone, the screen disappears, remember? Just pinch and flick if you want the menu back again. Geez, Mum, you're only fifty, not a hundred and fifty."

I walked back into my bedroom, not only to speak to Selena privately, but to get away from Ryan. It was all too much. He couldn't possibly be my son, could he? We looked nothing alike and any son of mine would surely have a classier appearance and less burping tendencies.

The ringing on the line persisted, until a click ensued, followed by a stranger's voice in an American accent.

"You've reached Ms Westley, personal assistant to Selena York. I'm currently unable to take your call, please leave a message with your name, access number and reason for your call. Alternatively, please contact Ms York's agent at The Fulton Agency in West Hollywood, on 555-6772."

Access number? Reason for my call? I just want to speak to my friend!

Beep!

"Crap!" Oops, didn't mean to say that out loud. "I mean, hello! I need to speak to Selena urgently, this is Kelli Crawford, er... McSnelly. I seem to have misplaced my access number, but she knows me, we're best friends, so if you could have her call me that would be awesome, I mean, wonderful." I tried to change my speech to better reflect a fifty-year-old woman. "It's regarding a rather pressing matter relating to something that happened twenty-five years ago and if I could only speak to her as soon as possible, that would–"

Beep!

Geez, they didn't give much time to leave a complete message. And since when do I need an access number to speak to my friend?

"No luck, huh?" Ryan asked, peeking into my bedroom.

I shook my head and slumped onto the bed.

"Well, it was nice of Miss Two-Time Oscar Winner to send flowers; at least Hollywood hasn't completely swept her away."

Selena was an Oscar winner? But she was a model. They didn't have Oscars for models. *Maybe they do now, how would I know?* "What were her Oscars for again?" I asked.

"Really, Mum, your memory is totally shot today. She won best supporting actress in *A Mother's Choice* and then best actress in *Glimpse*, ten years ago, don't you remember? You went overboard telling all the parents at my school that she was your friend, even parents you'd never met before; you totally embarrassed me."

"I did? Well, sorry about that." Wow. I couldn't believe my best friend was an Oscar-winning Hollywood actress! I never even knew she wanted to act. How did she end up there and I ended up here? It didn't make sense. It wasn't fair. Why didn't I get transported to a future where I was married to Grant, living in Italy, gracing the catwalks in Milan and banking millions of dollars in income? The future I was headed for. The future I wanted. And what could have caused this... cosmic shift thingy anyway? Everything in my life was going perfectly, well, besides the argument with my sister, but I was used to those.

"Anyway, Mum, time's a wastin' and I haven't given you your birthday present yet." Ryan pulled me up from the bed.

I stood still, unable to fathom getting through this day, unable to accept who I was and what my life had turned out to be.

"Your present's not here though, I have to drive you to it."

I wasn't listening. Desperately in need of a familiar face, I pinched the e-pad and summoned the menu, scrolling through my list of contacts. Grant was nowhere in the list. He was not part of this life. Selena had a personal assistant standing guard like her own secret service, while I was trapped behind the bars of this unwanted future.

"Mum?"

Like a plucked guitar string I shook, the reality of my situation overtaking my muscles with fear, but instead of music, a moan made its way up from my belly to my lungs and out of my mouth.

"What's happening to me?" I cried. "Why can't I remember the last twenty-five years?" I brought my trembling hands to my head and clutched at my hair, almost pulling out a few strands.

"You mean, you really don't remember?" Ryan held on to my arms, his unfamiliar touch only exacerbating my shakes.

"Nope." I shook my head from side to side.

Ryan looked at his watch/e-pad thing and then up at the ceiling, pursing his lips to one side. "I think I should take you to the doctor, Mum. Just to check things out. I want you to have a fun birthday, not be upset."

I nodded. "Yes, a doctor is a good idea." Maybe there was a medical reason for this. Or maybe there wasn't. But either way, I needed to search for an answer and most importantly, a way to get my life back.

Chapter 3
What's up, Doc?

"Looking fifty is great – if you're sixty." – Joan Rivers

"I NEED to see Dr Ford right away!" The receptionist's hair puffed backwards from the sudden burst of air as I practically slammed into the reception desk, knocking a pile of brochures onto the floor.

"Dr Ford?"

"Yes, I must see her now!"

"But Dr Ford retired years ago."

"Huh?" Oh yeah. She'd probably be about seventy by now.

"Mrs McSnelly, are you all right?"

God, my name sounded even worse out loud. "No, I'm not. I really need to see a doctor. I'm supposed to be twenty-five but I woke up this morning a middle-aged housewife and have no idea how I got here! I don't know if I'm sick, or crazy – or both! I need answers!" I thumped my fist on the desk, my breaths coming short and sharp.

"Okay, just a moment, Mrs McSnelly." The receptionist put on a headset and spoke into the microphone as I tapped my foot impatiently and glanced around the waiting room. A man eyed me with pity, but when I locked eyes with him he quickly looked away. Ryan stood behind a fake pot plant, fiddling with its leaves. My eyes turned to the floor and feeling slightly guilty, I picked up the brochures and replaced them on the desk.

"Dr Vischek can see you in a few minutes," the receptionist said, lifting off her headset. "Take a seat... and try taking some deep breaths, okay?"

Deep breaths, yeah right. Like that's going to get me out of this nightmare.

"Would you like a paper bag?" the receptionist asked.

"What for? Do you mean to put over my head? Geez! I know I'm not looking my best but have a little compassion!" I fumed. Oh, the nerve of the woman.

Her eyes widened and she spoke softly, "To *breathe* into. So you don't hyperventilate."

Oops. "Oh. Sorry, um, no thanks, I'll just..." I gestured awkwardly to the row of chairs.

I sat down and a moment later Ryan sat next to me. Unable to stifle my foot tapping and hand trembling, I picked up what looked like an iPad from a small table and looked at the menu on the screen. I pressed the icon for magazines and then the icon for *Domestic Delight*. I flipped mindlessly through articles about home improvements and decorating, until an advertisement for a homewares company caught my eye. KC Interiors. Interesting... when I was younger, I used to play around with sketches of beautiful lamps, mirrors, vases and candle holders, and joked that I could start my own business called Kelli's Designs.

That was until one of my mother's 'episodes' where she ridiculed my artistic passion and I lost all confidence, gaining confidence in my appearance instead. Why waste the gift of a photogenic face and perfectly proportioned figure? That's what

Mum used to tell me as she dragged me from one photo shoot to another. At first they were boring, but I soon grew to love the whole thing – photographers calling me beautiful as lights flashed around me, make-up artists complimenting my almond-shaped eyes and high cheekbones as they brushed colours onto my face. There was nothing more rewarding than seeing the finished product – a glossy professional photo of yours truly.

"Mrs McSnelly?" A man, presumably Dr Vischek, emerged from a nearby room. "Please come through."

I put the iPad thingy back on the table and bolted into the room, pacing back and forth until the doctor made me sit down.

"I saw you only a month ago, Mrs McSnelly. What seems to be the problem?"

Oh good, maybe he knew something. Maybe I was being treated for a brain tumour and was experiencing one of the symptoms or side effects. "I'm fifty!" I blurted out.

Dr Vischek looked at the file on his computer screen. "Ah, so you are. Happy birthday!"

"Happy? I'm not happy. I'm horrified!" I stood up again. "Only yesterday I was twenty-five. This can't be possible! How is this possible?"

Dr Vischek tugged on my arms to encourage me to sit down again. What was it with sitting down, how was that supposed to make everything all right? I was a model and used to standing, godammit!

"I know how you feel, Mrs McSnelly, it seems only yesterday I was a new doctor, newly married with a newborn baby and now I've been in practice for fifteen years and have three kids. Time sure flies, doesn't it?" Dr Vischek gave me a knowing grin.

"But you don't understand! I really was only twenty-five yesterday... well, twenty-four to be exact. Today should be my twenty-fifth birthday, but I woke up and... well, look at me!" I stood once again and waved my hands around my degenerative body like I was demonstrating a new kitchen appliance. I pressed my belly, allowing it to wobble, lifted my drooping breasts out of the southern hemisphere for a moment and pointed to the rugged landscape that was my face. "I even have wrinkles on my lips!" I shoved my face close to his so he could see. "Before too long I'll be power-walking down the pathway to the retirement village wearing a pink velour leisure suit!"

"Mrs McSnelly, try to stay calm," the doctor said, lifting his hands and facing his palms towards me as though I might be a bomb about to explode any second. "Are you telling me you're having some memory issues, or are you just stressed out about turning fifty?"

"Of course I'm stressed about turning fifty, but the thing is, I don't remember being forty-nine yesterday, or forty-eight the year before. The last thing I remember is having drinks with my friends last night. But last night I was twenty-four." This time I sat down of my own accord, suddenly tired and wishing I could lie down. Lie down, close my eyes and wake up in my own bed.

Dr Vischek leaned forward in his chair, deep furrows drawing a V into his forehead. "Do you remember bumping your head, or falling, or having any sort of pain, tingling, or numbness?"

I shook my head and he shone a bright light into each of my eyes.

"Taken any medications, drugs – marijuana even?"

"Of course not!"

"I have to ask, Mrs McSnelly, to rule out all possibilities."

"I don't want to rule things out, I want to rule things in! I want to find out what's causing this." I'd started to get sick of my own whiny voice, but what else could I do but complain? I was supposed to be with my friends, celebrating my birthday, but here I was doing the very opposite. And who in their right mind would let themselves get to this dilapidated state without intervention? I hung my head to my knees and then jerked upright upon seeing the purple, spider-like bulging of varicose veins around my ankles. "Argh!"

"Have you had any dizziness, or shortness of breath?"

"Well I did faint twice this morning, but that was after I looked in the mirror. And I guess I'm a bit out of breath, but I have had an awful shock."

Dr Vischek inflated a cuff around my arm to take my blood pressure, which was normal, and took hold of my hand while a cold swab tickled my finger. Then he pressed a little stick into my fingertip. "Ouch!" A tiny blob of blood emerged and he soaked it up on some other sort of stick, then inserted it into a handheld device.

"What happened to your arm?" he asked.

The cuts from the glass had dried into raised red lines. "I knocked over a vase in the bathroom and it shattered."

Dr Vischek eyed me curiously.

"No, I didn't throw it, if that's what you're wondering. It was an accident," I said.

The handheld device beeped and Dr Vischek looked at the screen. "Blood sugar's normal," he said.

Well, there goes the low blood sugar hypothesis. "Should I go to pathology and have other blood tests done?"

"You just had them done," he replied. "Let's see if anything's of concern." Dr Vischek scrolled through the screen on the device.

"You mean, one drop of blood is all you need?"

He gave a single, sharp nod and continued reading the results as I peered towards the screen, not that I understood what any of the numbers meant.

"Everything is in normal range for someone your... age, Mrs

McSnelly," Dr Vischek announced. "No sign of infection or inflammation and your cholesterol levels are good."

"Must be those yolkless eggs, huh?" I suggested, managing a brief smile.

He performed various other tests on me and all were normal, except I failed the one where he asked me who was currently running the country. "You really don't know?" he probed, shaking his head in apparent disbelief. That was when he decided to refer me to a neurologist and a psychiatrist.

"Shouldn't I get an MRI first?" I asked.

The 'V' in Dr Vischek's forehead deepened. "Mrs McSnelly, MRIs are no longer used. I can do a PBS now though, if you like, but it'll be an extra charge on your account."

"A PBS?"

"Portable Body Scan. I can check there're no lesions on the brain or spinal cord, just for peace of mind. Or you can wait till you see the neurologist and the cost will be covered under the consultation fee."

"I don't care about the cost, just do whatever you can now to find out what's going on."

As instructed, I lay down on the examination table as Dr Vischek placed a tunnel-like frame contraption over my head and torso, and connected another handheld device to it. He stood back and pressed a remote control, and the device began moving side to side on the contraption, from my head to my waist, like a boring mini-rollercoaster without the twists, turns and loops. With all the new technology available now, if they couldn't tell me the reason for my apparent time travel/age change scenario, then I had no idea what, or who, could.

Dr Vischek removed the contraption when the procedure was finished. He pinched the device and out popped a holographic screen, just like with the e-pad. Despite his instructions to remain lying down while he looked at the scan results, I slowly sat up. "Wow," I whispered, admiring the three-dimensional image floating next to the stark white wall. A convoluted mass of tissue held up by a long tapered stem appeared to be staring back at Dr Vischek as he studied it, pinching sections at a time to zoom in and analyse. Noticing my amazement, he pointed to the image.

"This is your brain and spinal cord, and so far I haven't seen anything amiss. The scan didn't detect any focal areas of heat or increased metabolism, no clots or bleeds and no alerts have been uploaded."

I didn't understand what he was talking about, but it seemed safe to say I didn't have any tumours pressing on the brain cells responsible for sense of time, or age perception – if such cells even existed.

"Your scan is perfectly healthy. And along with your other results, I can't see any physical reason for your symptoms."

"Are you absolutely sure?"

He nodded, helping me off the table and back to my chair. "Physically, you're in great health. But I'll give you a referral to a neurologist just in case and if you still feel this way in another week or so, book a consultation." Dr Vischek intertwined his fingers as he propped his elbows up on the desk. "I would like you to see a psychiatrist though. It could be related to stress or a repressed traumatic memory... I know it was a long time ago, but what happened to your mother might be affecting you in a subconscious way. It would be good to get a specialist's opinion."

The mention of my mother sent a jolt of pain through my heart. Surely her untimely death couldn't somehow be triggering this? I dealt with that... incident... years ago. I'm over it, aren't I? "You know about my mother?"

"Of course, I've been your doctor for years. It's my job to know your family medical history."

"How soon do you think I'd be able to see the psychiatrist?"

"There might be a bit of a wait, but I'll mark the referral as urgent." He typed on the virtual keyboard on his computer screen. "In the meantime, try to enjoy your day. Make the most of it – have some fun, do something different! You never know, by the time the day's over, everything might just make perfect sense."

"I hope so."

"Here," he continued, taking hold of my wrist. "I'll upload these referrals to your e-pad." Dr Vischek withdrew a USB drive from his computer and connected it to my e-pad, before acknowledging my confusion. "Do you remember how to work your e-pad?"

I shook my head. "I hadn't even heard of them till this morning, but my, um... Ryan showed me how to make a call."

Dr Vischek showed me all the basic functions, including how to retrieve the referrals, how to access my virtual driver's license, credit cards and other important cards that would normally fill up my purse, and he also showed me how to scan my e-pad when making purchases. Apparently I was now living in a cashless society, it was kinda cool.

I stood and shook the doctor's hand. "Thank you very much, Dr Vischek, for seeing me right away and for your advice."

"You're welcome. I'm sorry I don't have any definitive answers, but I think everything will be all right. I wouldn't be surprised if the next twenty-four hours makes a world of difference, and if not, the specialist can advise you further."

I nodded and turned to leave, before turning back again. "Dr Vischek?"

His eyebrows rose.

"What does e-pad stand for?"

"Electronic Personal Assistant Device," he replied with a smile.

Hmm, I wonder if it has a time travel function...

I returned to the reception desk and expertly scanned my e-pad the way Dr Vischek had showed me and the receptionist assured me my rebate had been applied directly to my bank account. She even commented that because I was now a 'senior', my consultation fee was less than usual. Nice to have some sort of compensation for the crap that being fifty had given me today, I guess.

"So, you've been given the all-clear?" Ryan asked as we walked back to the car.

"Guess so," I replied.

"And he definitely said you're in good health, no cause for concern?"

"Just stress, he thinks. But physically I'm fine. He said I should go and enjoy my day."

"Oh good, we better hurry then." Ryan picked up his pace as he walked alongside me. "Do I have a surprise for you!"

Chapter 4
Surprise!

"Life begins at the end of your comfort zone." – Neale Donald Walsch

"You've got to be kidding?" My mouth gaping, I stood rooted to the ground as Ryan tried without success to usher me towards the *Ben's Bungy Jumping* sign. What did he expect me to say, 'Oh yippee, just what I've always wanted'?

"I've booked us both in for a jump. It's gonna be awesome!"

"You can't be serious? There's no way I'm letting someone tie rope to my feet and throw me off that thing!" I pinned him with a determined stare.

"Mum, remember at your birthday dinner last year you said you wanted to do something adventurous for your next birthday?" Ryan enquired. "Something different, to feel alive again."

I shook my head.

"Oh, that's right... sudden memory loss and all that." He dropped his head and looked back up a moment later. "Well, you did say it and I listened, and I've had this planned for ages, and it's non-refundable so you can't back out. Mum – you'll thank me for this, it's going to be something you'll never forget." He clamped his hands together as though in prayer.

"Never forget? This is the thing I'd want to forget! I can't do this. Besides, I'm... fifty," I stuttered, still in shock of my situation. "Surely they wouldn't let seniors like me go bungy jumping?" I planted my hands defiantly on my hips and jutted out my jaw.

"Of course they do. It's perfectly safe and you've been given a clean bill of health by the doc, so there's no reason you can't do it. They even jump people who are in wheelchairs, you know."

Yeah. Probably adrenalin addicts who were in wheelchairs *because* of bungy jumping. I'd rather have William's third present than go through this.

"What if the rope breaks? They could forget to tie it on properly and only realise once I've plunged to my death!" Hmm, on second thoughts... at least then I wouldn't have to put up with this awful day anymore.

No, I couldn't think like that. *Pull yourself together, Kelli!*

"They won't forget. I know Ben, he's a professional," Ryan assured me.

Professional what? Professional idiot?

I looked at the huge purpose-built structure, completely out of place in the lush natural rainforest and imagined myself launching off the edge to hang precariously above the water. I shuddered as I envisioned all my saggy bits sagging upside down, my loose turkey-neck skin falling over my face, covering my mouth and nose and cutting off my air supply. This could be fatal in more ways than one.

"I can't do it... I'm not dressed for it!" I looked down at my curved hems, which would curve all the way over my head if I was hung upside down. "Look, I can't bungy jump in this outfit."

Ryan simply smiled, zipped open his backpack and pulled out a pair of pants and a singlet.

"You brought a change of clothes for me?"

He nodded. "I grabbed them before we drove to the doctors. I didn't want to say anything about what you were wearing in case you got suspicious." Ryan stepped in close and looked me in the eye. "I've bungy jumped four times already, it's exhilarating! You can do this, Mum. It might be just what you need."

Could he be right? Could this be some sort of challenge I have to go through to get back to my twenty-five-year-old self? Maybe it would shock me back to my real life. Hmmm, if I didn't do it I could be stuck in this terrible life forever. But if I did it, there's a chance it'd create another cosmic shift thingy and transport me back where I belong.

I alternated my weight from one foot to the other and Ryan continued to encourage me with his determined eyes. What was it the doctor had said? *Try to enjoy your day. Make the most of it – have some fun, do something different!* Aha! He could be in on this whole charade and that might have been a subtle way of telling me how to fix it, without saying: 'Mrs McSnelly, I'd like to prescribe a treatment of bungy jumping. Go jump off a ledge and call me in the morning.'

"Okay," I mumbled, eyes on the ground, barely believing what I'd just agreed to.

Ryan planted his hands on my arms. "So you'll do it?" His eyes widened and his breath quickened.

"Quick, before I change my mind." I walked towards the towering monstrosity and Ryan followed like a puppy anticipating a game of fetch.

"Yes! I knew you'd come round. You won't regret it, Mum."

My legs became weak and I was sure a rock star drummer was inside my chest, banging on the wall of my heart. But I forced the vision of my young self, lazing in bed in my own apartment to the front of my mind. Soon, with any luck, it would no longer be a vision but a reality.

Chapter 5
Leap of Faith

"You have to take risks. We will only understand the miracle of life fully when we allow the unexpected to happen." – Paulo Coelho

AFTER MEETING the legendary Ben and going through the required training, as well as signing a holographic legal form (almost signing my surname as Crawford instead of McSnelly), Ryan completed his bungy jump first. I didn't know whether watching him would make me feel better or worse, so I half watched through fingers covering my face. He came up to me afterwards all hyper and bouncy, like he'd had ten cups of coffee in one hit and reassured me I'd be fine.

By the time they'd attached me to the rope via the padded ankle harness, I thought I had made the biggest mistake of my life. Well, the second. The first would have been letting my body get to this visibly aged state. I looked longingly at the direction from which I'd come, wanting desperately to go back down and huddle under a blanket in the car. But Ryan was there, urging me on.

"You can do it, Mum! Just think how great you'll feel afterwards."

Right. Yes. Afterwards. It'll all be over soon. *Breathe, Kelli.*

"Now, just do a little bunny-hop over to the edge, like we practised, Kelli," Ben said, his hand on the small of my back.

Easier said than done. I couldn't find the strength to hop, the bones and muscles in my legs seemed to have disappeared. Using all the effort I could muster, I bunny-shuffled instead, the long distance between me and the water below becoming frighteningly more apparent.

Twenty-five. Twenty-five. Won't be long now and I'll be back home. Yes, back home. I fixed my mind on the desired outcome, rather than the heavy metal concert going off in my chest cavity. My toes met the edge and it was time.

"Take a deep breath, Kelli," Ben instructed. "And then allow yourself to simply fall forward."

I didn't know whether to cry or vomit, or both. I imagined my half-digested yolkless eggs going on a bungy jump of their own, only without the cord, landing in the water below with a big splosh. That made me want to vomit even more. I looked back at Ryan one last time, and his enthusiastic expression combined with his ridiculous hairstyle only reinforced the fact that I didn't belong here. Didn't belong in the McSnelly family. I needed to get back to my young, carefree, childless life. With Grant. I couldn't wait for him to wrap his arms around me again and get down on one knee to...

"Arghh!"

I lost my balance before I was ready, my arms circling frantically around in an attempt to stay on the ledge. But to no avail. My scream followed me down before, all of a sudden, the air inside my lungs whooshed out like someone had stuck a vacuum cleaner nozzle in my mouth.

I couldn't breathe. I couldn't scream anymore. I was surely

about to die. Something yanked at my ankles and my body flung upwards. Oh thank God, it must be over...

"Arghh!"

Here we go again. Whatever breath was left was sucked out again, along with what felt like all my insides. Yank. My ankles jerked again and my body went upwards. And back down again. I could feel my eardrums vibrating! Up... and back down again. Oh my God, it's never going to end! Up, down, up, down. Bounce, bounce, bounce. The eggs in my stomach were surely scrambled by now.

The dark water below swam into focus as the bouncing subsided and I hung there, desperate for something to hold on to. Now what? Were they just going to let me hang? *Help!* And then the best thing I'd seen all day caught my eye. A boat, yippee! I thought I'd died and was in heaven, but the putrid stench of body odour assured me it wasn't.

"There you go, sweetie. Wasn't so bad, was it?" Smelly man said as he pulled me into the boat.

I couldn't speak. I just lay there, limbs shaking. Wait. He called me *sweetie*. That's a name reserved for young women, isn't it? I must have changed back to... I jerked upright and looked down at my body.

"Arghh!"

My scream lasted longer than my bungy jump. Nothing had changed. I was still fifty-year-old Kelli Jelly Belly McSnelly. Or McSmelly, thanks to my deodorant-phobic rescuer, whose primal scent had rubbed off on my clothes.

All that for nothing? Talk about ripped off! When I got out of the boat and stepped onto the delicious stability of land, Ben and Ryan waved at me. Ryan gave me a thumbs up and climbed down the steps.

"You did it, Mum, you did it! That was freaking awesome!" Ryan ran over to me and threw his arms around my quivering body. I suddenly forgot my disappointment at remaining fifty and realised what I'd just done.

"I bungy jumped, can you believe it? I went bungy jumping! I jumped off the ledge and fell for miles... and hung upside down and bounced and bounced and bounced... and all the air went out of me... and I felt like I almost died but at the same time I felt so alive and... oh my God I can't believe I did it!"

"Whoa, slow down! There's a lot of adrenalin coursing through your body right now, take a breath." Ryan laughed. "But yes, you did it!"

My teeth chattered inside my dry mouth and I kept looking up at the huge structure and over to the water, back and forth, taking in the length I'd travelled. "I bungy jumped, I just bungy jumped," was all I could say, while my body vibrated like a jitterbug. No wonder Ryan had seemed like he'd had ten cups of coffee. I felt like I'd had fifteen, combined with a can of Red Bull, ten teaspoons of sugar and a truckload of red food colouring.

Not knowing what to do, say, or think, Ryan gave me my coral-coloured outfit to change back into and afterwards, led me back to the car. "So did you like it, do you reckon you'll do it again one day?"

"Me, um... don't know. Sort of, maybe, I don't know if I liked it. I mean at first it was horrific and then it was a relief... and now I feel all weird and jumpy and have heaps of energy." The words were bungy jumping themselves out of my mouth before I could process what I was saying.

"How about next year we go skydiving?" Ryan asked with a glint of anticipation in his eye.

"Next year? Let's just get through this day first!" I told him.

The passenger door of the car rolled up and over the roof and I slid inside, my skin still buzzing from the experience. Oh wow. I hadn't really noticed the details of the car before, as I'd been so anxious to get to the doctor and then Ryan had blindfolded me on the way to Ben's Bungy Jumping so as to not spoil the surprise. Not only did the doors roll upwards, like an eyelid opening, but the seatbelt embraced me from behind, sleeve-like arms stretched out in front that I had to feed my arms through, while two clasps locked together in front of my chest and hips. Ryan used his e-pad to start the engine and the car spoke in a strong feminine voice.

"Where would you like to go, Ryan?"

Holy crap. How did I not notice that before? My mind must have been so overflowing with fear and confusion that I blocked out everything else around me.

"City Point Shopping Centre," Ryan told the car.

"Route established. Estimated travel time: twenty-four minutes," the car spoke again. "Calculating optimal parking spot... stay tuned for directions when your destination approaches..."

My eyes darted all around the car. Holographic GPS map just under the windscreen, a small steering wheel that resembled an Xbox controller and a – what was that? I tugged on what looked like a straw and a smaller straw shot through the middle.

"Oh yeah, good idea. I'd love some coffee," Ryan said, sipping on the straw on the driver's side. "Not that I need any more stimulation, but who cares!"

The car had an inbuilt coffee machine? Pure brilliance! I sipped profusely, savouring the caffeine hit. Even though I felt like I'd already had fifteen of them, I was thirsty. And hungry. What was with my appetite? You'd think after the large breakfast I'd eaten I'd be set for the day. Or maybe I did throw up during the bungy jump and didn't even realise it.

"Go easy on the coffee, Mum. Save some room for your morning tea with Diora."

"Turn right," Miss Car said, and Ryan obliged.

"Morning tea? With who?"

"Yeah, I'm dropping you off so you can meet up with Diora." He glanced at me briefly. "You do remember your firstborn daughter, don't you?"

I stifled the scream that threatened to escape my lungs, figuring I'd acted like enough of a loony for one day. I had a daughter too? Just how many offspring did I bring into this world? No wonder my stomach was flabby as hell. Two kids. That'll do it. But still, you'd think I would have had some liposuction somewhere along the way, or a tummy tuck at least.

Wait. Diora. That was the name of my favourite doll I'd had as a young girl. I'd imagined calling my own daughter Diora one day, until I came to my senses and decided I probably wouldn't want children after all.

"Of course, I just forgot I was meeting her, that's all," I said to Ryan. Hopefully he bought it. Didn't want to freak him out too much in one day by saying: *actually, I don't remember her at all, or you for that matter. You, my son, are a complete stranger as far as I'm concerned.*

"I think she has a more passive activity planned for you, it'll give you a chance to calm your nerves after the bungy jump."

"Oh, good." Although, it would take something pretty powerful to calm my nerves right now. "Um, where am I meeting her again?"

"Dunno, she just told me to drop you off at the shopping centre. It'll be in your birthday itinerary though, just check."

Um... how?

My confused silence had him glancing towards me with that look. That *not again* look. "In the calendar, on your e-pad," he explained with a sigh.

I did the pinching thing and summoned the screen. Calendar, calendar... Aha! Here it was. Happy Birthday, the screen read, followed by a list of activities and their respective time slots. Eleven a.m. – Meet Diora at the south food court of City Point Shopping Centre.

A food court? What kind of daughter takes me to a dodgy food court for my birthday? She mustn't know me very well at all. And City Point Shopping Centre? That must be new, I'd never heard of it.

Whoa! "What are you doing?" I yelled, grabbing onto the side of the car.

Ryan had leaned back in the driver's seat, his hands behind his head. "We're on the freeway, so I've switched to auto-drive."

My eyes darted frantically around the car, my white knuckles bursting through my clenched hands. I expected to crash and burn at any moment, but the car remained on course and other cars remained in their respective lanes.

"So, it just drives itself?"

"Haven't you ever used the auto... oh of course, right." He cleared his throat, as though stifling his annoyance at my continual naivety. "Music please," he said.

A little twinkle sounded. "Album: Primal Prophecy."

And with that a strange sound emerged, which gradually got louder. Sounding very tinny and metallic, it irritated my ears. And then a sudden explosion of repetitive drums and a screaming singing voice made me jump up and bump my head on the roof of the car. So much for the seatbelt sleeve thingies.

"Ugh! What is that horrible noise? Turn it down. Or off, would be better." I covered my ears.

"Volume down by five points," Ryan instructed. The noise reduced. "Sorry, Mum. It was a bit loud. But what did you mean by horrible noise? Is that any way to respond to your own son's music?"

I tried to swallow a large lump of foot in my mouth, but it wedged in my throat. "That's your music?" I asked feebly.

He nodded. "It's my demo album."

Oops. "Of course, sorry. It was just so loud at first I didn't recognise it."

"Music off," Ryan said. "We don't have to have it on, you probably need a little peace and quiet before Diora talks your ears off."

A talkative daughter, huh? I bet she'd be more like me than Ryan was. "So, your demo album... any luck getting signed up yet?" I already knew the answer, but I had to start some sort of normal conversation that didn't involve me screaming or whining.

"Nope, but it's only a matter of time. And people are totally loving our gigs, so the word's getting out."

"Oh, that's good then." I looked more closely at Ryan, this young man who was apparently my son, with his black and pink hair, body jewellery and... oh, there's a tattoo of a cute little alien face on his arm. Was that what girls liked these days? Ben the bungy guru looked similar, although his hair was a yellow-blond crew-cut with a long wispy fringe.

"So, is there anyone special in your life... son?" Ugh. Too weird.

"Aren't you the nosy one today?" Ryan smiled and he switched back to normal driving mode as we exited the freeway and drove back into the city. "Possibly, I'm just not sure yet if the feeling's mutual."

"Well, have you told this special person how you feel?"

"Not exactly."

"Then maybe you should. Get it out in the open. Who knows, maybe she'll feel the same way."

Ryan took his eyes away from the road briefly to glare at me. "She?"

"You know, this girl you like."

He gave a high-pitched laugh. "It's not a she, it's a he."

"Huh?"

"I'm still as gay as I've always been, Mum." He laughed again.

My son's gay? Oh, okay. I just didn't expect it, that's all. "Right, um... yes. Well, maybe you should, you know... talk to him. See if he feels the same way?"

"I think he does, but I don't want to risk breaking up Primal Prophecy if it doesn't work out."

"He's in your band?"

Ryan nodded. "And before you ask, no it's not Davo, the guitarist. He's one hundred per cent straight."

No idea who that was, but anyway. "So who is it? You can tell me, I'm your mum." Ugh again. Did I just say that? Was I taking advantage of my motherly authority to get the upper hand on all the gossip? Yep.

Ryan hesitated, chewing his lip. "It's Ben."

"Do you mean... Bungy Ben?"

"The one and only. Bungy expert, kick-ass drummer and hot as chilli."

That was a little too much information, but I guess Ben *was* kind of good-looking, with an impressive physique. What was a mother supposed to say in this situation: 'Go for it, son. He's a catch!'?

"I guess if it's meant to be, it's meant to be." There, that should do it for my daily motherly wisdom.

"True, Mum. True." He drove in silence for a while and when Miss Car directed us to the best available parking spot (a four-hour spot right near the entrance), Ryan angled the car sideways alongside the other cars and said, "Park left."

A squishy sound emerged from underneath and the car moved directly sideways into the parking spot. Ryan didn't have to manoeuvre the car, it literally moved sideways, like the wheels had swivelled around. Cool!

"Only five minutes late," Ryan said, sliding out of the car and shrugging his shoulders. "Well, I'll leave you here and that way you can drive yourself to the meeting this afternoon."

I'd forgotten about the meeting. No idea what that would be all about, but with any luck, by then I may have figured out a way to get back to the past.

"Where are you going then?" I asked Ryan.

"Back home. Someone needs to be there to set up for your big party." He kissed me on the cheek. "Your jump was awesome, Mum. I can't wait to tell Dad about the look on your face! See ya!" He pressed something on his shoe and rolled off and out of the car park on his wheelie shoes.

I was suddenly alone. A gasp shot out of my mouth when I realised something. I was supposed to meet Diora, my daughter, right now in the food court of this shopping centre, but how would I find her when I had absolutely no idea what she looked like?

Chapter 6
Darling Daughter Diora

"Of all the haunting moments of motherhood, few rank with hearing your own words come out of your daughter's mouth." –
Victoria Secunda

THE CROWDS PUSHED past as I followed the signs to the south food court. Weaving my way between people, the e-pad vibrated against my wrist before the melodic beeping noise reached my ear.

Message received flashed on the small screen.

I pinched the e-pad and the screen appeared, showing a text message:

> Where are you? Am waiting and starving! I'm
> eating for two remember. Diora.

Oh good, I can narrow down my search to only pregnant-looking, twenty-something women. Hopefully there wasn't a baby boom going on or anything. But what if she's only a couple of months along and wasn't showing yet? Hang on, if she was pregnant, then that meant I was going to be... a grandmother. No way!

This couldn't be happening. Real grandmas knitted and had short curly mauve hair and stored tissues up their sleeves, didn't they? I was too young for this. Two children and a grandchild-to-be all in one day? I needed Valium. Preferably intravenously. Damn! I should have asked the doctor for a prescription.

I trudged onwards and came to the densely populated food court, where noisy kids ate greasy hot chips and drank cola while their mothers yelled at them to sit still and eat quietly.

Squish. I looked down to find a mangled chip stuck to my shoe, courtesy of the rosy-cheeked kid I'd just passed whose hot chips were spilling out of their container onto the table and floor. Shaking it off, I continued my trek, past a table of overweight teenagers sharing a pizza, one of them burping even louder than Ryan had this morning. Charming.

At another table, a woman with an exposed pregnant belly bursting forth from her skimpy singlet top, pulled out a cigarette and lit it. A security guard instructed her to put it out. She spat in his face and he promptly escorted her from the food court. Hopefully that wasn't Diora.

A cleaner frantically scrubbed one of the tables with some sort of electric cleaning brush, clearly unable to keep up with the demand, as patrons got up and left without taking their scraps to the rubbish bin. Disgusting. I was used to eating in fancy restaurants and hip tapas bars, but was now forced to endure what can only be described as... squalor.

I glanced around the crowd, eyeing the stomachs of young women like some weirdo. There was another pregnant woman, but her skin was too dark to be my daughter. A few other women sat by themselves, but I couldn't see their stomachs below the tables.

Diora, Diora, where are you? I know. I'll call her! Like a pro,

I opened the contacts screen on my e-pad and found her name. Diora Bellows. She must be married, or at least had the good sense to change her unforgiving surname. Diora McSnelly would be like fine wine served with baked beans. I pressed *call* and waited.

"The person you are calling is on another call. Please call back later."

Oh, why now? Which one are you, Diora? My eyes continued searching. And then I overheard an interesting conversation...

"No, I specifically ordered a deluxe pram, not a budget pram. What kind of mother do you think I am? As if I'd trust the safety of my unborn child to a budget pram, are you crazy?" The voice came from somewhere to my right. "Plus, they look awful. Why in the name of Dior anyone would want to buy an olive-green pram is beyond me. Or did the designers think it would go well with baby poo? Anyway, I expect your delivery driver to return to my house immediately to collect the mistaken item and deliver the correct pram. My husband will be there, I'll let him know to expect you. Goodbye."

I turned my head to the source of the confident voice; a beautiful young woman with glossy black hair, tied back into a sleek ponytail. Hoop earrings dangled at her cheeks and she shook her head, assumingly at the injustice of the budget pram incident. Understandably. Budget just meant crappy quality. Everyone knew that.

As I walked nearer, I could see a large mound at her front. She fiddled with her e-pad and spoke again. "Honey, I just called them. It's all sorted. They're going to deliver the correct pram within the next hour, so don't go anywhere, okay? Huh? No, she's not here yet. I'm bloody starving... okay, love you too. Bye."

Yep. Gotta be Diora. Either that or my long lost identical

twin. Minus the large abdomen of course. Actually, mine wasn't far off the mark.

"Mum, you're here, finally!" She tried to stand, but failed. "Come here, will you?" She gestured with her hands.

I leaned in and she kissed me on the cheek. It felt all tingly and weird and for a moment my legs became like jelly.

"Happy birthday! I hear you've had a bit of an adventure this morning?"

"I guess I have, after my freak-out, followed by the doctors and..."

"Wait, you went to the doctors? Are you all right? Is it your indigestion again? Or your hormones?"

Oh, so she meant the bungy jumping. I thought she was using the word *adventure* as a nicer alternative to mid-life-crisis. "I'm fine, just a little anxiety."

"So how was it... the bungy jumping?" Diora didn't wait for a response. "I can't believe you actually did it! My mum, leaping off the edge with no fear in the world! You're so brave. I'd chicken out for sure. Not that they'd let an eight-and-a-half-month pregnant woman do it anyway. Wouldn't want the baby coming out the wrong end!"

By the sounds of it she didn't need to bungy jump, words spewed from her mouth like she'd done three jumps in a row. I now understood what Ryan meant when he said she'd talk my ears off.

"I'm still a little jittery, but I survived, so that's the main thing," I said.

She nodded, then rubbed her stomach. "Well, if I don't eat soon I'll get grumpy and start telling people off for parting their hair the wrong way or having overgrown eyebrows. Let's eat, shall we?"

Yep. My very own mini-me. "You stay here. I'll get us something. What would you like?" I asked.

"Hot chocolate and a slice of chocolate mud cake. With chocolate ice cream on the side. And chocolate sprinkles."

Okay, the resemblance ends there. No way would I eat that amount of chocolate in one month let alone one day. Although at the mention of the word chocolate, my stomach grumbled and my previously dry mouth salivated. Chocolate cake would be nice, just this once. It *was* my birthday and this technically wasn't my real body. Besides, it's beyond help anyway, might as well indulge.

Within five minutes of bringing a tray of chocolate goodness to our table, Diora had wolfed down her cake and ice cream and worked her way through the hot chocolate. All while interrogating me for the details of this morning's adventures.

"Well, the adventures don't end there. The day's only just begun and you've got plenty more ahead of you," she said. "I can't wait for tonight. It's going to be so much fun!"

I'd already had quite enough for one day and it wasn't even midday yet, but what could I do? I just had to appear normal and keep an eye out for a solution, a way of getting back.

"Although," Diora continued, "if I'm going to be able to cope with your party, I'll have to have a nap beforehand." She rubbed her belly. "This little one's got me so tired I'm falling asleep at eight thirty most nights, only to be woken by a karate kick and triple somersault two hours later." She downed the rest of her hot chocolate, while I was only halfway through mine.

The conversation was easier than I'd imagined, as she did most of the talking. I mostly nodded and gave single syllable responses, then Diora looked at her e-pad.

"Wow, is that the time? We better go," she said, pushing her chair back with a screech and using her hands to propel her body up from the chair. "Whoa! Quick, Mum. Feel this." She grabbed my hand and shoved it onto her belly.

A wave of ripples met with my hand, then they moved

further to the side and I saw them. Little bumps rolled along her abdomen, as though a tiny creature was trapped and trying to get out. Well, I guess that was kind of true, although it was a tiny human.

But not just any human. My grandchild. And hopefully it wasn't trying to get out right now. I mean, of course it would eventually, but please, not today. I'm not ready to be a mother, let alone a grandmother.

"Does it hurt?" I released my hand.

Diora shrugged. "No, but I've been enjoying more Braxton Hicks lately, which certainly make me stop and take notice."

Braxton Hicks? Who's she talking about? Was he some kind of pop singer? And what did he have to do with pregnancy?

"How long did you have Braxton Hicks for before you went into labour with me, Mum?" Diora asked.

Crap. How the hell should I know? "Umm, I can't remember."

"C'mon, surely you have some idea. Was your pregnancy with me that unmemorable?" Diora planted an exaggerated pout on her face.

If only she knew the half of it. I couldn't exactly say: 'Actually, Diora, I don't remember it at all, nor do I remember giving birth to you and I certainly don't remember your (gulp) conception.' I shuddered at the thought of me with William. And then I remembered what he said about my other birthday present being later tonight. Oh God, I had to find a way back home before then!

"Um, maybe it was a week?" I hoped that was a believable answer and that she wasn't expecting me to say five months or anything.

"A week?" she exclaimed, holding on to her stomach as if for support. "I've been having them for about ten days now. I could pop at any minute!"

Please don't. Please.

"Oh well, my next doctor's appointment is only three days away, so I'll ask about it then. On second thoughts..." Diora pinched open the e-pad screen and typed something.

"What are you doing?"

"Foogling."

"What?" I peered towards the screen.

"Foogling. To see what the internet can tell me about Braxton Hicks."

A shriek of surprise shot from my mouth on seeing the search engine web page. It looked just like the Google logo, only it said Foogle.

"Oh look, three-hundred and forty-seven people on Facebook have been discussing Braxton Hicks in the last hour." Diora pointed at the screen.

This Braxton guy must be quite popular with young people these days. I wonder if his music's anything like Ryan's?

"Braxton Hicks contractions usually last anywhere from a few days to a few weeks before the onset of labour," Diora read from some website she'd found.

Contractions? Didn't contractions mean labour? Something told me she wasn't talking about a pop singer after all.

"And look, this blog tells the story of one woman who didn't have any Braxton Hicks at all. One day, her water just broke and bam!... Out came baby."

"Ah, Diora, maybe you should just wait until you see the doctor instead of relying on the internet." Well, whaddya know. My first piece of solid motherly advice!

"Yeah, you're right. And we better get walking," she replied, pushing the screen back into the e-pad and tugging on my arm, both to lead me in the right direction and to balance her weight.

"Diora?" I asked. "Why do they call it Foogle? I've forgotten."

"Seriously? And I thought pregnancy brain had fried *my* memory," she said. "Facebook bought Google, remember? So now it's Foogle."

"Oh, of course. Geez, the bungy jumping must have messed with my head." I attempted a light-hearted laugh.

We walked, or rather I walked while Diora waddled, moving at a snail's pace. Surely a bit of weight around the tummy couldn't make a person that slow? Getting impatient, I forced myself to walk slower, while inside I was still running around in circles after my bungy jump, not to mention the urgent desire to find a way out of this body.

As I waited for Diora to catch up, my eye caught a large poster displayed in the window of a beauty salon: *Take Ten Years Off with our YouthMagic Facial!* It had a before and after photo of a woman about forty, but in the after photo she looked about thirty. *Clinically proven to work** it said under the heading and there was some fine print at the bottom but I didn't bother with that. I pushed through the door and into the salon.

"Mum, what are you doing?" Diora asked, panting slightly.

"I must have one of these facials!" This could be it. I'd close my eyes while the beautician did her magic and when I opened them I'd be twenty-five – and it would be much more enjoyable than bungy jumping.

"Mum." Diora tugged at my arm again and ushered me away from the counter, much to the disappointment of the eager beautician. "I've already booked you in for a YouthMagic facial, remember? But not at this dodgy salon, at Queen of Beauty," she whispered.

"You have?"

"Uh-huh. For all three of us, remember?"

I was sick of people saying *remember*, but my eagerness for a magic facial overtook my irritation. Hang on. "Three of us?"

I hoped she didn't mean the unborn baby was having some

kind of pre-natal, trans-abdominal Foetus Facial. But this *was* the future and after experiencing yolkless eggs, e-pads, PB-whatchamacallit miracle brain scanners and talking self-driving cars – anything was possible.

"You, me and Elaine," Diora replied matter-of-factly. "Only I'm having the Pregnant Princess Facial." She smiled and raised her ample bosom with pride.

"Oh, right." I had no idea who Elaine was.

"And, they're going to do your hair and make-up. So you'll be all prepped for your big meeting this afternoon."

The only meeting I planned to attend would be my birthday party. With my twenty-something friends and no one even close to the age of fifty. I picked up my pace.

"Mum, can you slow down? Don't you remember what it was like when you were pregnant?"

No, I bloody didn't! I just wanted to hurry up and have this facial! Although, I had no idea where I was supposed to be walking to. "Yes, of course, sorry sweetheart." I was getting good at this mother talk.

Ten painful minutes later, we arrived at Queen of Beauty and I'd barely pushed open the door before a woman with a frizzy mop of blonde hair threw her arms around me.

"Oh, Kel. Happy Birthday! This is going to be so much fun!"

I jerked backwards and stiffened my shoulders at the intrusion.

"Mum's a little on edge after her bungy jump, Elaine," Diora explained.

"Yes, that's right. I can't wait to see the video!" Elaine said, before switching her embrace over to Diora and then placing a hand on her belly. "How are you, sweetie?"

Oh God, I'd forgotten they'd taken a video of the jump. Just routine, they said, for visual evidence if anything went wrong. Not that it ever did, Bungy Ben had assured me.

"Happy birthday, Kelli," a velvety voice said from somewhere behind Elaine's curly mop. Elaine moved aside and a large woman with hair rolled neatly into a bun on the top of her head stepped forward and grasped my hands in hers. "Welcome to your morning of pampering."

This must be the Queen of Beauty herself. A garland of tiny gold beads was strung around the base of her hair bun, looking somewhat like a crown. She wore a black and gold uniform, falling with a liquid-like drape over her curves.

"Thanks," I replied, glancing around the waiting area which resembled a palace. The chairs for guests to sit on and await their appointment were mini-thrones! Subtle ambient music permeated the air, as did a warm woody scent, while a triple-tier water fountain trickled peacefully in the corner. I'm sure I'm not the kind of mother to favour one child over another, but Diora hit the jackpot with this birthday gift.

I met my reflection in an elaborate gilt-edged mirror on the left wall and startled slightly, but was then drawn to the beautiful design of the frame. Its curves and swirls gave it a classic elegance, but with a hint of modern spark. A lamp stood below the mirror on a small table, the swirly design of the mirror repeated in the gold of the lamp base. "These are beautiful, aren't they?" I said, tracing the curved design with a finger.

"Of course they are, you designed them," Elaine said with a chuckle.

My finger froze and I looked up at Elaine, this woman I'd never seen before. "Huh?"

The Queen stepped forward again. "They've stood the test of time too, these classic pieces never go out of style. And although I adore your new season designs, I won't be changing the decor in a hurry. We get so many compliments from clients on the look of our salon and I always tell them it's thanks to KC Interiors."

KC Interiors... KC Interiors. The ad I saw in the virtual magazine at the doctor's! Do I really work for this company, designing homewares? Or could it be that I even own this company?

"My best friend certainly has talent, doesn't she?" Elaine said to The Queen, who nodded. "Anyway, are we going to get cracking on our YouthMagic facials or what?" She rubbed her hands together. "I think I'm beyond help, but it's worth a shot," she said, tipping her head back in a laugh.

"It's never too late, Elaine. Everyone can be a Queen of Beauty." The Queen glided towards a long red carpet that ran down the hallway and gestured for us to follow. When I caught up with her, she stopped for a moment and placed a hand on my shoulder. "You're going to feel like a new woman when you walk out of here, Kelli. I promise."

A hopeful smile stretched across my face. "I'm counting on it."

Chapter 7
Facials, Friendships and Fairy Tales

"Youth is a disease from which we all recover." – Dorothy Fulheim

AFTER CHANGING into black and gold gowns, the three of us took residence on our respective tables in the group treatment room. Apparently Diora had asked a few weeks ago if I wanted a private room, but I'd suggested we have a group session, so we could chat and catch up. Or more likely, so Diora could chat and Elaine and I could lie there quietly. Although, I got the feeling Elaine could probably give Diora a run for her money.

As I was the birthday girl, I was being treated by The Queen herself, who I found out had the rather unroyal name of Barb and had apparently been doing my waxing for the last ten years.

Elaine's therapist was Barb's daughter, Jilly, and Diora was to be given the Pregnant Princess treatment by Karina, a beautiful Asian woman with hair that appeared glued in place and who assured Elaine and I that we too would feel like Princesses after our YouthMagic facials. Hopefully, because the only princess I felt like was Princess Fiona from Shrek. The ogre version.

Elaine released a sigh as Jilly lathered cleanser onto her face and Barb did the same to mine. "That feels so good," Elaine moaned.

"Our YouthMagic cleanser has a proprietary skin-relaxing ingredient, which opens up the pores for deep penetration of the cleansing nano-particles," Jilly explained.

The creamy yet textured sloshing around my face sure felt great, but I hoped they would ensure my pores were closed on leaving the salon. Enlarged pores were unforgiving in certain light conditions, although they kept photographic airbrush artists in business.

Jilly continued her well-rehearsed script about the powers of Egyptian crushed micro-sand and then her tone lightened. "You know, one of my regular clients calls this the *Better Than Sex* facial."

"Jilly!" Barb scolded and I held back a laugh for fear of drowning in microscopic Egyptian sand if I opened my mouth.

Elaine had no such fear. "Honey, I'd be happy with a facial even half as good. I've practically been living like a nun since my divorce three years ago," she said. "Well, minus all the praying. Unless you count holy crap, bloody hell and dear God, why me?"

Okay, now I couldn't hold back the laugh. It burst out of me, splatters of cleanser spraying across the room. And then I snorted, inhaling a clump of cleanser and having to sit up quickly to cough it out.

"Sorry, Barb, maybe we should have booked private rooms after all," Diora said.

"Not to worry, love," she replied, wiping cleanser from the table, opposite wall and my gown.

"Must not laugh during facial," Karina intruded. "Skin must relax. Laughter not good."

"Sorry," Elaine and I mumbled in unison, and I sunk back into position, feeling like a naughty schoolgirl.

As Barb exfoliated the inner walls of my pores, I wondered who this woman – this apparent best friend of mine lying on the bed next to me – was. What happened to Selena? I mean, I know what happened to her, but who was Elaine? How did we become friends? She couldn't have been a model. No offence, but she didn't have the bone structure for it. And divorced too... the poor woman.

Elaine moaned some more and Jilly said, "See, my client was right, wasn't she?" Barb shushed her daughter again.

"I can't remember the last time I felt this good," Elaine slurred. "Actually, I think it was when my youngest finally began sleeping through the night. After three kids I knew I was done with babies and that blessed morning I woke after eight hours straight, I thought I'd died and gone to Heaven."

"So in your case it could be called the *Better Than Sleep* facial," Jilly suggested.

"Now that, my friend, would get you a truckload of business from all the sleep-deprived mothers out there."

"Speaking of sleep-deprived," Barb said. "Looks like someone hasn't been getting their forty winks lately."

An earthy snore sounded from one of the beds. Diora was fast asleep! So much for being the life of the facial party.

"And the baby's not even born yet," Elaine commented. "She won't know what's hit her, ain't that right, Kel? Remember what it was like when the kids were young?"

I'd only ever been sleep deprived through choice. Late night parties and early morning photo shoots – it wasn't that bad. You'd just make up for it later. No big deal.

"It was so long ago, I don't really remember," I said.

"The sleep deprivation must have fried your memory! You had a terrible time with Ryan. You said it was the reason you never had any more children after him. Turned you off for good."

Hmm, his overactive adrenalin must have started young then. Probably bungy jumped down the birth canal. "I guess I just shut out the trauma of it all." I faked a sniff. "Anyway, I'm sure Diora will cope fine, she's a strong woman."

I barely knew Diora but somehow I knew that to be true and not only because I'd overheard her giving attitude to the baby store representative, but because I could sense it. She exuded confidence, commanded respect and most likely got her way quite a lot. I smiled to myself as an unfamiliar sense of pride appeared.

More snores sounded from Diora's gaping mouth, despite Karina continuing her treatment. It must have been catching, because I yawned a big stretchy yawn and my mouth didn't seem to go back where it was supposed to. My skin elasticity, or lack thereof, really sucked.

Beep!

"Oh, Kelli, you really should mute your e-pad while you're in here," Elaine scolded.

"Yes, yes, sorry. In a sec." Not that I knew how to do that. I lifted my wrist to look at my e-pad. It was a message from William:

> Ryan said the bungy jump went well. I'm so proud of you!

I replied with a quick *thanks*, then pretended to mute the e-pad.

Beep!

Crap.

> Speaking of bungy jumping, it's given me some creative ideas for the bedroom *wink-wink*
> Looking fwd to trying them out tonight ;) ~ W

Double crap. Stunned, horrified and trapped in several other awkward states of emotion, I flung my arm back down, ignoring the message.

Beep!

"Kelli!"

"Sorry!" I squinted at the e-pad:

> Did you get my message just now? I said I'm looking fwd to trying out my bungy-inspired-bedroom-ideas tonight, after the guests have gone. xx

Arghh! He didn't have to say it again! My finger shook as I typed a reply:

> Yes, got your message loud & clear. Sorry, can't chat, having facial right now. ~ K

Beep!

> Of course, sorry sweets. Talk later. Mwah! ~ W

Geez, he even tried to kiss me through text message.

I placed my arm back down, hoping no one else would send a message. Then I wondered why my dad hadn't sent a happy birthday message yet. Oh well, it was still early.

Warmth spread across my face. "Time for the special YouthMagic regenerating mask," Barb said. "This will penetrate deep to target wrinkles at their core and work with the skin's own healing system to encourage collagen formation. In other words; reducing fine lines and adding firmness and radiance."

"Do you think you could put that on my whole body?" I asked.

Barb laughed. "We do have a YouthMagic body wrap, but that will have to be for another day," she said.

It didn't matter, I swore I could feel myself getting younger with each stroke of her hands, like she wiped away the old and revealed the young me. Warm blood circulated through my skin, as though I was lying on a Caribbean island, soaking up the sun. Whatever was in this mask must be doing the trick. In fact, it seemed to be spreading throughout my whole body. My gown suddenly seemed too hot, like I'd been lying in the sun a bit too long. Maybe that was how this mask worked, giving the skin a rush of heat to eliminate the evidence of age. Only now I felt like I was lying in the sun and someone had rubbed chilli on my face and then put me into an oven.

My heart raced and I squirmed on the bed. "What's in this stuff? I'm on fire!"

"Kelli, are you all right?" Barb removed her hands from my face and I sat upright, fanning my face with my hands, but they too were hot.

"What's happening to me?" My breathing quickened and Elaine sat up too. Diora stirred slightly then released another snore. "Arghh! I need water, or a fan, or ice – something cold, quick!" I stood and turned this way and that while Barb urged me to sit down and take a deep breath.

I didn't listen, but went to the sink and splashed water on my face, undoing Barb's handiwork. I continued until all the mask was off, my face a dripping mess, but still burning.

"Kel, calm down. You're probably just having a hot flush," Elaine said stiffly through a masked face, trying not to move her mouth.

"A what?" I kept fanning my face and Barb handed me a glass of water which I sculled instantly.

"Hot flush. You've been having them for a while now, since you started going through menopause."

Oh no, it couldn't be true. I was fifty, a mother, a grandmother-to-be *and* menopausal. I must have been a criminal in a past life to deserve this. *Why, oh why was this happening?*

"Breathe slowly, Kelli, in and out," Barb instructed, as she massaged something cool onto my temples and then onto my wrists.

"Don't worry," Elaine said. "They'll gradually reduce in frequency and severity. Mine only lasted a couple of years and then went away, about the same time as Peter left me. Funny that."

That's it. If I could wish for anything right now, I'd wish to be a man. They have it so easy, they don't even realise how good they've got it. Bastards. I slowed my breathing and drank another glass of water, and gradually the heat dissipated, relief flooding my body.

"Feeling better?" Barb asked.

"Much," I replied. "Are you sure it wasn't one of the ingredients in that mask?"

Barb shook her head. "If anything, the mask should have a slight cooling effect. I'd say it was definitely a hot flush, I've had them too, I'd recognise one anywhere. Why don't you lie down and we'll start again?"

"Well, if you're sure the product won't cause it to happen again, then all right." I wasn't about to lose my chance of becoming the real me again.

I shifted position to lie down again and Diora woke up. "Did I fall asleep?"

Everyone nodded.

"What'd I miss?"

"Oh, nothing much. Just another day at the office," Jilly said with a grin.

Diora settled back down and closed her eyes again, all of us silent as the facials continued. Drowsiness followed and for a moment I thought I'd even fallen asleep, but couldn't be sure. My mind drifted, thoughts and memories floated around, and I relaxed for the first time today. When Barb announced softly that it was time to get up and she would meet me in the next room for hair and make-up, I felt like telling her to get stuffed. I could lay here forever. And then I remembered.

Take Ten Years Off. Proven to work. I opened my eyes and stood. Elaine, Diora and the therapists were nowhere in sight. With haste I walked to the mirror above the sink and prepared to see my youthful glow again. My smile sunk into a frown as the same old Kelli McSnelly stared back. I was somewhat softer around the eyes, my skin moistened with a dewy glow, but there was no denying my age. It hadn't worked.

My frown lifted for a moment when I realised I still had my hair and make-up session to go and maybe that would be the final trigger that would shoot me backwards in time. Yes, I just had to stay positive. The facial was the primer and the make-up would do the rest. It had to. It bloody had to or I would consider jumping off that bungy tower without the rope this time.

I removed my gown, revealing my coral-coloured outfit, then, raising my chin I pushed open the door into the adjoining room to find Elaine showing Jilly photos of hairstyles on her e-pad and Diora sinking her feet into a footbath.

"We thought you'd never emerge," Barb said. "C'mon, it's time for your hair to get some attention."

I sat in a chair and Barb fluffed my hair about with her fingers. "I take it you've already washed it today, so I'll just style it. I hear you've got a business meeting soon. I'll make it professional yet feminine, classy yet sexy."

"What are you wearing tonight, Kel?" asked Elaine.

I almost said, 'the red shimmery dress I bought last week', but then realised that would have been twenty-five years ago and I'd bought that dress to wear to my twenty-fifth birthday party. Tonight was my fiftieth and with any luck I wouldn't be around to have to decide what to wear. "It's a surprise," I said. "What about you?" Might as well humour her.

"Oh, you won't believe what I picked up, I can't wait for you to see it," she replied.

The poor woman would have to wait because I wasn't going to see it.

"How many guests are you having?" Jilly asked.

Oh, she was looking at me. "Um..." Diora, help me out here.

"I think around forty people are coming," Diora revealed.

Thanks, Diora. Talk about mother-daughter mind reading. And forty people, huh? So that's how many friends I had in this life. Not bad. I wondered who they could be and if I would recognise them. But I wouldn't have to wonder, because tonight I'd be seeing my closest friends for a classy dinner, followed by Grant's proposal. I had to keep that in the forefront of my mind. The image of him on one knee (he was used to that, being a photographer and having to get into weird positions to get the right shot), popping open a velvet case and dazzling me with a shiny ring that could be seen from the moon.

"What are you thinking about?" Elaine asked. "You're smiling like you've just, you know..."

'Huh?" I snapped myself out of my visualisation. "Oh, I was just thinking about the man I love."

"Aww, how sweet. Will is so lucky to have such a caring wife."

"What makes you think I'm talking about William?" I snapped.

"Mum!" Diora shot me a fierce questioning look.

Oops. William was her father and I couldn't upset a

pregnant woman. "Just kidding!" Not. "Of course I'm thinking of your father. He's so... nice," was all I could think of to say.

"He's better than nice. That man's been an absolute winner of a husband in my opinion," Elaine said. "I wish I'd married him instead of Peter. Sorry, Diora." She laughed.

She could have him as far as I was concerned. The only man I wanted was Grant. Barb combed some gooey product into my hair.

"Oh well, there's no turning back time," Elaine mused. "Peter gave me three beautiful children and we did have a good marriage mostly. We just... grew resentful, I guess." Jilly slid a straightening iron over Elaine's hair, forcing her curls into submission. "If I hadn't given up my dreams for him so he could have his career, maybe things would have been different, who knows?"

"It's not too late to follow your dreams now, Elaine," said Barb.

"I'm fifty-three, love. My boat sailed out years ago."

"I'm fifty-six. And I think you can always catch another boat," Barb said, tipping my head forward and attaching a clip to the top portion of my grey-black head of hair.

"Hear, hear," Diora agreed. "Most women live to one hundred these days and men to about ninety-two, so there's plenty of years left in you yet," she reassured Elaine, while Karina rubbed something into Diora's feet. She'd opted for a pedicure instead of a hairstyle, since she apparently hadn't been able to reach her feet for the last two months and they'd been unacceptably devoid of coloured polish for far too long.

I almost told them about my plans for an international modelling career, but bit my tongue. That boat sailed out twenty-five years ago, but as soon as I could get back, I'd be on it, steering that boat to the future I wanted and no way in hell would I let any icebergs get in my way.

"There, what do you think?" Barb asked when she'd finished my hair.

My lifeless strands had been converted into a voluminous mass of windswept hair, brushed back from my face like I had a permanent high speed fan in front of me. It was an improvement and obviously the latest trend as I'd seen other women with a similar hairdo, but not what I'd choose for myself. Anyway, bring on the make-up.

I asked Barb to turn my chair around from the mirror so I could be surprised when she finished. If this worked, I'd be looking back at the real me in the mirror and Diora and Elaine would either not be there or would simply be strangers who'd come into the salon for a makeover like me.

I closed my eyes as Barb brushed the soft eye-shadow coated bristles of a make-up brush across my lids and then expertly slid an eye pencil across the junction between my eyelids and eyelashes. She applied some sort of gel to my cheeks and they tingled. I couldn't see what she was doing, but I swear I could feel my cheeks lifting and the crow's feet around my eyes walking away.

"You're enjoying this, aren't you?" Barb stated.

"Sure am," I replied. I was in my element. I was no stranger to having strangers create art with my face and I breathed a sigh of contentment.

After cooling my lips with a coat of moist lipstick, Barb had me close my eyes and she sprayed my face with a cool, refreshing mist. This had to be it. It was happening. I could feel it. The droplets of mist tingled like snowflakes on my face and I imagined them to be tiny fairies casting a spell of youth on my skin.

Finally, Barb spun my chair around to face the mirror. My youthful reflection smiled back, but then I realised my eyes were still closed, so I opened them. Oh my God. I couldn't believe it. A swirl of helplessness spiralled from within and a splutter escaped my throat. Then another... and another, until I was sobbing uncontrollably.

"Kelli, Kelli, what's wrong? Aren't you happy with the result?" Barb gripped my shoulders. Elaine came over and placed an arm around my back. Even Diora manoeuvred herself up from the chair and waddled urgently towards me.

"I'm... it's... why?" Words jammed in my throat and I longed to tell them, to scream from the top of my lungs that I was really twenty-five and didn't belong here. But I couldn't. They would send me to a facility for sure. That would be worse, because they'd make me wear an awful hospital gown with an exposed back, or a pair of orange overalls or something else hideous and if I kept insisting I was Kelli Crawford and had travelled a quarter of a century into the future, they might even call in an exorcist.

No. No matter what I did, I was stuck in this warped fairy tale and no Prince Charming would be coming to rescue me. I had to pretend. I had to come up with something, some reason for my outburst. Besides, Diora had given me this as a birthday present and I couldn't bear to upset her. If I did she might start having more of those Braxton thingies and she might have the baby in the footbath!

I forced air into my lungs and steadied my stomach muscles, resisting the involuntary pulsing that had overtaken me a moment ago.

"Mum?"

"Kel?"

"Kelli?"

They all looked at me with genuine worry on their faces.

"I'm sorry. It's just that, lately I've been feeling like my life has been passing me by. It's all happened too fast and I can't believe I'm actually fifty." Well, that was no lie.

"But I thought you'd feel great after having your hair and make-up done," Elaine questioned.

I glanced at myself in the mirror, my expertly coiffed hair exposing my painted face, with coral-coloured cheeks to match my outfit and coral-coloured eyeliner under... my eyebrows? Since when do make-up artists draw a bright coloured line under your eyebrows? Not only that, my lips were coral too – with a sharp gold outline. *What the hell?* I shook my head and almost laughed at the result.

The women around me still looked concerned and I had to reassure them. "When I turned around just now and saw my face, I cried because... well, because you did such a great job, Barb and... I wish I could look like this all the time." Ouch. That was hard to say.

Barb visibly softened and a hand flew to her chest in apparent relief. Elaine stepped back and smiled. Diora rubbed my back.

"Oh, Mum. You always look great and today you'll just look extra special."

Extra special indeed. If Selena could see me now, she'd laugh till she ran out of air and as for Grant, he'd... well, hopefully he'd stand by me and say it didn't matter what I looked like. Although, something inside told me it did matter to him.

"You're going to knock everyone's socks off at the party tonight, Mum. You don't even look fifty! I wouldn't be surprised if some of the guests bought fortieth birthday cards by mistake."

I must have taught my daughter the art of lying well.

"It's going to be a great night and just you wait till you see the birthday cake Dad's organised for you. It's gorgeous! You can look forward to that and to blowing out the candles, and making a wish," she said.

A wish, birthday cake... that's it! How silly was I to think that bungy jumping or a facial could turn back the clock. The idea seemed ludicrous now. But making a wish on one's birthday cake? That's what happens in the movies – they make a wish and something magical happens. And in my case, well, I knew exactly what I'd be wishing for.

All the helplessness spiralled back down into oblivion and I knew the cake had to be it. I just had to get through this day as best I could and await the inevitable singing of Happy Birthday, dancing flames from the candles holding the key to my dreams.

I stood. "You're right. It's going to be a great night. And a great day. And I cannot wait to see my birthday cake!"

"That's the spirit!" Diora cried out. "Well, don't waste this day of yours, Mum. When are you meeting Kasey for lunch?"

I'd forgotten about my sister! Selena may be far away and Grant nowhere in sight, but Kasey must be here somewhere... and she would be forty-seven years old!

"Um, I can't remember."

"That's the damn menopause again," Elaine said. "Not only do you get to experience four seasons in one day and the surprise of finding random hairs growing from odd places, it kills your memory too."

Hmmm... this couldn't be just a severe case of menopausal memory loss, could it? I shook my head. Of course it couldn't and Dr Vischek would have said something if that was even remotely possible, wouldn't he?

"Permanently," Elaine continued. "The hot flushes may be gone from my life but the shoddy memory remains. The only thing I seem to remember these days is my credit card number."

A knowing laugh emerged from Barb's mouth. "Well, use it or lose it – so they say."

Elaine laughed too. "And boy, do I use it!" She held up her e-pad. "Speaking of which, here you go." She positioned the e-pad near Barb's payment scanner and Diora approached with hers too. "Put half on my VISA. Diora and I are sharing the cost for today."

"Thanks, girls," I said.

"Our pleasure." Elaine then gestured to my e-pad. "Look in your calendar, Kel, to remind you when to meet Kasey."

Of course. It seemed one couldn't live without these e-pads. They stored everything and did everything. I pinched the screen and pressed Calendar on the menu. "In twenty minutes, at City Junction Cafe."

"Oh, I love that place," Elaine said. "Peter and I used to go there quite a lot, until... until we didn't anymore." She looked sad and then shook herself out of it. "Anyway, enjoy! And order the most expensive meal, no doubt Kasey will be paying."

I hoped she wasn't still angry with me. I turned towards the door. And then I realised our fight would have been twenty-five years ago and with any luck we hadn't had another one recently. As in, recently in the future. The past of the future. The – *oh, I'm confused!* Anyway, if she hated me she wouldn't be meeting me for lunch. Ooh, I couldn't wait to see her!

Beep! A new message from William:

> Hope facial was nice. Hey do you know if the hardware store sells some sort of heavy duty rope that's stretchy? ~ W

Heavy duty stretchy rope? Why would I know anything about that, or hardware stores? He was the man of the house, shouldn't he know that kind of stuff? Oh wait... he's not really the practical, outdoorsy, whip-up-a-masterpiece-with-a-hammer-and-nails-and-wood kind of guy.

I typed *no idea, sorry* then gulped. He couldn't be serious about the bungy bedroom activities, could he?

Beep!

> Don't worry, I'll have a look. Just about to go on my lunch break. If not, one of those stretchy exercise bands you have at home might do the trick.

My God, he *was* serious. I gulped down my gulp and turned to Diora. "Will you be okay getting back to your car?"

She flicked a hand at me. "Of course, Mum, the baby may be slowing me down but it's not stopping me from getting where I need to go. I just need double the time. Or maybe triple. Go and enjoy your day and I'll see you tonight." She gave me a quick hug, followed by Elaine's.

I walked out the door and turned left.

Elaine poked her head out the door of the salon. "Kel, where are you going? It's that way." She pointed right.

"Oh, whoops!" I waved to her and walked in the other direction. I had to find a map or something.

At the top of what seemed to be a cross between an escalator and a lift was a large floating screen with a layout of the shopping centre. I typed in a search for City Junction Cafe and a red flag appeared, followed by a green flag showing me where I currently was, and the route I'd need to take to get to my destination. I imprinted the route into my mind and began walking.

Just before turning a corner that would lead me to the cafe, a store drew my attention. It was one of those new-age shops, with the smell of incense in the air and brightly coloured tie-dyed outfits displayed on a rack at the front, next to a sign that read: *Psychic Expo Here Today: Fri-Sun Only!* I could see four psychics sitting in makeshift cardboard booths, each with their name written above and a sign saying *15 Minute Psychic Readings - $300.*

Three hundred bucks? They had to be kidding! It looked like I wasn't the only thing inflated in the future. Three hundred dollars was probably equivalent to about fifty dollars back in my time. Back in my time? I was starting to sound like a grandmother.

I glanced at the time on my e-pad. Fifteen minutes exactly till I was to meet Kasey and two of the four psychics were currently available. I wouldn't normally have considered seeing a psychic – they were probably quacks – but what I was going through right now wasn't exactly normal, so maybe there was something in this stuff. Maybe they could tell me what was happening to me and why I'd skipped ahead to the future.

Could be a waste of time, or it could help me make sense of everything. It was worth a shot.

Chapter 8
Past, Present and Future

"To know the road ahead, ask those coming back." – Chinese proverb

I ENTERED the shop and assessed the two psychics with a twist of my lip – Liliana, or Rosie? Rosie gave me a look that said *please pick me*, so in sympathy, I did.

Once payment was confirmed on my e-pad, Rosie drew in an excessively deep breath through her teeth, almost whistling, and then released it so violently I thought her teeth might fly from their sockets. In fact, I think my windswept hairdo was more like hurricane-swept now.

"You are going through a period of transition right now, yes?" she asked.

I nodded. If only she knew the extent of that transition. Well, maybe she did.

"I sense that you are feeling... what's the word..." she circled a hand repeatedly, "... ambiguous about a situation at the moment. You're not sure which direction to go in, yes?"

"Um, not really. I know which direction I want to go in, but I can't seem to get there."

"Yes of course, that's what I meant. You're torn between where you are and where you want to be."

No, she definitely said I wasn't sure which direction to go in. Strike one for this psychic. She drew another deep breath and I held on to the edge of the table, leaning back, bracing myself for the onslaught. Whoosh! There we go.

"You have children, yes?"

"Yes."

"Beautiful children, I can see." She smiled. I shrugged and tilted my head. "Oh wait, I'm sensing something... yes, that's it... you're wishing you got a chance to have another child and you're feeling like you've missed out, yes?"

Was she for real? I never planned for any children and certainly didn't want another one. "Actually no, I don't wish that I had another child." Strike two. Another strike and I'd be outta here.

I shifted in my chair and Rosie did the same, and then she inhaled again, sucking the oxygen from our immediate environment. I gripped the table and wondered if oxygen masks might drop from the ceiling and a *fasten seatbelt* sign would flash in preparation for the impending turbulence. Whoosh! Oh, dear God. I'd paid three hundred big ones for this?

"I feel that deep down you did wish to have another one, but you're hiding this in your subconscious. Sometimes we are not ready to accept our deepest desires."

I knew very well what my deepest desires were and a crying, messy, totally dependent miniature human being was not one of them!

"Okay, I'm sensing something else now..."

That I was not particularly satisfied with this reading?

"Your mother."

I sat up tall and pricked my ears. Maybe she'd been warming up and was actually onto something now.

"I feel you haven't spoken to her in a while."

Well, that's true.

"I'm getting the sense that you need to give her a call, perhaps take her out for lunch. Have a good old mother-daughter catch up."

Strike three. That was it. I pushed my chair back and stood, shaking my head. Rosie was a dud and in fact, I could probably do a better job.

"Wait, what's the matter?" Rosie asked, standing up.

"Just how am I supposed to take my dead mother out to lunch, huh?"

Rosie's face went rosy and she sat back down in defeat. I turned to walk away but someone's hand stopped me. Long purple fingernails gripped my wrist and my gaze followed the length of an arm until it met with the other psychic's face. Liliana.

"Wait. I can help you."

I tried to shrug her hand away but it wouldn't budge. "No, no! You people are frauds!"

"It's your birthday, today." It wasn't a question, but a confident statement.

I narrowed my eyes at Liliana. "How did you know that?"
She smiled.

"No, someone could have told you, or you could have been following me. I'm going now." Again I tried to move but this woman sustained her grip, even stronger than the breath from Miss Hurricane who was now dabbing at the corner of her eye with a tissue.

"This birthday has not been what you expected, has it?" Liliana asked.

I shook my head and looked down at my feet. "No, it hasn't."

"It's strange, when I read your energy, instead of getting a continual flow, I sense a sudden interruption. Like a big chunk of your life has gone missing – it's strange, I tell you."

Intrigued, I looked up into her bright blue eyes. "Go on."

"Come." She gestured to her booth. "Take a seat and let me see what else comes up for you. What's your name, dear?"

"Kelli." As though hypnotised I obliged, setting my backside down onto the chair, much to the dismay of Rosie, who escaped from her booth into a room out the back of the store.

Liliana took a normal breath like a normal person and continued. "It's as though you're living two different lives. I get a sense of the person you were in the past, when you were younger – very strong willed and determined, with your whole life planned out. And now, the person you are at present is more... flexible. More creative. More spontaneous. And yet, it's like there's this string trying to pull you back to the past and another one trying to pull you forward. You're stuck. Stuck in the middle and you wish more than anything that you could go back and live the kind of life you used to live. Is this making any sense to you?" Liliana's eyes searched mine.

The tingle of goose bumps appeared on my arms and tiny hairs stood up on end. "Yes, it makes perfect sense." Finally, someone who understands.

"Do you have any specific questions you'd like to ask me?"

Did I have any questions? Boy, did I have questions! Where would I start? How was it possible to wake up twenty-five years in the future, why did I marry William of all people, why did I have children when I couldn't even handle a pet, and why am I not the world's most famous supermodel?

I lowered my voice to a whisper. "Liliana, do you believe in..." I glanced around surreptitiously to make sure there were no men in white jumpsuits getting ready to whisk me away to a facility for middle-aged menopausal psychopaths. "... time travel?"

Liliana didn't gasp, or bring her hands to her mouth, or call security – she didn't even flinch at the question, as though asked this kind of thing every day. "I'm not totally convinced that it's possible... in the sense that a person can travel to the future, or the past for that matter, and remain the same age like you see in the movies."

Damn. And I thought she'd believe me.

"But," she leaned in close to me over the table, her eyes darting right and left as though checking for eavesdroppers, "I have heard of a phenomenon known as a *fast forward*, in which a person is transported to the future – their future – but their age adjusts to what it would actually be in that particular time."

A loud bell sounded in my head as though I'd just hit the jackpot and my jaw dropped further than it had during my morning bungy jump. "Seriously? There's such a thing and it has a name?"

Liliana nodded. "But I only know of a few cases through my spiritual colleagues. It's all very hush-hush, as a couple of people who reportedly experienced a fast forward and were brave enough to share their story, were publicly ridiculed. So-called experts classed them as delusional. They were turned away by their families and friends and left to wonder if they truly had gone crazy."

"Holy cow." Blood thumped hard in my veins and blue bulges lined my hands as they gripped the table.

"Wait... are you telling me you've experienced one of these?" Liliana's eyes were like needles, piercing into my soul.

I cleared my throat and took a breath almost as epic as Rosie's. "I believe I *am* experiencing one right now."

The cardboard booth wobbled as Liliana suddenly leaned

backwards, her chair bumping into the back of the booth. "Now? As in... you're in your future, right now?"

I bit my bottom lip and nodded.

"Well, I'll be damned!" she said. "Never thought I'd live to see the day. So tell me more..." She leaned forward again. "I get the feeling you were a young woman when this happened, say early twenties?"

"Twenty-four. Today was supposed to be my twenty-fifth birthday, but, well... look at me. I'm no spring chicken! Today's my fiftieth."

"And you remember nothing of the last quarter of a century? You went to bed twenty-four and woke up fifty?"

"Uh-huh."

Liliana kept shaking her head. "And is this future – your life – how you thought it would be?"

"Not at all. It's completely different!" I filled her in on my normal life and my life as it was right now. She laughed when I told her I was so desperate to get back I even bungy jumped. "Why me, Liliana? Why did this happen to me?"

"Only you can know that, dear. But all the reported cases had something in common. According to them, their life was going perfectly, or so it seemed, when the fast forward propelled them into the future and a life they didn't recognise. And also, they each had lost a parent prematurely." She placed her purple finger-nailed hand on mine. "Your mother was sick, wasn't she? I can feel pain in my joints and a deep depression in my heart."

"Yes."

"But it wasn't the illness that killed her, it was something else."

"Yes." I lowered my head, my grip on the table softening, hands now trembling. "She had rheumatoid arthritis. Severe enough that she couldn't follow her dream of being a professional dancer."

"She wasn't that old when she died. She had you quite young, yes?" Liliana enquired.

I nodded. "She still had hopes and dreams she wanted to pursue. The symptoms subsided somewhat during her second pregnancy apparently, but after she'd had my little sister she..." I searched my mind for the words.

"Became a different person?"

"Yes, exactly. There were times when she was in a sort of remission and would frantically rush about doing things, taking me shopping and to photo shoots, but then the condition would flare up and the mood swings would start again." I shifted in my chair at the uncomfortable memories. "She'd get angry, yell and then cry, sometimes for hours. I never really knew if it was from the stress of the disease or the piles of medication she took."

Liliana patted my hand. "She began relying on certain things to numb the pain... physically and emotionally."

"Alcohol, mostly, and sleeping tablets. One day I found her on the couch. I thought she was asleep, but when I approached her she was pale, so pale. Her chest wasn't moving. An empty bottle of wine and containers of medication were on the coffee table. Some of the pills had fallen to the floor and I knew she was gone. The only thing I didn't know – still don't know – is whether it was an accident or..."

My voice cracked and I couldn't bring myself to say the 's' word. I mentally pushed down on the swollen bubble of sadness rising in my chest. "Anyway, that was a long time ago. I haven't thought about that day for a long time. It's probably best if I forget about it."

"Dear, your mother wants you to know that it was indeed an accident. She didn't realise what she was doing and only wanted the pain gone," Liliana spoke softly. "She also wants to tell you that she's sorry and she's showing me a piece of paper being ripped up. Does that mean anything to you?"

I rubbed my ears as I heard the painful rip of paper, as though it was my heart being torn in half, but before I could respond to Liliana a beep sounded from my e-pad. It was a message from Kasey:

> How close are you? Am at the cafe, see you soon I hope. Kasey.

Oh no, I'd completely lost track of time! Liliana's reading had gone over the fifteen minutes, compounded by Rosie's incompetence and there was so much more I wanted to talk to her about. I glanced behind where several people waited in line for the psychics. "I have to go, but thank you so much." I grasped Liliana's hands and stood. "Can I come back later, what time do you finish?"

"I'm here till five, then off to my daughter's engagement party." Liliana smiled. "I'll be here over the weekend as well." She then leaned close to me. "Don't be scared, dear, I'm sure you will return to your normal life, but you were sent here for a reason. When you've realised what that reason is, go back to your life armed with the knowledge of how to make your life the best it can be."

I clamped my lips together and nodded, before turning away and walking out the door. Away from the one person who believed me and knew I wasn't crazy. I took another of those breaths that everyone says to take and checked the time on my e-pad. I was determined, that by the time the birthday cake was placed in front of me I'd be ready to go home. I'd understand why I'd been sent here and it would all be over.

I could do this. I could get through the rest of this day. It would be a piece of cake, pardon the pun. Only five hours until the guests would arrive at my party and then they'd sing Happy Birthday, and I'd make my wish. Only five hours. What could possibly go wrong in that amount of time?

Chapter 9
Five Hours to Go

"If we could be twice young and twice old we could correct all our mistakes." – Euripides

A MAN in a suit nodded at me as I walked through the doors of City Junction Cafe. "Good afternoon, madam, do you have a reservation?"

"I'm meeting my sister, Kasey, it might be under Crawford?"

The man removed one of his hands from behind his back to press a screen next to the door. "There's no Crawford, could it be under another name?"

It couldn't be under McSnelly, could it? I was too embarrassed to ask. In fact, by the looks of the opulent interior with mahogany tables and crystal chandeliers I doubt they'd let anyone by the name of McSnelly inside.

A woman from one of the tables by the window glanced in my direction, her rounded cheeks reflecting the light from outside. She was definitely my little sister. Just twenty-five years older. She waved at me and I waved too, taken aback by how classy she looked. Her once dishevelled mop of hair was moulded into a sleek bob and she was actually wearing lipstick!

"Don't worry, I see her," I said to the man.

He glanced towards Kasey and with a sweep of his hand, ushered me through before returning to his vigilant stance. All sibling rivalry dissolved as I approached the table, my tense muscles relaxing at the sight of a familiar face, even though somewhat different. "Kasey, Kasey, it's so good to see you!" I flung my arms around her and she laughed.

"I saw you yesterday, why so happy? Ah, you've had one of those better-than-sex facials, haven't you?"

"I sure have." I sat down on the suede chair.

"Happy birthday! I heard you've had a lot of fun so far?"

"Well, apart from my trip to the doctor's this morning, that's never fun."

"Doctor? What's wrong?"

"Oh, nothing, I think I just came down with the common cold, but it's mostly gone now." I managed a tiny fake sniff for effect.

"The common cold? Good one, sis!" Kasey faked a hearty laugh. "You know how many times I've heard that joke?"

"Joke? What do you mean?"

She laughed again. "Oh yeah, tell the person who found a cure for the common cold that you *have* the common cold. Seriously, Kelli, the joke's so old now, but I'll humour you because it's your birthday." She winked.

I faked a chuckle, while inside I racked my brain to process what she'd just said. *Tell the person who found a cure for the common cold that you have the common cold.* Was she serious? Did she actually mean that she'd...?

"Hey, Doc, fancy seeing you here!" A grey-haired man said as he walked past our table.

"Yes, fancy that," Kasey replied with an exaggerated tone of sarcasm. The man continued on his way to a table of similar looking men in boring trousers, shirts and terrible ties.

Doc? I eyed Kasey curiously.

She thumbed over her shoulder in the direction the man had passed. "He says that all the time. It's getting a tad old. Most of the staff from FutureTech Labs eat here at least three times a week."

"Old... like the joke about the common cold, huh?" I tried, hoping to extract more information from her.

"Yeah, and the one where people tell me they have some kind of bug. I mean, it's been over five years since my discovery." Kasey took a swig of water from her glass.

Wow. She was serious. "Well, um... I'm very proud of what you've achieved."

"Thanks. Who would have thought that a common household bug would hold the key to the eradication of the cold virus, eh? I still shake my head in disbelief when I think about it."

Holy crap... my sister found The Cure for the common cold! No wonder she looked all flash and we were meeting in a place like this. She must be worth a fortune! Okay, if I ever get back, I'll never tease her about her bug collecting habit again.

Beep! A message on my e-pad.

Hi hon, the hardware store was all out of heavy duty stretchy rope I'm afraid. But I picked up this neat multi-pocket tool storage belt that I can wear. I'll fill it with the supplies we'll need: a can of whipped cream, jar of chocolate spread, a feather and one of those massage roller things. Off to buy them! xxx

Please, ground, swallow me up right now.
Beep!

> P.S Can't wait to see you at the meeting. Love you – W.

I opened my calendar. Meeting – 3:30 p.m. Okay, it looked like I would have to attend this meeting, since the YouthMagic facial wasn't so magic after all. I had no idea what the meeting was about... and what was that UK man's name again? Mr Tulson... Mr Turret... Mr Tugboat? Damn, I had no idea. *One step at a time, Kelli.* Right now, I was having an extremely long overdue catch-up with my sister. There was plenty of time before the meeting.

"So, what are you having?" Kasey asked, pointing to the inbuilt e-menu in the mahogany table. "Pick anything you like – my treat of course."

A bottle of wine would be good. But I should probably have some kind of protein on the side to make it a complete meal. Actually, it could be best to avoid alcohol until tonight. I wanted to keep my wits about me and I did have to drive... unless my talking and mostly self-driving car had an option for taking complete control due to birthday-induced intoxication. Nope, better not take the risk.

"Let's see..." I eyed the e-menu, but the words blurred slightly under my gaze. I leaned in closer, but they blurred even more, so I tucked my chin to my chest and leaned back. That made things clearer, but I could barely make out the words.

"What are you doing?" Kasey giggled.

I must have looked like a right idiot. "I can't seem to read the menu. Is yours blurry too?"

"Put your glasses on," she replied.

Glasses? I wouldn't be seen dead in glasses and besides, I'd never needed them.

"Honestly, Kel, I know you hate wearing them, but

presbyopia is a normal condition for people your age. You need the glasses to help focus on things up close."

Geez, not another bodily defect. I'll add that to the list of thirty-seven other afflictions for the middle-aged, shall I?

I pinched my e-pad and reopened William's message. I had no problem reading that, but the text was three times the size of the e-menu, so no wonder. "I forgot to bring my glasses."

"Then enlarge the screen."

"Oh." I tentatively pinched the screen on the table and hoped it functioned like the e-pad. It worked and a listing of the available food choices came into focus. "Hang on," I looked up at Kasey. "You're not much younger than me, how come you can read the menu so easily?"

"I had the surgery, remember? The surgery you were too chicken to have, so you opted for the glasses which you're too chicken to wear?"

"Ah yes. Well, if everything can be enlarged, why even bother with the surgery or glasses?"

"Not everything in the world is written in holo-ink, Kelli. Technology hasn't come that far."

I stifled a chuckle. Kasey may have grown with the technology, but when you've been shoved into the future suddenly you realise how far it had come. I assessed the menu options and resisted the urge to express shock at the prices. Not to mention some of the strange food combinations. By the looks of it, genetic modification really did take off, despite all the protests. Turken, cranberry and camembert melt on broccolato rosti. What the heck was that? Turken... aha! Turkey Chicken. Broccolato... ah, so someone had found a way to genetically combine a potato with broccoli, huh? Ingenious for all the vegetable haters/potato lovers out there.

"What will it be, madam?" the waiter asked me as he approached.

Madam – or in other words... old woman. I was used to being called *Miss* and *Love* and *Sweetie*.

"I'll have the turken, thanks." I swallowed a giggle.

"And I'll have the steamed salmon with roast vegetable salad," Kasey said.

Wow. She was much healthier than I remembered. She'd always ordered things like fish and chips, pizza, or hamburgers. Salmon and vegetables? I was impressed.

The waiter disappeared into the kitchen and for the second time that day my stomach grumbled. Geez, what was wrong with me? Before, I could go all day without eating and now I couldn't even last a couple of hours.

"So, how's business? I hear you're meeting *the* Mr Turrow this afternoon," Kasey enquired.

Mr Turrow... that was the guy's name! I still didn't know who he was or what the meeting was for but at least I wouldn't call him Mr Tugboat now. "Yes, that's right. Um, it's going well I guess." For all I knew, business could be on a downward spiral and Mr Turrow could be some kind of debt collector.

Hang on... business... assuming she meant my business, then I must actually own KC Interiors!

"Who would have thought all those years ago that it would turn out so successful, huh?" Kasey added. "Must be the fantastic name we came up with." She winked.

We came up with it? But it obviously stood for Kelli Crawford, my maiden name.

"I'm glad you eventually surrendered the 'Kelli's Designs' idea and went with mine. I mean, KC Interiors – it's just so brilliant how we combined our names. Poor old Will, not getting any naming rights, but he does own more of the company than I do and keeps the boat floating so to speak. We couldn't have done it without him." Kasey leaned forward. "Although, he couldn't have done it without us. Your talent, my money and his business skills… perfect!"

So much information circled around my head trying to be processed, new revelations continually added to the proverbial merry-go-round in my mind. So, my sister was part owner of my business… and William and I were not only husband and wife, but business partners. Whatever happened to not mixing business with pleasure? And the name, KC… aha! Kay-Cee… Ka-sey… Kasey Interiors! We used our initials which just so happened to sound like Kasey's name. It *was* brilliant.

Despite momentary pride at my success and the relief that I wasn't just a housewife after all, I still didn't understand why I hadn't become a successful model. Mum would have loved it… would have been so proud. I remembered what the psychic said about her being sorry and I felt all weird inside, so I made the effort to push the memory from my mind.

When the waiter arrived with our meals I was anxious to check out the turken and broccolato. I immediately sliced off a tender chunk and pierced my fork into the flesh, along with a fragment of the crispy rosti.

"Holy crap!" I exclaimed after a deep moan. "This is freakin' delicious."

Kasey's loaded fork paused near her open mouth and her eyes widened. A serious looking woman with lips like a taut rubber band glared my way from the table near us.

"What?" As I asked the question I realised I had spoken like a twenty-five-year-old as opposed to a mature woman of a certain age. Oh, and *freakin'* probably wasn't the word of the moment in the future… although had I heard Ryan saying it earlier? I couldn't remember. Nothing new there.

From then on I used more appropriate words like divine, mouth-watering and heavenly, while Kasey simply said her meal was great as usual. When we'd finished our lunch and a dessert of – get this – oyster ice cream on honeycomb wafers, I downed a mouthful of the rich, warm liqueur-free affogato I'd decided to indulge in, despite having had more than enough caffeine and adrenalin for one day. Not to mention dairy. Whether it was the melted cheese on the turken or the oyster ice cream or the affogato I didn't know, but my stomach was bloating like a balloon. Well, considering the fact that I woke up with a balloon-like stomach anyway, it was filling up like a large helium-filled balloon. With any luck it would continue inflating and float my cumbersome body back to the past. Hopefully it wouldn't suddenly deflate with a high-pitched squeal.

"Did you forget to take your enzyme tablets?" Kasey asked, gesturing towards my stomach as I rubbed it a little. "You've probably overdone the lactose."

"Damn." I nodded. I didn't know where to find any tablets as I wasn't even carrying a handbag. No one seemed to carry handbags. Poor Prada must be out of business by now. Just me and my e-pad. Unless the e-pad also stored tablets, as well as glasses for my failing eyesight? It could be like a Mary Poppins e-pad.

"I'm sure it'll pass," Kasey said, indulging in an affogato too and for the first time since I sat down opposite her at the table I noticed the diamond glinting on her left hand. On *the* finger... as in the engagement-wedding-marriage finger. A single stone cradled by a spiral of gold melded perfectly alongside a plain gold band.

My sister was married! I couldn't believe it. Kasey... a wife? I never thought I'd see the day. Well I'd guessed it was always possible, but I never saw her as the marrying type. Once, when she was about seventeen, I even thought she might be gay because she seemed to brighten up whenever my friend Rachel came over. But it turned out she just wanted to be one of us, although she never was. She was and always would be in my eyes, Kasey the bug-obsessed tomboy... which, as it seemed, had worked out well for her.

"How's hubby?" I couldn't resist asking. I wanted the goss.

"He's great. Busy with his new anti-skin cancer campaign. I'm so proud of all the awareness he's raised."

Twenty-five years later and skin cancer remained a problem by the sounds of it. Probably due to that global warming stuff. Kasey's husband was probably a medical type too, some kind of doctor or researcher perhaps? I bet he and Kasey were like twins. Two little (well, not that little) scientific types discussing bugs and... holo-ink over the breakfast table.

"Sounds like he's been a busy boy," I added, hoping for more details.

"Yes, but not too busy to come to your party tonight, of course. We're both looking forward to it."

Oh yay, I'd get to meet her husband. How cute! I smiled at my little sister, feeling suddenly protective and big-sisterly and guilty for the many times I'd made fun of her as a child.

"Why are you looking at me like that?" Kasey asked with one eyebrow cocked.

"It's just, well, do you remember the night before my twenty-fifth birthday (last night to be exact, but what could I say?), when you got upset at the bar and stormed off during my speech?"

Kasey's eyebrows drew together and she tapped at her chin. "Oh yes, you were talking about your fantastic life, while I was thinking how crappy mine was."

"Well, I can't remember if I ever apologised for whatever it was that upset you and for any times I made you feel left out. So, I'm apologising now. I'm sorry."

Kasey flicked her hand towards me. "Oh, don't be silly, it's all in the past. And besides, I was really only upset that night because of Dad."

"Dad?"

"Yeah. You would have been a mess too if you'd just found out the father you thought was flesh and blood wasn't your biological father after all."

Whoa, what?

A splatter of coffee escaped my lips and I wiped it away quickly with my hand.

"I didn't want to disturb your birthday celebrations by telling you I was only your half-sister, which is why I waited till the day after your birthday to tell you."

I wanted to yell out at the top of my lungs, *Mum had an affair?* and *We have different fathers?* but it took all my effort to remain composed. Besides, if I let loose my stomach probably would too.

Kasey looked concerned at my spluttering, so I lied and told her some coffee went down the wrong way.

"So I wasn't really upset with you at all that night, I was just feeling... like a reject, I guess. But at least it all made sense after that. I mean, you and I, we were always so different. And with Dad being a builder, a practical man who never finished high school, and Mum not having a scientific bone in her body, it was strange how I didn't resemble them. Even though I had Mum's genes too, I obviously took after the scientific, enquiring mind of Mum's physiotherapist."

Oh man, I couldn't believe it! Mum had an affair with her physio and the result of that was Kasey. Dad probably believed she was his child.

"So when did Dad find out about the affair again, I can't remember?"

"Just before Mum died she confessed. Said she didn't love the other guy, just fell in love with the pain relief he was sometimes able to provide."

"I can't believe he waited so long to tell us."

"Yeah, but I guess he was only looking out for me in his own way. Not wanting to tell me until I'd finished school and got my degree. But then I told him I was going to keep studying for my masters, followed by a PhD and the poor guy probably thought he'd never find a good time to tell me the truth!" Kasey took a quick sip of her coffee which had now melted the ice cream in the affogato.

"So," I began tentatively, "do you know if he's coming tonight?" I really wanted to talk to Dad and understand everything that had happened all those years ago.

Kasey looked at me with morbid disgust. "What do you mean is he coming tonight?"

"I mean, I'm not sure who's on the guest list so I was just wondering..."

"Stop joking around, sis. I wish I could see him again too sometimes but at six feet under, I doubt that'll be happening anytime soon."

It was as though my heart was in an elevator that had just plummeted from top to bottom of a thirty-storey building.

"Dad's... dead?"

Chapter 10
Four Hours to Go

"The man who views the world at fifty the same as he did at twenty has wasted thirty years of his life." – Muhammad Ali

"KEL, ARE YOU OKAY?" Kasey leaned forward and placed her hand on my arm. "Will texted me earlier to say you were feeling... vulnerable."

"I... I don't understand how Dad could have... died." My voice shook.

"Kel, the pancreatic cancer took him a few years back. I know we haven't discussed it much, but I feel bad too, not having been there to say goodbye."

"Why? Why did this have to happen?"

"Just life, I guess. If he hadn't expanded his building company overseas to work on those commercial developments, maybe we would have got to him sooner. But there's no point feeling guilty now." Kasey gave my arm a light squeeze.

I shook her hand from my arm, too raw for human touch.

"The disease came on so fast there was nothing we could

have done to help. He wouldn't have wanted us to see him suffer. It's understandable he didn't contact us till it was close to the end." Kasey shook her head slowly from side to side. "It's such a shame that he'd gone by the time we arrived at the hospital, I often wonder... if only we'd left a day earlier."

The emptiness sat heavy in my chest like a brick, weighing down my lungs, unable to breathe. Both my parents. Gone. I had never felt so alone in all my life.

"Oh, sorry, Kel. I shouldn't be dredging up the past on your birthday," Kasey said, a look of concern on her face.

"No, it's okay," I replied. "I need to talk about it. I don't want Dad to be forgotten." I paused, silent for a moment. "When did I last see him?" I asked, tears threatening to spill from my eyes. "I need to remember the last time I saw him."

"I think it was about a year before he died, when you took that quick trip? I didn't go of course... too caught up in my work."

"Oh, yes. That's right." How could I have let a whole year go by without seeing him again? Kasey must have been absent a lot longer. "Did you ever actually visit him, overseas?" I asked with a curious eye, as though it had simply slipped my mind.

My sister shook her head. "The last time I saw him was before he moved away. The damage had already been done by then. We'd gradually grown distant since he revealed the truth about Mum's affair." Kasey's chin dropped to her chest. "I think it hurt him to see me. To be reminded of Mum's infidelity. I don't think he felt paternal about me anymore."

My chair screeched as I stood and pushed back tears. "I'm sorry, I have to go," I said. How could our family have become such a mess?

"Wait, Kelli, talk to me. Why are you so upset after all these years?" Kasey stood too.

"My father died! I haven't even said goodbye! I wish I could see him, I miss him. It can't be true, it can't be! I just want to go home!" The tears flooded my face. Overwhelmed with the desperate need to escape, my eyes darted to the exit.

Kasey grabbed my arm. "I know it's an emotional day for you and it's normal to be reminded of the fact that Dad's not here. Not to mention Mum," she began. "But you need to be thankful that *you're* here, that you're healthy and make the most of your life. Dad wouldn't want you to be upset."

With tears burning in my eyes, I looked at my sister, now an elegant yet blurry blob in front of me... and saw Mum's eyes. We may be half-sisters, but we came from the same womb.

"I'm sorry, I don't know why I'm so upset." I tried wiping my tears with my hands but the sleek liquid only spread further around my face. Kasey handed me a napkin and I dabbed at them, no doubt messing up Barb's handiwork. "You're right, I'm just emotional today and..." I realised the whole cafe was staring at us and felt bad for Kasey who probably knew most of the people, "... and I'm going to make the most of my birthday. I just need some time alone to clear my head and get back to normal." Whatever that was. "I have to go, but thank you. Thank you for a... beautiful lunch." I gave her a brief hug but my body was desperate to move, to get away and let off steam.

"Will you be okay?" she asked.

I puffed out my chest. "I'll be fine, don't worry. I'll see you tonight." I forced a smile and thanked her once again for my birthday lunch, before scurrying out the door with an audience of concerned onlookers. Poor Kasey, I'd left her in the lurch again. Alone, to fend for herself.

But I had to, I couldn't do anything else right now but mourn my father and I needed to be alone to do it... which was extremely hard in a busy city on a Friday afternoon. I ran off towards an exit which led to an overpass; an enclosed pathway connecting the shopping centre with another building. The walls and roof were transparent, and the city crowd and traffic buzzed below. I stopped in the middle of the overpass to catch my breath, leaning on the wall.

"Oh, Dad," I whispered to myself, tears rolling down my face.

A stranger stopped next to me to ask if I was okay, handing me a tissue, and I nodded. I remembered the uncontrollable sadness that had washed over me when my mother died, and this was no different. Except I had seen my mother. I had said goodbye. I didn't have any closure with Dad.

A tiny bubble of hope surfaced then, when I realised that this life may not be hanging around too much longer. If I could go back, I would call my dad, go and see him, throw my arms around him and tell him to never move away from us. Tell him to sort things out with Kasey before they drifted apart. They may not be related, but they still loved each other. Dad raised her as his own, she was as much his daughter as I was.

What if his cancer was somehow caused by unresolved emotions? If I could make things better between them when I got back, it might – just might be possible – to save his life. Couldn't it? Those two hardly ever had a proper conversation and now I knew why. Come to think of it, Mum had treated Kasey differently too. Parents say they don't have a favourite child, but I was definitely Mum's favourite. I think Kasey was not only a reminder of Mum's infidelity to Dad, but a reminder to Mum of her betrayal.

My grief at Dad's death merged with the relief of knowing that in my real life he was still alive and my urgency to get home intensified. But to do that, I had to keep it together. If I kept losing it, someone was sure to schedule an intervention. I had to keep pushing the emotions deep down inside and close the lid on them. I drew in a sharp breath and dabbed at my eyes with the stranger's tissue. I had to get on with the day as planned and keep my eye on the prize: The birthday cake... my wish.

With resolve I stood tall and my blurry vision cleared. I turned to walk back into the shopping centre when I caught sight of someone down in the street below. A man wearing a stylish grey suit, with balding grey hair and black-rimmed glasses sat at an outdoor cafe with a pretty woman half his age. He had one leg crossed, bouncing his foot up and down. As though he couldn't sit still. Just like someone I knew...

"Grant!" I screamed, all composure going AWOL as I rapped furiously on the glass wall of the overpass. "Baby, it's me! I've found you!"

The people walking through the overpass gave me strange looks but I didn't care, I'd found my man! My eyes scanned the layout of the vicinity in which I stood, and then the street below, as though I was a cop on surveillance and had to plan the best available route to catch a criminal.

I peered down into the street. There was an exit just under the overpass, not far from the cafe where Grant was. Pinning his location in my mind, I ran back into the shopping centre and towards the escalator/lift thingy, excusing myself past a slow group of people to get inside the closest compartment. It took me downwards in a smooth, almost instant ride and when the doors opened I pushed through excitedly. "Excuse me... sorry... excuse me," I kept saying. I hurried to the exit on the left, almost colliding with an automated wheelchair-vehicle of some kind driven by an elderly man.

"Grant!" I called as I launched myself outside, turning towards the cafe. He was gone. Grant was gone!

My eyes practically exploded from their sockets as I searched to find him in the crowd. On trembling legs, I ran swiftly to the cafe table where he'd been sitting. I spun around one way and then the other. Passers-by bumped into me from all sides and I had no choice but to move with the crowd. Then I saw him...crossing the road.

"Grant!" I called out, but he didn't hear me. "Grant!" I yelled louder.

I looked left, right and stepped onto the road. A car narrowly missed me. The driver slammed on brakes and beeped the horn. Waving an apology, I stepped onto the sidewalk on the other side of the road and rushed up behind my boyfriend.

"Grant!"

He turned around, his framed eyes connecting with mine. Only they didn't completely connect; his held uncertainty for a moment. "Yes?"

"It's me! I'm so glad I found you!" I clasped my hands around his wrists and leaned close to him. He had a paler look about him and fine creases hung at the corner of his eyes, but he was still my Grant.

He pulled back, releasing my hands and the woman next to him glared at me. "Who..." he began, but just as the words came out of his mouth realisation dawned in his eyes. "Kelli?"

I nodded excessively and stretched a wide smile onto my face. "Yes, it's me!"

"It's been a long time. How are you?" he asked in a businesslike tone.

I kept trying to wrap my arms around him but with each step forward, he took one step back.

"I'm great now I've found you," I replied. At his curious glance I realised I must look a mess after all the crying. I gestured to my face. "Oh, I just had lunch with my sister and, whoa!" I made a fanning motion with my hands, "the amount of chilli they put in the meal, you wouldn't believe."

"So what have you been up to lately?" Grant asked,

checking his e-pad briefly and I winced as the woman next to him slid her hand into his.

I looked up at the sky that was trying and failing to compete with the attention of the crowded high-rises. "Wow, where do I start?"

I held up my hands and let them fall back to my thighs with a slap. I wanted to tell him everything and tell him not to worry, that I would be back in the past soon enough and we could be together again.

What would be happening in the past, right now? Would my birthday be happening without me? Maybe Grant had filed a missing persons report. Or maybe some other version of me was there, living out the day as planned but without my awareness. But I couldn't tell him the truth. I had to choose my words carefully, even though they were all lining up at the door of my mouth, ready to barge through like customers in a Boxing Day sale.

"I woke up this morning, shocked to find that I'm fifty years old and..."

"Oh, it's your birthday?"

I felt like saying: 'Of course, you beautiful idiot! You were with me last night,' but bit my tongue. "Yes."

"Happy birthday," Grant said with a nod of his head. His companion shifted on her feet and looked longingly at the direction they'd been travelling in before my intrusion.

"Thanks! Anyway, my son gave me a bungy jump for my birthday, can you believe it? So I actually did it and then I met my daughter for the first time, er... in a week, and after that I had a facial that was better than sex... oops, I mean, not better than you of course, but, well, it's just a gimmick sort of thing, you know..." Damn. Said too much, and now the woman was carving my eyes out of their sockets with her laser glare.

Her glare shot towards Grant. "You... slept with this woman?"

Grant's cheeks flushed pink and I could see the veins throbbing in his neck. "No, of course not! I mean, not recently..."

"What?" The woman planted her hands on her hips and stamped a sharp high-heeled foot onto the sidewalk, possibly triggering a catastrophic earthquake or tsunami somewhere in the world.

"What I mean, honey, is that I was with Kelli a long time ago, when she was young."

When we *both* were young. Why were women seen as young or old and men were just seen as... men?

The woman's hands relaxed a little. "Before we were together then? And before your... other wives?"

Grant gripped her shoulders. "Yes, as I said, a long, long time ago. It was nothing, there's nothing for you to worry about."

She nodded and raised her chin as she slid an arm territorially around his back.

It was nothing? Other wives? The gap between Grant and I widened, and I wished there was something nearby to hang on to as my legs became jelly. Well, at least now they matched my belly. How could he say our relationship was nothing? He was... *is*... going to propose!

But in this life – this weird, warped, ridiculous existence that was the life of Kelli McSnelly – Grant had lost his way. He'd become, by the sounds and looks of it, a millionaire photographer with a history of marriage and divorce to rival Ross Geller's from *Friends*. Only I bet he didn't marry a lesbian and I bet he didn't say the wrong name at his wedding, or marry his friend in a drunken haze in Vegas.

Grant wasn't like that. Couldn't be like that. He was my generous, affectionate, caring soon-to-be-fiancé and we were soulmates. Now I wanted to get home more than ever, not only to see my dad, but to marry Grant and stop him becoming this, this... imbecile who'd been searching for me in every woman he met and never finding true happiness because the woman he loved was married to William McSnelly. How did the universe get this so wrong?

"Sorry, Kelli, I should have introduced you two. This is Charli, my fiancé."

Charli Schmarli. She was just a possibility in this future, a hologram projected onto this existence by some giant e-pad controlling the universe. They'd got it wrong. When I got back I'd be able to change the future and Charli would play no part in it. Even her name was close to mine. I wouldn't be surprised if his other wives had been Kyli, Karli and Karali. In the real future, I'd become Kelli Mills, his one and only wife.

We tentatively shook hands and I turned to Grant with a smug smile. "I know you and I will be together again, Grant. You wait and see. I know you still love me, but don't worry, when I travel back to the past I'll make things right. In twenty-five years it'll be you and I standing here arm in arm."

A shrill laugh escaped Charli's mouth and if she hadn't been holding on to Grant, I was sure he would have fainted with embarrassment as she looked at him and said, "You were actually with this loony?"

"Ah, Kelli, I think you ought to go home and lie down, okay?" He held out two hands, palms downward, as if he was trying to calm a wild animal and stop it from coming any closer.

I just smiled and said, "I'll see you soon... honey." Then I winked at him and turned away. It was kind of fun teasing him a little and scaring the daylights out of Charli, but I knew Grant wouldn't remember this when I really did see him again. Because it would be from a future that would never happen.

Liliana! I suddenly remembered that I'd planned to go back

and see her. She might be able to shed more light on my relationship with Grant and possibly even pass on a message from Dad. As I crossed the road, back towards the shopping centre, my e-pad rang and I pinched and pulled the virtual cord to my ear. "Hello?"

"Kelli! Where the hell are you?" a young female voice asked in a whispered yell. "It's 3:35! Will is doing his best to keep Mr Turrow entertained but we need you here right now!"

Oh God. The meeting! *I'm late, I'm late, I'm...* "Arghh!"

In a cruel twist of fate, I tripped on the chair leg at the table Grant and Charli had been sitting at. As I fell forward onto a large middle-aged man with his shirt untucked, I was bombarded by an unsightly bulge of fat and an inch of bottom crack in my face. Unbalanced by my unfortunate momentum, he fell forward, sandwiching a teenage boy between himself and the pavement.

"Get off me!" the boy said.

I struggled about trying to find my feet again and hoped the curved hem of my skirt didn't ride up as much as it felt like it had. "I'm sorry, so sorry!" I said to the man and the innocent bystander who was flailing about underneath the mass of flesh.

I held out a hand and it took all my effort to help the heavier man up. Eventually he made it, his shirt now even more untucked but thankfully hiding the revolting bottom crack. The kid ran off like it was the zombie apocalypse and I turned my attention to the voice on the phone.

"Kelli, are you all right? What's going on?"

"I just tripped in the street, that's all."

"In the street? You're not even in the car yet?" Her voice escalated in tone but remained a whisper in volume. "Right, I'll tell Mr Turrow that you've been caught in an unfortunate traffic incident that's out of your control and you'll be here in about ten minutes, okay?"

"Okay. I'll be there as soon as I can!" I raced back inside as fast as my old legs would carry me and found my way back to the car. Automatically reaching for non-existent keys in my non-existent handbag, my hands then flew to my cheeks. *How do I unlock the car? Not only that, but where in the name of Dior is this bloody meeting?*

Chapter 11
Three Hours and Twenty Minutes
to Go

"The secret of staying young is to live honestly, eat slowly, and lie about your age." – Lucille Ball

THINK, Kelli, think! How did Ryan open the car earlier? Okay, okay. I circled the car, while memories from this morning circled around my mind... the e-pad, he did something with his e-pad. I held my e-pad out and scanned it along the side of the car, hoping for a scanning device, or a miracle. Nothing.

Maybe it just opens the normal way? I glanced around to see if anyone was watching and then, hoping I wouldn't set off an alarm, lifted the handle on the front door. The door stayed closed, but a slight beep sounded. I bent over to get a closer look at the door handle. A thin red laser protruded from underneath and I held my e-pad to it.

Click! I opened the front door and slid into the driver's seat with relief. Problem one solved. Now, to drive this thing properly and find the location of the meeting. I tilted my head and looked to where the ignition would normally be and of course, in its place was a small round scanning device. I held my e-pad to it and the engine purred. Geez, what would stop someone from stealing my e-pad and then my car?

Something flashed on the dashboard: *Please activate approved driver fingerprint recognition.*

Huh? I glanced around for somewhere to roll my thumbprint onto, but nothing appeared to be for that purpose. I placed my hands on the small steering wheel and the words disappeared from the screen, replaced by: *Welcome Kelli McSnelly.* Oh, why thank you.

After a few moments of getting my mind around all the controls, making sure I knew where the brakes were, the car spoke to me: "Where would you like to go, Kelli?"

"Twenty-five years into the past?" Hey, it was worth a shot. "KC Interiors," I said when the car failed to respond to my time travel request.

A map formed on the screen, little flag symbols popping up. "There are five results for that location. Can you be more specific?"

"Um... KC Interiors..." I tried to think of something more specific than that. That was all I knew about where the meeting was. Hang on, five results. That must mean KC Interiors stores. Huh! Maybe I have franchises scattered around the city or something. This little business must be doing all right.

"There are five results for KC Interiors. Could you be more specific," Miss Car repeated.

Of course, duh! I slapped my forehead. "KC Interiors Head Office," I said.

"Calculating route..." I thrummed my fingernails on the steering wheel. "Estimated travel duration: nine minutes and forty-seven seconds."

About half an hour late. Damn! I was about to put my foot on the accelerator and veer out of the parking spot when I realised the car was packed in tight. When Ryan drove into this spot the car moved directly sideways. I turned the steering wheel as far as it would go to the right and ever so lightly pressed my foot down, but it began to move diagonally. Not enough to ease out of the spot.

Bugger! I thrummed my fingernails again, my eyes scanning the car's interior for a solution. There was a button on the dashboard with an arrow pointing to the right and another to the left. I pressed the right arrow and the car moved by itself out of the parking spot. Awesome!

But it looked like the rest was up to me. I followed the signs around to the other side of the lot, careful not to over-steer the steering wheel, as it seemed to have super-sensitivity. I approached the exit and while I waited for the gate to rise up, I leaned over and wrapped my lips around the straw I'd used before and warm coffee ran down my throat.

"Turn left," Miss Car said.

Okay, this wasn't too bad. I was doing it. I was driving the car of the future. Young Grant would be so jealous! I continued to follow the car's directions, opting against auto-drive along a straight bit of road, preferring to keep control.

Nine minutes and forty-seven seconds later, I arrived at another car park, this time underneath a tall building. The car manoeuvred into a parking spot and I stepped out, automatically turning to point my key and expecting the characteristic high-pitched beep of the lock. Oh, the e-pad. I held it underneath the door handle and it beeped twice, which hopefully meant it was locked. Not that it mattered. It appeared that you needed to be pre-approved by fingerprint verification in order to drive the car.

I scanned the lot and a sign up ahead said *entry*. I went to push open the door but it sensed me and opened by itself into a narrow foyer. I spotted the information desk against the back wall of the room. I couldn't exactly ask the young man at the desk where the KC Interiors head office was. He might recognise me and wonder why I didn't know where my own office was.

It had to be upstairs somewhere, so I'd walk up the stairs until I saw a KC Interiors sign. Hopefully we were not the kind of posh business that identifies itself by some sort of wordless symbol.

I lifted my foot onto the first step alongside the information desk, but the young guy peered over at me with a frown. "You're not seriously walking up thirty flights of stairs are you, Mrs McSnelly?"

I removed my foot. "Oh, no of course not. Well, I could if I wanted to..." I puffed out my chest and tensed my non-existent arm muscles defensively. "I bungy jumped today you know. I'm not as old as I look, either." I spoke like a proud child who had just learned their ABC's.

"Oh that's right, happy birthday!" he said.

"Thanks. And I don't even feel forty."

He eyed me in a way that suggested he knew I was well over forty, but at least I didn't lie. It was true. I didn't feel forty. Heck, I didn't even feel fifty, more like sixty-two or sixty-three, but probably only because there'd been such a sharp jump in age from yesterday to today.

"Well, I'll just take the elevator," I said, swinging my arms in anticipation and also to detract from the fact that I didn't know where it was. All the walls were stainless steel, it was as though I was lost in a maze of blurry mirrors. Until... *Ding!* A curved part of the wall opened up and out stepped a woman in a red suit. "Hold the elevator!" I held up my hand and dashed inside the circular capsule.

"Hey, hon. Happy birthday! I'm looking forward to tonight. See you there!" The woman winked at me and sashayed her voluminous butt out into the foyer, where she embraced another woman entering the building.

I wondered if she worked for me. Nah, she wouldn't have called me *hon* if that were the case. Unless I was simply the world's best boss, which was totally possible of course.

"Which floor?"

I jumped at the sudden voice as the door curved closed. So elevators talk too. Nothing new I guess, they sometimes said 'Going up' or 'Women's Apparel', or at least that's what I remembered the most.

The guy had asked if I was walking thirty flights of stairs, so it must be on level thirty. I touched the number on the screen. Moments later the door opened again. The ride had been so smooth and fast. *Ding!* I stepped out of the elevator and there it was: *KC Interiors - Everyone deserves to be surrounded by beauty.* Ha! I bet I came up with the tagline. I'd barely entered through the glass door that swished open, when a young woman launched herself at me.

"Where have you been?" she said in that whispered yell I remembered from the phone. "It took you twice as long to get here! Mr Turrow is on his third cup of coffee and getting jumpy!"

"Sorry, there was... car trouble," I said.

"Here's your presentation," she said, shoving some kind of remote control into my hand. "Now get in there and give it your best. You'll have to be brilliant to make up for your lateness, now go!" She pushed me into the meeting room.

William was in there and his face turned from white to pink in relief as I walked through the door.

"Glad you're finally here," he said, giving me a quick embrace. "Lucy told us there was a streaker running through traffic on Main Street. Was anyone hurt?"

I stifled a giggle. *That* was the traffic incident she was going to mention as the reason for my lateness? A bit crazy, but at least they bought it and now I had an excuse if I appeared a bit flustered during the meeting.

"No, a few near misses and general chaos, but the police eventually escorted him away under a blanket." I faked an amused chuckle and turned to the short bald man next to William, who was rising up and down on his toes. "You must be Mr Turrow," I said, taking his hand and making every effort to appear charming.

"Indeed, and what a pleasure to meet you, Mrs McSnelly." He sandwiched my hand between both of his and shook it to the point I thought it might fall off. "Well, let's get started. What have you got to show me?" He took a seat and clasped his hands together on the table in the centre of the room and William followed suit.

Tell me and then we'll both know... I looked at the device in my hand. *Your presentation,* Lucy had said. *Okay, so I'm giving a PowerPoint presentation or something. Shouldn't be too hard, I'll just read everything on the screen.*

"Right... well, firstly, I'd like to welcome you to KC Interiors and what an absolute pleasure it is to have you in our office, Mr Turrow." I hoped the pleasantries would buy time while I figured out how to use this device. I waved it about as I gestured and complimented him on his lovely tie (which was an awful tangerine colour) and the shirt that brought out the green tinge in his eyes. He looked rather flattered, but soon his expression became businesslike again.

"Why thank you," he said. "But I'm looking forward to seeing your presentation." He pointed to the blank wall in front of the table.

There wasn't any projection screen, projector, or a laptop. Just this device in my hand. I pressed a round button and pointed it at the wall, and a square shaped blue screen appeared. Phew! Okay, it was similar to a TV remote. I pressed an arrow button and a soothing piece of music drifted through the room, followed by the KC logo.

Right. This shouldn't be too hard. Except, I still didn't know who Mr Turrow was and what I was trying to achieve with this presentation.

I clicked the arrow button again and a KC Interiors heading appeared, followed by the tagline and some text, which appeared to be a history of the company.

I cleared my throat and stood side-on with legs crossed and one hand on my hip as they'd taught us in modelling class. If I didn't have a clue what I was presenting I could at least look confident. William gave me a curious glance.

Here goes. "KC Interiors is a family owned business and has been operating for seventeen years. Longer than many of our competitors," I began. The screen only showed keywords but I was able to string them together. It was all about putting on a show. I could do that. "We combine creative design with optimal business practices, going above and beyond industry standards." So far so good.

Mr Turrow lifted the coffee mug to his lips and tipped his head back, shaking the remaining drops out. He plonked the mug down and clasped his hands together again on the table. "Now tell me, Mrs McSnelly, why Harrods London, would choose your products as opposed to your competitors. What makes your company unique?"

Whoa, he must be a buyer from the iconic department store. Sitting in front of me, listening to my presentation! An engine of nerves revved up inside me, as I realised the implications of this meeting. If Harrods were to become buyers of KC Interiors' products, the business would become very well off indeed.

What made us unique? I hoped the next slide would tell me and him. I pressed the arrow button.

An animation began, showing an old-fashioned mirror, a little like the one at Queen of Beauty, merging with a modern safe and forming a decorative piece of storage for valuables. Carved swirls danced around the frame and each golden flourish was a hinged cover which opened to reveal a compartment for trinkets and jewellery. There were no words on the screen, so I winged it.

"KC Interiors combines modern technology and design with classic style." Yay, good one, Kelli. "And I'm sure 'thy valued Harrods customers' would appreciate our... allegiance with history and tradition that merges forth into contemporary living." Man, I was good. Shakespeare who?

Mr Turrow nodded. "I see, I see. Now, tell me what your highest selling product is."

Crap. I pressed the arrow button but the next slide only continued showing transformations of old products into new.

I tapped my finger on my chin, as though trying to conjure the last financial year's sales figures. Of which I knew nothing about. "Let me think... oh, it's escaped my mind," I blabbed on. "You see, all our products sell so well, it's hard to remember which one the stand-out is."

William tried to tell me something with his eyes and he kept jerking his head forward as though to remind me of what to say, or trying to catapult the information from his brain to mine. Eventually, William stood, just as a strange gurgling presented itself in my stomach. I'd been holding it in of course, trying to look slim, but now it was expanding again, like it had done earlier at the cafe.

"Kelli's right, all our products are successful. But, our smart-lamps are definitely our best-selling item."

Thank God William was here.

"Their innovative design and intelligent computer program provides the right amount of lighting for any given situation,"

William continued, as my stomach continued to churn and I couldn't resist giving it a firm rub with my hand. Oh man, I really should have gone to the toilet beforehand.

"Plus, the energy-saving, infra-red powered light source lasts for years, so they are both stylish and environmentally friendly."

Gurgle... Gurgle... bloody hell. I had to get out of here! "Um, I'll be right back!" I raised a reassuring finger and turned for the door. "Right back," I repeated with a forced smile, while William glared at me with a 'what the hell are you doing' expression.

Lucy eyed me curiously too as I dashed past her desk and towards the toilet sign. Once in the privacy of the bathroom I breathed a sigh of relief and then bolted to the cubicle. Damn lactose. It never bothered me before, why now?

I washed my hands (after figuring out the taps worked just like the faucet-free shower at home) and emerged from the bathroom. How would I explain my sudden departure from the meeting? Poor William was probably sick of my incompetence and attacks of the crazies by now. I needed a reason to have left that didn't involve bodily functions. I scanned the reception area and my eye caught the shine of light on a spiral-shaped object on the coffee table in the waiting area. Without thinking I grabbed it and dashed back into the meeting room.

"I'm sorry to run off like that, but I just had to show you this..." What the hell was this thing?

"... this... particular piece, which as you can see, forges traditional class with modern innovation. A perfect example of our exquisite products which are like... the past, present and future all rolled into one." Nice one.

William stifled a chuckle. "Yes, our automated, decorative, tissue-dispensing machines are definitely unique, but the smart-lamps will be quite a hit in Harrods, I'm sure. Especially since our deluxe smart-lamp also doubles as a heating device."

Sure enough, when I pushed on the top edge of the spiral a tissue popped out and I plucked it out and dabbed at each of my temples in a show of post-exertion. I really was good at this. I knew I should have taken up the offer of being a model on *The Price Is Right* when I had the chance. I gave a little hand flourish around the tissue-dispenser before placing it on the table. As if I had somehow anticipated needing to dab my temples with a tissue, a wave of heat rolled up from my toes to my head, my cells jumping in shock as a tsunami hot flush drowned my body and left behind a sea of carnage.

"Kelli, are you all right?" William asked.

"Yes, yes, I'm fine," I said, sweat drenching my face as I dabbed at it with a tissue. "See, getting a tissue when needed has never been so easy with our dispensing machine." I glanced around the room for something to fan myself with.

Why was there no bloody paper in this office? It was worse than the bathroom with no towels.

I sidled up to a fake plant in the corner of the room and surreptitiously stroked the large plastic leaves, leaning slightly forward and flapping the leaf around my face, as William and Mr Turrow looked on with confused expressions. "I, ah, I was just thinking... that um... we could create a plant that has an in-built fan function!" I flapped the leaves a little harder, swishing blessedly cool air around my face. "Yes, the leaves could..." flap, flap, flap, "swivel, or vibrate and create a cool environment for the home or office!"

Both William and Mr Turrow jutted out their bottom lips, turned the corners of their mouths downwards and nodded.

"That's not a bad idea!" said Mr Turrow.

William murmured his agreement as he cocked his head towards the screen. The message in his expression said it all: *Now get back to the bloody presentation and quit doing weird things!*

I gulped down a glass of water in as dignified a way as possible and resisted the strong urge to tip it over my head. I clicked through more of the slides, ad-libbing as I went and sprinkling various compliments here and there for Mr Turrow's ego.

My e-pad beeped and I glanced at my wrist to see *Selena calling* on the screen.

Selena! I was about to answer it when I realised I couldn't. The future of KC Interiors' international expansion depended on this meeting and I couldn't let William down. I could see he was eager to please Mr Turrow – he probably thought I didn't notice, but he kept wringing his hands under the table. My poor husband was probably more nervous than me. Damn it! I wanted to speak to Selena but couldn't. I pressed *decline* and got back to the slides.

"Something that sets KC Interiors apart is the fact that we give regularly to charity. Ten per cent of our net profits to be exact." Well, there you go.

"Oh, right. Wonderful. Which charities?"

I pressed the arrow button and thankfully, I, or whoever designed this presentation pre-empted this question. "We support disadvantaged youth by providing opportunities for creative expression and skill development." I pressed the arrow again. "Last year our funding allowed teachers to travel to Africa to teach design and construction of useful household equipment, as well as creative expression workshops which provide enjoyment and camaraderie among youth." I was on a roll.

"You can turn off the presentation now," Mr Turrow said.

Huh? I thought it was going well.

"Enough about the company, I want to hear more about you."

Me? William was obviously wondering the same thing as he shifted awkwardly in his chair.

"I understand this business was born of your desire, tell me what led to the birth of KC Interiors. Why did you start it up?"

Crap. All I knew was that Kasey had provided money and stuff, I designed stuff and William managed stuff. What more could I say?

I really wished Lucy would barge in with some urgent phone call I simply had to take, or an announcement, like the building was on fire, or... the crazy naked guy from Main Street had escaped from police custody and followed me here, holding the poor guy from the information desk hostage until he could see me. Okay, maybe not that, but I was fast running out of words and couldn't think of a single thing to say.

William stood. "You know, Mr Turrow, when Kelli first showed me the preliminary designs she'd come up with – just as a hobby at first, while our kids were young – I not only saw an amazing talent expressed on the paper, but an amazing glow on my wife's face. Drawing, creating... it lights up her eyes. I knew she was onto something good. I knew her ideas were unique and that it would be a mistake not to pursue this as a business."

Wow. Now I was more speechless than before. Hearing William talk about me like I had really been there when Diora and Ryan were young was strange. His eyes seemed to be back in the past, seeing the events that took place. Like it was real. Only it wasn't real to me. I didn't remember that time, but I did remember what it felt like to create something out of nothing. To take a blank piece of paper and produce a design that hadn't existed before. I hadn't drawn for years, not since I was thirteen, but the pure bliss when I was in the zone? There was nothing like it. So I began telling Mr Turrow this.

"And I knew that I wanted to do this for the rest of my life. That creating beauty was a part of me, an expression of my soul and a passion that couldn't be suppressed." Only it had been. Not long after my thirteenth birthday in fact, when I'd finished creating a design I was particularly pleased with and –

Clap. Clap. Mr Turrow's hands slapped together, interrupting my flow of thoughts. "Mrs McSnelly, what an inspiring story. I thank you immensely for sharing your deep passion for the creative process." He stood and grasped my hands again, shaking them with even more enthusiasm than before. "However, this will of course be a decision based on business, so I will consider your proposal and that of the other companies I've met with today and advise you of my decision when I get off the plane at Heathrow."

I nodded. "Of course."

"Thank you both for your time." He shook William's hand, who ushered him outside, giving him his personal number and explaining that the office would be closed tomorrow but he could contact William directly so plans could begin immediately.

After he'd left, William led me into another room, which housed a kitchenette, table and chairs, and by the looks of it, one of those smart-lamps which brightened upon us entering. He closed the door behind him and then pressed what appeared to be a lock button.

"I think you won him over," William said, coming towards me with arms outstretched.

"*We* won him over," I corrected.

"Yes it was a team effort, wasn't it? And even though you didn't tell him half the stuff we'd planned, I think overall it went well."

He slid his arms around my back and leaned his head into my neck, nuzzling it with his nose.

I tried to push him away gently. "What are you doing?"

He brought his face in front of mine. "We've got some spare

time, why don't we enjoy one of your birthday presents now?" He resumed nuzzling into my neck.

Oh God. "But, isn't that supposed to be for tonight? And... Lucy's out there." I pointed to the door.

"Lucy will be busy finishing up the week's admin work, she won't bother us. Besides, the door's locked."

He tried to press his lips onto mine but I turned my head and they landed on my cheek. So he kissed that instead, then my ear, then the part of my neck just below my ear, his lips making squelchy sounds.

This was wrong. "William, I think you should stop."

"Why?" He continued the kissing. "And what's with all this 'William' talk? You haven't called me that in years."

"Right. Will, honey, I think it would be better to... save ourselves for tonight. You know, make it more special?"

"What's more special than celebrating a successful business meeting, on your birthday, in a private staff room, on the spur of the moment?" He ran his hand down my cheek and then across my lips, and then down my neck, tracing the neckline of my top with his finger.

"As much as I..." gulp, "...want you right now, I really think tonight is best, when everyone's gone home and we can have our comfortable bed to ourselves."

Damn, why couldn't Selena have chosen this moment to call?

"I really have to call Selena back. She rang before, in the meeting." I looked longingly at my e-pad and noticed the time. It was a few minutes past five. Liliana! I shoved William, er... Will, back quickly, much to his disappointment. "I just remembered, I'm supposed to meet someone, right now!"

I adjusted the left sleeve of my top which he'd slid part way down my shoulder. "Sorry, honey, but I really have to go. I'll see you at home, yeah?"

"Who do you have to meet?"

"Just an old friend I bumped into at the shopping centre today, that's all. I don't have time to explain, I'll see you back home in time for the party." I would not be late for that. So I left Will and his pouting puppy dog face in the staff room, and dashed out. "Bye, Lucy, sorry you had to make up a story to cover for me," I said without waiting for a response as I pulled open the door and escaped into the elevator.

I could make it back by 5:15 p.m. and with any luck, Liliana would still be there. She said she'd be there until five, but surely she wouldn't leave on the dot, not having seen me again, would she?

Chapter 12
Two Hours to Go

"You can only go halfway into the darkest forest; then you are coming out the other side." – Chinese proverb

I RAN from the car park to the New Age (ha!) shop where I'd seen Liliana before and skidded to a halt at the entrance. Two people stood expectantly in the queue and only one psychic was left in the booths. Rosie. Damn! I doubled over to catch my breath and looked up as a woman in a white cheesecloth dress approached me.

"Are you okay, madam?"

I exhaled my disappointment and scrunched up my lips. "I was really hoping to see Liliana. She's not out back, is she?"

The woman shook her head. "I'm sorry. Liliana has left for the day."

"Do you have her number, can I call her?"

"I'm sorry, madam, we're not at liberty to disclose our psychics' personal phone numbers." The woman went to walk away, but stopped. "Oh, you're not Kelli by any chance, are you?"

"Yes, that's me. Why?"

The woman scurried off to the sales counter and back again with a small card in hand. "Here, Liliana said to give this to you if you came back."

My eyes fled to the card as I plucked it from her hand. *We Know The Truth–www.FastForwardExperiences.com.* I turned the card over and along with a barcode there was a handwritten message:

Good luck! ~ Liliana xo

A tiny smile found its way to my lips and I couldn't wait to check out the website. Maybe I could find out more about what was happening to me. "Thank you!" I hugged the woman who stiffened in surprise. "Please thank Liliana for me."

"Will do." She smiled. "We still have another psychic here if you're in need of a reading?" She pointed towards Rosie whose client was shaking her head as if to say: 'No, I didn't have a dog called Scruffy.'

"Thanks, but I'll pass." I walked away, my eyes still on the card, narrowly avoiding a collision with the side of the door. Why was there a barcode on the card? I held it next to my e-pad out of curiosity and it beeped, the screen flashing. I pinched and flicked so the holographic screen would appear.

Do you want to save document? Yes. No.

I pressed yes and a list of folders became visible. I then pressed business cards, resulting in a confirmation message.

Document saved to business cards folder.

How cool. No need to house an overgrown collection of business cards anymore. I scrolled through the other folders out of interest: credit cards, debit cards, reward cards, membership cards... this device was a virtual purse. My e-pad was fast becoming my BFF. Although, I sure would miss my Prada handbags, unless… could there be Prada e-pads?

A loud clang from the roller door of a nearby shop broke my fascination with technology for a moment. Everyone was closing their doors for the day, except the New Age shop where Rosie was probably doing unpaid overtime for incompetence. I walked in the direction of the car park (too buggered to run again), as lights dimmed and doors closed around me. Returning to my car, I pinched open my e-pad screen again, selecting the Foogle icon.

In the address bar I typed fastforwardexperiences.com, which opened an intro page with an image of a swirling tunnel, along with the words: *If you want to know the truth, click here to enter.* I pressed my finger to the screen and the next page appeared.

Welcome! This is a site for those interested in studying the Fast Forward phenomenon and those who have been chosen to experience one.

I clicked on 'About Fast Forwards' and it pretty much said what Liliana had told me. I then clicked on 'Experiences', which brought up six listings. Most under aliases, but a few used a first name. I clicked on 'Jessica' and my eyes scanned through the words as quickly as they could. She was twenty-nine when her fast forward happened and just about to leave for a backpacking trip around Europe. On the morning of her departure, she woke to find herself forty-one, unmarried and childless, living on the streets, addicted to drugs and alcohol. Her experience lasted three days and sounded awful, going from completely sober and clean to desperate for a fix.

When she returned to the past, she still left for her overseas trip but did one thing differently. She avoided getting involved with the man who introduced her to drugs and kept up her supply of alcohol. Her fast forward had shown her who this man was and despite his charms the second time around, she resisted, knowing too well the outcome if she didn't. An update posted at the bottom of her entry on the website said that Jessica was now thirty-nine and working as a drug rehabilitation counsellor, married to a wonderful man with her first baby on the way.

Rob's story was also interesting. An aspiring guitarist in a band with his friends, he'd just finished a business degree at twenty years old when his father died. Not long after, he quit the band, deciding to focus on 'doing his father proud' by following in his footsteps in the business world.

A year into his new job, his fast forward sent him ten years into the future to a life of success but without the freedom and happiness he desired. On anti-depressants, he had gained a pile of weight and found it hard to get up in the morning. He lasted a week in the future, struggling with the demands placed on him at work, in a job he barely understood, causing his boss to call him into his office for a final warning to prove his competence. Not only that, his old band mates had recruited a new guitarist and were now topping the charts with four albums having been released so far.

When he woke aged twenty again, he realised his father wouldn't have wanted him to end up unhappy like that and he'd only done the degree because he thought it was expected of him. So he took a year off to focus on his music, encouraging his band mates to record a demo album which went on to become signed by a big record label. Rob was now thirty-one and, although I didn't recognise the name of his band – Sons of Silver – apparently everyone else in this day and age did!

My heart raced on reading the next experience. Someone calling themselves Polly had not only jumped ten years into the future, but was still *in* the future. She didn't say which year it was so I didn't know if she was in my here and now, or even further in the future, just that after turning forty she woke up fifty. Hallelujah! Someone besides me who knew what a shock it was, not that she had as far to go as I had, though.

She'd been an up-and-coming politician, only to be wrenched from her impending success to a future where she was no longer a politician, but a political journalist. And after four years in her fast forward – yes, four! She was still there, clueless as to why and resigned to the fact she may never get to go home to her old life. *What if I was stuck here for months or years, like Polly?*

I read through the rest of the experiences, spellbound by how interesting and varied they were, although none of them had jumped as far ahead into the future as I had. I clicked on 'Submit an experience', opening a very detailed form. It had to include my name and contact details in order to be considered for publication on the site, no doubt to prevent frauds from making something up, not that it would totally deter them though. I was tempted to write something, to tell of my experience so far, but it wasn't over yet. I vowed to remember the website name if – no, *when* – I returned home. I realised that the website might not exist twenty-five years in the past, but it would be worth checking anyway when the time came.

But what if I never got back? Fear and doubt took residence in my mind, pushing out some of the hope that sat there earlier. No. No, I couldn't let negative thoughts take over. Most of these people got to go home and improve their lives. It had to happen for me too. Only, I couldn't think how to make my life better. It was already what I wanted, although I'd certainly keep up a consistent exercise and beauty regime throughout life from now on.

I glanced around the car park, which was fast emptying as customers left and before I knew it my finger had pressed on Selena's phone number in the contacts list. I still hadn't spoken to my best friend and longed to talk to her.

It went straight through to her assistant's voicemail again. Some assistant, never even answered the bloody phone! Frustrated, I drew in a sharp breath and leaned my head back on the seat. A wave of sadness rolled through me as I remembered what Kasey had told me about Dad. If only we'd stayed in contact more often, if only he hadn't moved overseas, if only he hadn't gotten sick, if only...

An idea struck me. If he's dead, then he might be buried at the same cemetery as Mum. I turned on the car and told her I'd like to go to Goldwood Cemetery. Miss Car asked me to clarify whether I wanted Goldwood Cemetery North or Goldwood Cemetery West. I didn't know for sure, but North seemed more likely. I'd know it when I saw it, unless they'd revamped it beyond recognition, which didn't often happen with cemeteries, did it? Well, they must have run out of room for all the bodies, because at Mum's funeral there'd been heaps of land available and now there were two cemeteries. I even imagined myself being buried there one day, near Mum – and now, Dad – but it seemed I'd have to settle for the West location instead.

I followed the directions and arrived just under ten minutes later. I glanced at the dashboard. There was still time to make it back home to get ready for the party, as long as I didn't stay here too long.

Goldwood Cemetery looked different from what I remembered, although it still lent some recognition. It still had my insides twisting up inside me on entering the grounds and I was right about them running out of room. A sign at the entrance said the cemetery was complete and showed a map of its western counterpart, almost as though it was flashing a neon 'no vacancies' sign, like on a motel.

Sorry to those on their deathbeds, we're all out of rooms. Why don't you try down the road at the other place, I hear the view is to die for.

I shook the ridiculous thoughts from my mind as I stepped from the car and wandered down the main pathway, instinctively remembering the approximate whereabouts of Mum's permanent abode. The large tree in the centre of the cemetery still stood and I turned to the left just beyond it, passed seven graves until I stopped at the foot of my mother's.

Diana Crawford – Now at Peace.

Glancing at the empty vase, I cursed at not thinking to stop off to buy flowers. They should have flower vending machines here; it was the future after all. Staring at Mum's grave, I almost forgot why I was there, until I allowed my gaze to drift to the grave on the right.

Malcolm Crawford – Forever at Peace.

The shock of seeing it for the first time took my legs from under me and I crumpled forwards onto my knees, my hands grasping the foot of the grave.

"Dad," I whispered, my voice shaking at the realisation. "It's not fair," I cried, leaning forward and resting my cheek against the cold stone. "Why did you have to go so soon?"

A warm tear slid down my face and onto the grave where it cooled into a tiny puddle against my cheek. I knew that in my old life he was still alive but right now I was here, in the future, in a world my dad was no longer a part of and the pain was just as real as it had been after Mum's passing.

I lifted myself from the grave and wiped at my face with the heel of my hand, my legs tucked under me on the ground. "I'll come back for you, Dad. I'll make sure you never leave us."

I caught a glimpse of the candy pink sunset on the horizon before I closed my eyes and my mind travelled back in time – way back in time – to when I was a kid hanging out with my dad on a building site. They weren't as strict about hard hats and safety back then, and Dad would often bring me along to check out his current projects on the weekends. We'd walk through the timber forest of the house-in-progress, as Dad explained the frame was like a skeleton that would hold everything else up. It was the most important part of the house, yet once completed it would be invisible, just like our own skeleton. "Sometimes it's what you can't see that's most important," he'd say.

We'd bring a picnic bag of sandwiches and eat them on the floor of the dining-room-to-be, and I'd tell him where all the various pieces of furniture should go. Once, he lifted me up to the second level of a house, as there were no stairs built yet and then he caught me when I jumped back down. He was strong, my dad. His shoulders could carry a mountain if they had to. Thinking about what Kasey had told me, they probably had in a manner of speaking. He'd stuck with Mum throughout her illness and addiction and the subsequent knowledge of her betrayal. Despite all this, he never left. He kept our home intact, never daring to rock the foundations.

"What colour should this room be, Kelli?" he'd ask me, as we walked through bare rooms.

The colour wheel I'd learned about in school would spin in my mind and then it would stop right on the perfect colour for each room. I just knew what would look right, what would feel right. I'd imagine curtains, lamps, tables displaying candles and photo frames, fluffy rugs on the floor, and beautiful framed pictures on the walls. While Dad focused on the skeleton of the house, I'd see the skin, the body of the house come to life before my eyes. Those times with Dad were my happiest memories of him.

After one such day, I couldn't wait to get back home and add more designs to the scrapbook I'd been making. On the front I'd written 'Kelli's Designs' in pink and purple swirling letters and inside were drawings of all the things that made a home beautiful. I'd been so pleased with myself, I went to show my scrapbook to Dad but he was on the phone, so I peered into the lounge room where Mum lay on the couch in front of the television.

"Whatcha got there?" she'd asked.

Pleased she was showing interest, I sat next to her and held out my scrapbook as the scent of alcohol floated around me from her breath. I didn't mind, I was just glad she was paying me some attention. Until she took the book from me and turned each page over with a sharp flick.

"What are these all about?" she'd asked, to which I'd replied, "I'm designing homewares and maybe one day I can actually get them made. I'd love that, it would be my dream." I'd twirled a strand of my straight hair around my finger until it slid from my grasp when she looked at me with what appeared to be anger.

"Why are you wasting time on this? Forget about following a silly dream, Kelli. Life doesn't turn out how we want it to." My heart had raced and I'd stood up defensively. "Look at you!" she'd continued. "You shouldn't waste your looks by hiding away in your room with paper and pencils. You're meant for the spotlight, Kelli. Not for this... childish hobby!"

In her moment of anger – or possibly even jealousy – she tore the page from my book and ripped it in half with a jarring sound that made me shudder. It still made me shudder every time it intruded on my memory. In that moment, all confidence in my ability and sense of achievement was ripped in half too.

Glancing at Mum's grave, my lips clamped tight, I picked up a clump of dirt from the ground and threw it at the headstone where it dispersed into a spray of dust. On that awful day, I'd run from the room in tears to my dad, who'd calmed me down before going into the lounge room and shutting the door.

Muffled shouting travelled through the walls and then Mum's sobbing. She must have taken some tablets because she slept the rest of the day. Dad taped my pages back together but it wasn't the same. Nothing could patch up what had happened. The picture I could draw again but I couldn't redo that moment.

My lips trembled with sadness and my nostrils flared with anger as I stared at the dusty headstone. Within seconds, I brushed off the dust with my fingers and blew it away with whatever breath was left in my lungs. Liliana's words echoed in my ears... *she wants to tell you she's sorry*. I knew Mum wasn't herself that day. I knew she was in a bad way and was frustrated she couldn't follow *her* dreams. I knew she probably envied me, which was why I went along with the modelling jobs. It made her happy, at least for a while. She kept saying how proud she was of me and I kept wanting to hear it. *She wants to tell you she's sorry.*

"I know you are, Mum. I know," I said out loud, my finger tracing the frame around her photo. I wrapped my arms around the headstone, allowing a few remaining tears to slide down my face. "I forgive you." A light breeze circled my body as though embracing me too and for a fleeting moment I believed that Mum would be proud of me – and of KC Interiors.

Even though I didn't know anything about the company until recently, in this life I'd obviously worked hard to get it to where it was today. My muscles softened and a slight sense of achievement brushed over me. The achievement I'd felt after working on my scrapbook. It had been buried away but was now rising from its grave.

My tears dried and I stood, glancing at the sky which had transformed from candy pink to dusty salmon. I checked the time on my e-pad. I'd only need to change into something nice for the party, considering my hair and make-up had already been done. Although after all the crying, I'd need to touch it up a little and that shouldn't take too long. Before heading back to the car, I opened Foogle on my e-pad screen and searched for KC Interiors.

Pages and pages of results showed up, but I clicked on the main website. It repeated what I'd told Mr Turrow in the meeting, but also had a gallery of pictures of all our products and information on upcoming designs that were currently in production. There was a listing of all our stores, as well as stockists of some of our most popular products. Our latest news section revealed that beginning the following year we would be implementing an in-home decorating consultation service and there was a form for people to register their interest.

There was also a photo of our head office staff; a smiling team of fourteen – including yours truly. Diora was in the photo too and scrolling down to the staff profiles I discovered that she was head of the marketing team – a surprise, but it made sense considering her personality – and was currently on maternity leave. No surprises there. Ryan wasn't in the photo, so he obviously spent all his time bungy jumping and making – ahem – music.

Maybe I could get back in touch with designing when I got home to the past. I mean as well as the modelling. I still wanted to grace those catwalks and revel in the familiarity of flashing lights. A woman could do both, couldn't she? Especially now I knew I could do it.

Maybe Grant would invest in the business with me? He

could take all the photos of the products and bring out the best in them, like he did with me. But would the business have the same success with Grant a part of it? Would he even want to be a part of it? My mind flashed back to Will at the meeting and how nervous yet eager he'd been. How happy he was afterwards on winning Mr Turrow over. KC Interiors was his life, his passion.

I closed the website and the door on my thoughts, and tried calling Selena. Met once again with voicemail, I typed her name into Foogle and clicked on images.

Holy cow! I was surprised to see what she now looked like. Still beautiful, but... well, you could tell she'd had some work done. Her lips appeared stung by a bee and her eyebrows were in a permanent state of surprise. I clicked on one of the pictures which led to an article titled: *I should have Stopped after Three Surgeries*, where Selena openly confessed regretting the fourth procedure, saying it had gone too far. I also found a video of Selena accepting her Oscar and felt a twinge of pride at her achievement. In the video her eyebrows were about half an inch lower than the post-surgery brows and I agreed she should have left it at that.

A text message beeped and flashed on my screen, followed immediately by another one. The first was from Ryan.

> When will u be back? Hope u have enough time to get ready. R.

> On my way now.

The second message was from CareLab:

> This message is to confirm your appointment for a mammogram at 9am on Tuesday.

Oh joy! So there's a fancy brain scanning device available in the future but nothing so advanced for boobs. Wonderful.

I brushed specks of dirt from my clothing and walked to the car, but not before glancing back at the graves, now sheltered from the setting sun by the tall tree to the left. Its branches cast skeletal patterns across the stone, just like the timber in the houses Dad used to build. "See you soon, Dad."

Chapter 13
Forty-Five Minutes to Go

"Life is just one damned thing after another." – American proverb

THANKFULLY, Miss Car remembered where I lived and safely helped me navigate home. If I'd gone into the past instead of the future I would have had no hope, unless there were carriages driven by horses with photographic memories.

Despite living fairly close to the city, my house was situated in suburbia heaven. I pulled into Bellbird Drive, welcomed by rows of round, silver encased lights forming a dotted edge along each side of the road. I frowned on noticing there weren't any power lines. None at all. Maybe everything was solar powered, or maybe someone – my sister, probably – had discovered an unlimited source of renewable energy and electricity had been given the flick. I chuckled at the thought.

I drove into the driveway of number nine. A middle-aged woman in leggings and a top too tight for her figure stopped trimming her rose bushes to wave at me from next door. The garage was closed and I didn't know how the heck to open it, so I parked on the driveway and stepped out of the car.

"Hi, Kelli," she said.

"Hi..." *strange woman I've never met.*

"Nice evening, eh?"

I nodded. "Sure is."

"You got a party on tonight or somethin'?" she asked with a frown, gesturing to the house with her hedge clippers.

A low hum of music drifted from inside and a van marked *Big Night Caterers* was parked alongside the house. My guess was my Lycra-clad neighbour was a bit miffed that she wasn't invited.

"Ah, just a small family gathering," I replied, edging away from the side fence in case she was planning on using her gardening tool as a weapon. "Well, I'd better get inside. Have a good night!"

I walked on before she could reply and pushed open the unlocked door. The kitchen and living room had been transformed from an average family home into something resembling a movie set. An animated movie set. Which didn't really make sense because they didn't have sets for animated movies, did they? It's all done on computer screen, but anyway, it looked cartoonish. Brightly coloured paper flowers hung from the ceiling with glossy balloons, long streamers hanging from wall to wall and fancy multi-coloured lighting. Delicious savoury smells wafted past my nose as I looked towards the kitchen where four people in white chef outfits scurried about like elves, busying themselves with food preparation.

"Mum, you're here! You better go and get ready, but first, let me take you on a quick tour of my creation." Ryan, dressed in some ridiculous outfit, flourished an arm towards the living room. When he turned, I almost tripped on a tail-like thing attached to his back and dragging along the floor.

Was this the kind of clothing young people wore these days? How bizarre!

"Over here we have the Bliss Garden, where guests can sit down on one of the pods and enjoy a drink and relaxing conversation," Ryan explained, as he pointed to the far corner where giant origami lotus flowers lay around the seating pods, similar to bar stools but lower and shaped like cylinders with a little round cushion on the top. Origami butterflies dangled from the roof and tiny lotuses floated in a birdbath.

Ryan led me outside, the summer night air sharpened by a hint of cool. "Out here on the patio is The Galaxy, an out-of-this-world space for fresh air and warm food." A grey cushioned outdoor setting took up most of the space, above which hung tiny fairy lights that resembled stars. A colour-changing, heat-radiating lamp took centre stage, casting a sinewy rainbow on the tiled floor and holographic models of the planets floated in mid-air, powered by a small device attached to the wall.

"And the main area where guests will mingle," he said as he led me back inside, "is the Party Hub, hence all the streamers and balloons and bright stuff everywhere."

"Wow, you've done a really great job!" He had. Selena and Grant would love this!

"Well, I have to get as much practise as possible before I launch KC's in-home decorating service next year," he replied. "Plus, the photos I've taken here will be awesome for my final year university portfolio."

Ah, so he did work for my company, or at least, would be once he finished his studies. A family business indeed. I looked at the time on my e-pad. "Well, I'd better go and get ready, huh?"

Ryan shook his head as though waking from a dream. "Oh yes, sorry I got carried away with my new world." He pushed my lower back with his hands, walking me to the hallway near the kitchen. "Can't wait to see what you're wearing!" he said with a smile.

Wow. Not many twenty-something sons would give a flying hoo-ha what their mother was wearing to her birthday party.

I moved past the caterers – who were moving about like little robots – and entered the sanctum of my bedroom. Mine and Will's bedroom. An image of us sliding underneath the covers together flashed in my mind. Almost as quickly, I shook it out.

Okay, now... what to wear?

I slid open the wardrobe but didn't hold out much hope for a decent outfit. Not after this morning's search produced only the coral-coloured atrocity. I flipped through the clothing hanging on thin metal hangers, silently scolding myself for allowing my fashion collection to be hung on such flimsy structures, instead of curved wooden hangers that kept the shape of the outfits, preventing that telltale pointy shoulder edge. Didn't KC Interiors do coat hangers?

In frustration I sighed and leaned against the frame of the wardrobe, when suddenly the clothes began moving by themselves. They slid sideways on the rack, before curving around and disappearing into the wall behind. New clothes gradually appeared on the other side, coming out of the wall and curving around to the front. A rotating wardrobe!

Eventually it stopped and I had a whole new selection of clothes to choose from. These ones were much nicer, although a little mature for my taste, and I flipped through the choices. My lips formed a pout as I remembered the red dress I'd bought and was planning on wearing to my twenty-fifth birthday party and now couldn't. I'd even bought matching underwear; a cute balconette bra with sequined straps and lacy bikini briefs. Well, hopefully I'd still get to wear them.

I continued appraising my options, pulling a few from their

rack and holding them up to my body in front of the mirror, momentarily shuddering at my smudged make-up and artificially windswept hair. Scrunching my lips, I put the outfits back on the rack and looked through the selection again. A protective slip hung on the rack and I lifted the bottom of it to reveal what it was protecting.

My red dress! I'd kept it all those years! I lifted the slip off and slid the dress from the hanger, holding it up in front of me. The sequins adhering to the soft figure-hugging fabric twinkled under the bedroom lamplight and I smiled, pleased to have something with me from the past. Something to remind me that my old life wasn't just some dream fast disappearing from my consciousness.

I held the dress up against my body and looked in the mirror. My smile sunk downwards as I eyed my dress – and then my body.

I lay the dress on the bed and examined it with my hands. It was stretchy, it might fit. I could possibly squeeze into it if I had some sort of figure-squishing support underwear underneath. Or even a portable liposuction machine.

I pulled open the drawers of the dresser and rummaged through each one, quickly closing the first one when I came in contact with Will's underwear. The third one housed various singlets and stockings... and voila! This looked promising! I pulled out an unopened cardboard package with a picture of a slim woman wearing a skin-coloured support suit on it.

SlimFX Magic Suit – drop a dress size and reveal your slim inner Goddess!

It must be related to the YouthMagic Facial, I thought, as I peeled off the plastic and withdrew the beige suit, which looked tighter than the red dress. I might need support underwear to be able to fit into the support underwear and that could go on and on. I'd be my own Russian doll.

I turned the package over to see if there were instructions for the suit, but all it said was to lift it over the head and roll it down the body like so. A diagram showed a woman – who clearly didn't need the suit – happily putting it on. It also said to put on the bonus SlimBriefs before putting on the dress-shaped magic suit. I tipped the package upside down and shook out the hidden briefs. They looked like they might just fit a seven-year-old.

Okay, here goes. I was going to fit into this dress if it killed me.

I kicked off my shoes and took off my curved hem outfit, opting to leave my bra on even though it wasn't exactly employee of the month in the breast support department. I stepped into the briefs, the fabric stretching to three times its size and pulled them up towards my hips where they abruptly stopped like a car in back-to-back traffic on the highway, or in this case, the 'thighway'.

"Ugh," I grunted in effort, pulling the briefs upwards. They only moved a smidgen, so I grunted and pulled some more. Bungy jumping would have come in handy right about now. "Ugh," I continued, jumping up and down on the spot in the hope of forcing the briefs over my hips, probably causing the hors d'oeuvres in the kitchen to spring up and down on their platters, while the robotic caterers watched in confusion.

"C'mon!" I pulled harder and the briefs shot up over my hips and squashed my jelly belly into oblivion. Well, apart from the upper abdomen where the rolls billowed out like a giant mushroom. The magic suit would fix that.

"Done." I breathed a sigh of relief until dread washed over me as I realised each trip to the bathroom would be an Olympic feat. I'd just have to go easy on the drinks and anyway, I only had to survive until cake time.

Now for the suit. I held the tiny thing in front of me and

pulled at it. It stretched quite well. I lifted it over my head, fed my arms through it and it sat in a horizontal clump across my collarbones.

Right, step one – check! Now to pull it down over my body. I drew in a deep breath and exhaled, quickly pulling down at the suit, but it only went halfway over my breasts. I breathed deeply again and, letting as much air whoosh out of my lungs as I could, yanked it further down my chest, flattening the boobs on the way. I might as well cancel that mammogram appointment as the SlimFX Magic Suit obviously had its own in-built mammogram function.

"Phew," I said, the suit now clumped across my ribcage.

Step two – check! The last step was to squeeze it down my abdomen and hopefully dissolve the spare tire wrapped around my middle. I shouldn't have glanced in the mirror at that moment but I did, shocked to see I almost resembled a Christmas cracker; pinched tight at top and bottom but thick in the middle.

"Okay, let's do this." I grabbed the suit with both hands and dragged it down my waist, squeezing my torso like a tube of toothpaste and eventually it slid over my hips where it ended just above my knees.

"Mission accomplished." I nodded in satisfaction. Except... why were my breaths coming in shallow bursts?

The suit was constricting my ribcage and I couldn't draw a deep breath. This awareness only made things worse and I panicked. *Oh no, oh no, I'd better take this thing off!*

I reversed my previous steps and pulled upwards at the suit, guiding it up over my hips and belly, and with one giant grunt, up and over my breasts which almost slapped me in the face from the effort. I took a few breaths of relief as the suit sat under my armpits for a moment. I crossed my arms, delivering my hands to opposite armpits and proceeded to pull the suit upwards over my shoulders and head. Only it got stuck halfway at my elbows, my face obscured by a blanket of beige and my arms up in the air, trapped alongside my head inside the suit that sure as hell wasn't magic.

"Argh!" This thing was like a bloody straitjacket! I'd like to see Houdini get out of this one. I yanked and yanked, but the suit wouldn't budge, and now it was almost cutting off my air supply, like I had envisioned my turkey neck could have done during the bungy jump. "Argh!" I panicked, the suit muffling my voice. I twisted and turned, swivelled this way and that, all the while trying to pull the suit up over my head, but there it stayed. In my furious efforts, I bumped into the edge of the bed and toppled over to the floor. My legs flailed about as I tried to get up without using my hands, which were waving about helplessly above my head with my elbow joints locked in place by the 'miracle rip-proof triple-woven fabric' of the magic suit.

Magic Suit my arse. More like Death Suit – this thing was killing me!

I grabbed the edge of the fabric again, pulling as hard as I could, but only managed to squash my face, my upturned nose now practically touching my forehead. I must have looked like one of those criminals who cover their face with stockings. I could rob a bank in this thing, only I'd need an accomplice – or a guide dog – to show me where the hell I was going and possibly an oxygen tank feeding me air through a straw.

Oh my God! What was I going to do? My mind swirled in one chaotic haze, as panic rose within and the chances of getting out of this predicament alive seemed slimmer by the minute. Unlike my abdomen.

Crazy images flashed through my mind of Will finding me passed out on the floor of the bedroom, the magic suit still covering my head, arms still stuck up in the air... paramedics whisking me off to hospital... Will waiting anxiously outside the operating room and the doctor emerging with an expression of defeat, pulling the mask off his face in resignation.

I'm sorry, Mr McSnelly. We did everything we could. We managed to remove some of it, but couldn't get it all, I'm afraid. The situation was too far advanced and she couldn't fight any longer. I'm very sorry.

Will would collapse in tears and the doctor would go back to the operating room and sign my death certificate. *Cause of death: Asphyxiation by SlimFX Magic Suit.*

A lawsuit – ha! how appropriate – would ensue and, if the suits weren't taken off the market, they would at least come with a warning on the packet like cigarettes: *Use magic suit at own risk. May cause death, deformity, or post-traumatic stress disorder.* They'd have a grotesque picture of some poor woman – probably me – trapped in the suit. Others would show gangrenous arms from the circulation being cut off and faces permanently disfigured from the pressure exerted by the suit during its attempted take-off mission. I realised then that I'd have to have a closed coffin at my funeral so as to spare my family from the trauma of seeing me like that. Speaking of coffins, I'd probably need an extra-long one to accommodate my arms, permanently extended above my head from not only the stuck magic suit but also rigor mortis.

Before my mind got carried away further with ridiculous visions from the lack of oxygen, I knew I had to get help.

"Help!" I yelled in a muffled voice, trudging blindly towards where I remembered the bedroom door to be. "Ryan, help!" I screamed through the door and, unable to open it, I banged it with my raised fists, adding a kick of my foot for good measure. The door swung open and banged me on the head, only adding to my dizziness and disorientation.

"Mum! Oh my God!" Ryan's voice exclaimed, as he yanked at the top of the suit.

"Get it off me!" I yelled.

"I'm trying, I'm trying!" He continued yanking.

The poor kid, I'd probably scarred him for life. Thank God I had the good sense to keep my bra on underneath, otherwise this situation would be a whole lot worse with those two buggers on the loose.

"Ugh!" Ryan grunted and then spoke in a muffled voice.

"What did you say? I can't hear properly!" My arms were stuck against my ears so not only could I barely breathe, speak or move, I was half deaf as well.

"I said: you'll have to pull it back down, okay?" he yelled.

"No! I have to get it off, right now!"

"I know, but I've tried and I can't. Let's just pull it back down so we can figure out what to do!"

Except I couldn't pull it back down since my arms were stuck and all blood had most likely drained out of them. Ryan pulled at the suit and it rolled gradually down my arms, over my head, and past my shoulders, until my face was free and I rapidly drew in wonderful, delicious gulps of air.

"There, at least you can catch your breath," Ryan said.

"I... I've... got it... from here, thanks." I turned away from my son and dragged the suit back over mammogram land, and then over my belly and hips. The shallow breaths I took were a welcoming contrast to the strangulation I'd experienced.

"Should I get some scissors?" Ryan asked, pointing out the door where two of the caterers looked on in horror.

"No, I'll just have to leave it on for now. It's okay, I can breathe. It's a little tight, but not too bad. I'll attack it with scissors once the night is over." Which I probably wouldn't need to do because as soon as that cake appeared I was out of here! At least I hoped I would be. I couldn't take any more. This was the last straw. If worse came to worst and I was still here after the party, then at least the magic suit would be a deterrent to William's advances and he'd probably give up and go to sleep.

"You sure?" Ryan asked, and I nodded.

"Although, could you help me into my dress, just in case?" I flashed him an apologetic smile as I stepped into the dress, my body squishing further as he slid the zipper up at the back. There was a moment when I thought it wouldn't go all the way up, but it did. Just.

After the most traumatic moment of my life, bar the bungy jump, I stood dressed and ready for my party. Apart from my hair which appeared starched in an upward fashion, and my lipstick which was now on my nose and my eyeliner which now graced the lines on my forehead.

"Why are you wearing this dress anyway, Mum?" Ryan asked, lines of confusion on his face.

"Why? Don't you like it?" Were red sequined figure-hugging dresses some sort of fashion no-no in the future?

"Of course I like it, but it's a bit old fashioned and anyway, it's not exactly a costume."

"A what?"

"A fancy dress costume. Your birthday event is a costume party, remember?"

Oh, crap. Crap. Crap. Crap.

All that hard work and I could have just worn a big white sheet, easily covered all my bits and called myself a ghost. Ryan's eyes were awaiting an answer, so I racked my brain for an excuse.

"I... I'm... dressing up as my twenty-five-year-old self." *Brilliant, Kelli!*

Ryan's mouth formed an 'o' shape. "Right. Okay, it's different I guess, but great idea, Mum."

Phew. Drama averted.

"So did you wear shoes back then?" He glanced at my bare feet.

"Oh shoes, yes I need shoes!" My toes hooked under the handle of the bottom draw of the wardrobe and pulled it open. Thankfully there was a decent array of shoes to choose from, so long as my feet hadn't gained weight too and needed their own support briefs. There were no red shoes to match my dress, so I plucked out a pair of plain nude heels, slipping my feet inside them.

As I did this, Ryan pulled some kind of mask over his face and I tipped my head back in realisation that his tail was part of a fancy dress costume and not the latest fashion as I had originally thought. "So, what are you dressed as?" I asked.

"Seriously?" he said. "You don't know?"

I shrugged and held my palms up as if the answer might fall into my hands.

"The Lizardile," he said in a teasing manner.

"The what?"

"You know... The Lizardile, from the book and movie series?"

I stared at him blankly.

"The mutant lizard-slash-crocodile who defeated the Lord of Zarcan to free the inhabitants of Drokon Island? The only book and film franchise to outsell Harry Potter?"

"Oh, *that* Lizardile, of course!" How the heck could a mutant lizard crocodile creature thingy outsell Harry Potter?

"And Ben's dressing up as The Frake, my accomplice." I stared blankly at Ryan again as he spoke. "Frog. Snake. Frake?"

"Yes, that's right. It's been a long time since I've seen it." God, I hope it wasn't released just last week or anything. I should really learn to think before I speak. "So, Ben's coming, huh? Have you thought any further about telling him how you feel?"

Ryan dipped his head and sat on the bed. "I was thinking about telling him tonight, but I'm still not sure. What if he doesn't feel the same and then storms out and our band breaks up and he never speaks to me again and I can no longer get discount bungy jumps?"

I sat next to Ryan on the bed, touched that he could talk to his mother about these things. I must be pretty cool. "You'll never know if you don't try," I said.

"I know. I'm just... scared." He picked up his tail and fiddled with the spikes protruding from it.

Awareness of how important this was to him hit me like a slap on the face. All day I'd been concerned only with myself, but somehow, this future was real, even if it wouldn't eventuate again once I got back home. Ryan needed my help, my words of wisdom, if I could summon any.

I drew a sharp intake of air, still somewhat in oxygen debt from the recent trauma, and said, "If you truly love someone and want to be with them, you can't waste any time wondering. You have to take a risk, take the opportunity when it arises and tell them how you feel. Because one day you might wake up and they could be gone. Don't let the chance of happiness slip through your fingers."

Ryan's wide eyes looked at me from beneath his crocodile mask and he smiled. "You're absolutely right, Mum. I'm going to tell him. Tonight."

I seriously hoped I'd given him the right advice and didn't just dig a proverbial grave for his ego. I said what felt right and the rest was up to him. He was a grown man, er... Lizardile.

"Are we having the party in here instead?" Will pushed open the bedroom door and walked through, lifting his tie over his head, kicking off his shoes, and placing a shopping bag – no doubt containing our bedroom supplies – in the corner of the room.

"Mum and I were just having a chat, but I'd better get back out there before the guests arrive," said Ryan. "You should get a move on with your costume, Dad."

"Yep, I know. It won't take long, it's a one-piece suit," he said and Ryan and I burst out laughing. If only he knew what I'd been through with *my* one-piece suit.

Will eyed us with a curious smile and I flicked my hand at him. "Private joke, don't worry."

"Fair enough." He unbuttoned his shirt then paused to glance at his e-pad. "Bugger, I won't have time for a shower." He withdrew a deodorant bottle from his bedside table, giving each of his armpits a quick spray, a warm spicy scent filling the room. "Hey, why aren't you wearing your costume?"

"She's going as her twenty-five-year-old self," Ryan explained, smiling and exiting the bedroom, leaving a whiff of fruity aftershave in his wake which battled with the opposing scent of Will's deodorant.

"Is that so?" Will sidled up to me. "In honour of the age you were when we first met again, huh?"

"Yes, I thought it would be a nice idea."

"And you're even wearing the same dress you wore that night." He ran his hand down my arm and eyed the length of my body. "Looking good, honey." He removed his shirt and shoved it into a chute like the one in the kitchen, revealing a light layer of hair on his chest and surprisingly sculpted abs. Not model material, but he obviously looked after himself. For an old guy.

"Thanks," I said as he undid his belt and, realising I'd see a whole lot more of Will than I was used to if I didn't act soon, I shuffled my tightly enclosed body over to the en suite and opened the door. "I, ah, I'll just fix up my hair and make-up." I slid the door closed behind me just as the pants slid down his legs.

I rearranged my make-up back to its correct geographical

locations and found a brush, hair elastic and bobby pins in the bathroom cabinet to pull my hair back in as close to a chignon as I could manage. I finished off with a spray of some perfume I'd never heard of, but smelt divine, and opened the door a fraction to make sure Will was decent. My jaw dropped as I opened the door to find Will in a Superman outfit, standing with his fists planted firmly on his hips and the moulded muscles of his suit making him appear bigger than he was.

"I've come to rescue you," he said, scooping me off the ground and into his arms then collapsing on the bed with me in laughter. "Okay, my superpowers might kick in a bit later. I need to get warmed up first." He smiled and I couldn't help but smile too. He was such a dork. But a cute dork nonetheless.

Ding, dong!

"Sounds like our first guests have arrived," Will said.

"Can you help me up? My dress is a little on the tight side."

He pushed on my back to lift my rigid body from the bed and I took a preparatory breath.

"Shall we?" He offered his crooked elbow and I linked my arm with his and headed to where the party was about to begin.

Chapter 14
Party Time!

*"Not until we are lost do we begin to understand ourselves." –
Henry David Thoreau*

"It's a bird, it's a plane, it's–"

"It's your father, now come here and give me a hug." Will wrapped his arms around Diora. "How's baby?"

"Kicking like mad, having its own party in there, I'm sure." Diora waddled into the living room, the soft netting of her pink fairy outfit wafting side to side. The fancy wings attached to her back didn't provide any lightness as she trudged towards a seat.

"Hey, man, all ready for fatherhood?" Will asked a man in a wizard costume, presumably Dumbledore as he wore thin glasses, a long white beard pulled into a ponytail at the front and fancy robes trailing on the floor.

"As ready as I'll ever be," he replied.

A short caterer approached carrying a tray of drinks which looked like test tubes. "Can I interest you in a glass of champagne, sir?" he asked Will, who lifted a tube and took a sip.

"Thanks."

"And you, sir?" the caterer-turned-waiter asked Diora's husband.

"No thanks. Permanent on-call taxi duty for me." He pointed to Diora and her protruding belly. "Any day now."

The waiter nodded. "Perhaps you'd like a sparkling mineral water, soft drink, or juice?"

"Lime mineral water please," he said and the waiter disappeared to the kitchen, returning with two tubes of green-tinged liquid, handing one to Diora also.

"And what would the birthday girl like to drink?" The waiter turned to me.

"Champagne, please." I regretted my decision as soon as he'd handed me the tube and I'd gulped half of it in one hit. How I was supposed to get through this party without needing the bathroom and an entourage of assistants to help with my underwear I had no idea.

Diora's husband kissed my cheek and handed me a small gift. Will took it from me and whisked it away to a dedicated gift table, on which sat a vase containing the flowers Selena had sent and an envelope propped against it. I wondered if I'd designed the vase myself. It was unique, shaped like a spiralling splash of water wrapping around the stems. Nice.

"Thanks," I said with a smile and walked to Diora in the Bliss Garden to give her a motherly hug, which triggered a five-minute talking spree about the three stages of labour and the types of aromatherapy oils she planned on using, along with matching music to maximise the effectiveness of the uterine contractions. I expected her to whip out a remote device like the one I'd used in the meeting and give a PowerPoint presentation, complete with graphs and animations and sound effects, but was saved by the bell.

"Happy birthday to our favourite daughter-in-law!" A woman in a green dress with a large blue beehive hairdo and big fake eyes came through the front door, along with a large man with the same eyes wearing a white T-shirt which was obviously filled out with extra padding around the stomach.

"Doh, I forgot the present!" The man ducked outside and returned moments later with a wrapped gift.

Well, well, well... looked like my parents-in-law were Marge and Homer Simpson. So, *The Simpsons* were still popular twenty-five years in the future! They hugged me and asked why I wasn't in fancy dress, so I told them I was the twenty-five-year-old Kelli and they too, like Ryan, thought it was a good idea.

Marge walked through the living room 'ooh-ing and ah-ing' at the decorations and her beehive got caught in a string of origami flowers hanging from the ceiling. "Oh dear, what have I done?" She tugged at the string and instead of coming loose from her beehive it came loose from the ceiling. "Oh, I'm terribly sorry," she said, glancing at Ryan, then at her husband. "I knew I should have come dressed as Madonna." She continued tugging at the flowers stuck to her beehive but they didn't budge.

"Leave them in, I think they look good," Ryan said, snapping a photo of Marge. "Now, you two, over here." Ryan gestured for Will and me to stand near the Bliss Garden. He took a photo with his e-pad and did the same with Diora and Dumbledore, and my parents-in-law who I'd be calling Marge and Homer until I discovered their real names. Or, I could always call them Mum and Dad. Daughters-in-law often did that, didn't they?

I wondered what Grant's parents were like. I knew they were divorced, but apparently still co-owned an investment company and lived in the same street. I was due to meet them tomorrow afternoon on our way to the luxury cabin we'd booked for the weekend. Perfect timing, considering Grant and I would have an announcement to make.

"Can I offer you a drink, sir?" In true Homer fashion, my

temporary father-in-law accepted a beer from the waiter and wandered to The Galaxy outside. Marge followed, getting stuck on another flower on the way.

I downed the rest of my champagne as the doorbell rang again. Kasey walked in baring a little too much flesh than was appropriate for someone of her size. She wore a brown dress – or more accurately, piece of fabric – wrapped around her body like a diagonal sash and her hair was messed up on purpose. "Me, cavewoman," she said gruffly.

"And me, caveman." A man walked through the door after her, nothing but a brown sash covering his groin and a scruffy fake beard attached to his chin. If he was a scientist, he looked like he spent more time outdoors than in and more time at the gym than the lab. He was toned and buff, he was hot, he was...

Max Sheldon! The underwear model Kasey had a crush on since forever and who would have been joining me at my twenty-fifth birthday party.

Kasey married Max Sheldon? How did she score someone like him? He'd had women falling at his feet, could have any woman in the entire world, yet he chose... my sister?

I lifted my jaw from the floor and welcomed them into the house with a kiss on the cheek, and a lingering embrace for Max, because I wanted to feel if his muscles were as firm as they appeared. They were. "It's great to see you, Max, you're looking... very natural."

He gave a caveman grunt, then laughed. "The outfits were Kasey's idea and a good one too. Especially considering today's warm weather."

Kasey sidled up to her husband. "It's going to be even warmer tonight," she whispered, but not soft enough that I couldn't hear, and Max flashed a cheeky grin and wrapped an arm around her, drawing her in for a kiss.

Crash! My champagne tube fell, the shards of glass reflecting flickers of light from the fairy lights around the room.

"Damn! Sorry," I said to the nearest caterer, who deftly scooped up the broken glass and extended some kind of mini sucking machine which eliminated the remaining shards.

Kasey approached and leaned into my ear. "Are you okay? You were pretty upset at lunch, is everything all right?"

"Yes, of course. Sorry about that, I've had a long day, that's all." I pulled a confident smile. "But tonight's going to be great, isn't it? And you and Max, wow, I can't believe..."

Oops.

"Can't believe what?"

"Can't believe how... great you both look. Age has been kind to Max, hasn't it?"

"Hasn't it ever." She winked, before discreetly placing a gift on the table.

I explained once again why I was wearing normal, if somewhat old-fashioned, clothes and lifted champagne from the passing tray. Ryan turned up the music volume, which was obviously not his creation as it sounded nice. Relaxed, ambient, cruisy music, but not too relaxed to be doze-worthy. I bopped my head and tapped my toe so I looked to be enjoying myself and gave thanks that if I didn't know someone's name I could call them by their fancy dress persona. So long as there weren't any more surprises a-la The Lizardile.

A kerfuffle of voices burst through the door, as two men entered wearing police officer costumes – okay, for a moment I thought they actually were police officers – and I startled on seeing the figure of a woman in an elaborate ghost costume. Layers upon layers of floaty white tulle covered her whole body except for her face, painted white with grey shadows under her eyes.

"Recovered from your hot flush yet?" the ghost asked.

"Elaine?"

"My costume's that good, eh? You don't even recognise your best friend?" She winked.

"It's fantastic, very spooky." I nodded, chuckling to myself that she probably dressed as a ghost to avoid wearing a SlimFX Magic Suit like me. Smart woman.

The policemen gave Will a friendly slap on the back then approached me with a hug, which I returned rather pathetically, my arms unable to extend above shoulder height thanks to the restriction of my outfit. A woman entered the house and slid an arm around one of the men, then a familiar-looking woman entered and approached Ryan. She gave him a loud squelchy kiss on both cheeks, which by the look on his face he despised. She wore a soft white halter dress, blond wig and blood-red lipstick, now imprinted onto the small part of Ryan's cheeks that were visible through his mask. She was obviously Marilyn Monroe and I recognised her as the woman from the lift that had spoken to me on my way to the KC Interiors meeting.

"Regina, long time no see, huh?" Will's voice held a tinge of sarcasm.

"Yet I've missed you so much." She repeated her kissing fest on Will's cheeks, before she sidled up to the two men that entered earlier. "And who are these gorgeous beings?" she asked them, holding out her hand. By the looks on their faces, they didn't know whether she expected them to kiss her hand or shake it, but on grasping her hand, Regina pulled one of the men in close and kissed him on the cheeks too, the red lipstick right at home on his flushed face.

"Kelli, honey." Regina kissed me too. "Sorry I didn't stop to chat earlier today, but I knew you had that important meeting. How'd it go?"

"It was... interesting," I replied. "I think it went well."

"And don't you look ravishing tonight? Your dress, what a

lovely vintage piece." She placed her fingers on the shoulder strap.

Vintage? This was new season Vera Wang!

"Now who is that gorgeous guy I had the pleasure of embarrassing?" She pointed to one of the fake policemen. "I only got his name... Steven. But how are you two connected?"

"Um... well, ah..." *How the heck should I know?*

Will came over and propped an arm around each of us. "I hear you've been flirting with my little brother, Regina?"

"Steven's my brother-in-law." I nodded as if I'd known this all along. Phew! *Thanks, Will.*

"And the other one?"

"That's my older brother, John," Will replied. "And," he emphasised, "that woman next to him is his wife."

"I see, well I won't bother with him then, unless... would you say their marriage is strong? Or is it on the rocks, even just a little?" She pinched her thumb and forefinger together in the air.

"Don't even think about it." Will wagged a finger at Regina and as a waiter held a tray in front of her, she swiftly took a glass and tipped her head back.

More people filtered into the house, dressed in various costumes ranging from cowboys to clowns. No one had thought about coming as their younger self and I felt quite proud to be the stand-out among a crowd of people looking like idiots.

"Kelli, happy birthday!" said a woman about thirty or so, swathed in a Cleopatra garment and with long black hair that actually appeared real. "So what did you think of Maurice's proposal on Monday? I mean, what did you really think?"

Huh?

Maurice. Proposal. Okay, I could wing this.

"Well, I thought it was... sweet."

"Sweet?"

"Yeah, sweet. Didn't you? Proposals are always sweet."

She narrowed her eyebrows and tilted her head. "I've never thought of them that way, but I guess, they could kinda be seen as sweet. Considering they're trying to win you over."

"Of course."

"So are you going to say yes?" she asked.

I almost dropped my champagne tube again. "What? Me?"

"Well the decision rests with you of course. You are the creative director."

Ohhh, right. A business proposal. Not a marriage proposal. *Duh, Kelli!* I cleared my throat. "I'll, ah, have to discuss it with Will and have a long hard think about it."

"Right, well I look forward to your decision." She smiled and turned away, greeting a man dressed as a sandwich. A sandwich, can you believe it?

Will, er... Superman strode back to me, one arm outstretched and his fingers curled into a fist as though he was flying. I couldn't help but giggle. "Party's off to a great start, isn't it? The costumes are fantastic," he said.

I nodded, but with all these strange people surrounding me I felt overwhelmed and out of place. "Hey, how about we have the birthday cake now and get it out of the way. What do you say?" I longed for the flicker of birthday candles and the smell of melting wax, the precursor to making my wish and hopefully going back home. It had been kinda cool to experience the technology of the future, but my legs ached, my brain hurt, my boobs were painfully compressed to within an inch of their life and I was tired of putting on a facade. I was ready for home.

"Don't even think about it, the cake will be the highlight of the evening, so naturally we'll leave it until the end of the party. You'll just have to wait." Will tapped me on the nose like a child wanting to open their presents on Christmas Eve.

"But–"

"No buts, just enjoy the next few hours and before you know it the cake will be in front of you, and you can officially kiss forty-nine goodbye."

Goodbye? Forty-nine and I had never officially said hello. And a few hours? Oh man, now my countdown had to start all over again. I pouted and sighed, but Will didn't notice as another guest arrived and took his attention.

Okay, I could do this. I'd been to my fair share of parties before, I just had to remember the Three Golden Rules and I'd be fine:

1. Smile and nod regularly during conversation, even if you have no idea what the person is talking about.

2. Always have a glass in hand (or in this case, a test tube).

3. And NEVER stand directly underneath fluorescent lights.

There. Easy peasy. A haze of white swam towards me. "The house looks great, doesn't it?" the ghostly Elaine said. "Ryan is so talented. I'm going to get him to style my place when he's finished university. If I can afford it." She looked at me hopefully.

"Oh, well of course we'd give you a discount, Elaine."

"Oh, thanks." She placed a hand on her tulle heart and sighed. "You and Will are so lucky."

"What do you mean?" My champagne tube hesitated near my mouth as I awaited an answer.

"I was watching you two before. He's just as much in love with you now as he's always been. You're very lucky." We both glanced at Will who was comparing fake muscles with someone dressed as The Hulk, even though Max Sheldon outdid them both hands down with his natural muscles.

"Um, thanks." I didn't know what else to say.

"You know what, Kel? I often wonder... if I could go back in time and make different decisions, would Peter and I still be together? If I'd followed my dreams instead of casting them aside in the hope of being the perfect wife and mother, maybe I wouldn't have resented him and myself and things would be different. I just wish I knew."

Elaine was more deserving of a fast forward than me, or in her case, a fast backward, or a random rewind or something like that, so she could live the life she'd wanted and possibly save her marriage. Why was this phenomenon wasted on me? "What were your dreams, Elaine?"

"You know, become a chef and open a restaurant, or even a little cake shop with cake decorating classes on weekends, make beautiful wedding cakes, birthday cakes, the lot. But Peter's important job with the police department and his unpredictable schedule would have made it impossible to manage that plus the kids, and it's not like we could have afforded a nanny." She took a swig of champagne. "It was easier to put my cooking skills to use in the home. Sometimes I wonder though, if my family knew how good they had it. How good they *have* it."

Wow, this woman had literally pushed her dreams aside for her family. She was practically a saint, but her sunken smile and tired eyes told me this wasn't something women should aspire to. What good was she to others if she wasn't totally happy with her own life? Women should go after what they want, and surely there were ways to manage a family and a lifelong passion. I'd done it, hadn't I? The future me, I mean.

"It's not too late, you know. What's stopping you from opening that restaurant or cake shop now that the kids are older?"

She flicked her hand towards me and chuckled. "Oh, not this conversation again. I'm just too tired now to start anything new."

"But if you're passionate about something, surely that passion would feed your energy?"

"Maybe… ah, I don't know. I should probably just let things be. I've got a good life, a healthy family. I shouldn't complain. Anyway, tonight's about you, so when are you opening your presents?" Elaine's face changed to a somewhat forced expression of excitement and I felt sorry for her. I almost wanted to give her my birthday cake and tell her to make a wish that would send *her* back in time.

"I'm not sure, I guess Will or Ryan will tell me when it's time for that. They seem to have everything under control." I attempted a deep breath.

"Are you okay?" Elaine asked.

I squirmed a little. "Yeah, it's just that I'm wearing this…" I leaned in close to her ear, "support underwear and it's a bit on the tight side. Plus I really need to go to the ladies room."

Elaine gave me a knowing smile. "Why do you think I wore this ghost costume tonight?" She laughed and I tried to join in but that only put more pressure on my bladder. "Well you better go now while the guests are preoccupied with each other." I shot her a worried look and her eyes widened. "Do you need me to… help?"

"Oh, God no." Was she serious? I mean, I was used to changing into different outfits with a small audience around me, but that was when my body easily slipped in and out of things. Now it would be like sumo wrestling with myself – not something I particularly wanted an audience for. "I mean, I think I'll be fine. If I'm not out in fifteen minutes, maybe you could come and check on me?"

"Deal." Elaine winked and I wandered off towards the bedroom en suite, which was the only bathroom I knew the location of in the house. As I passed the kitchen, a caterer cut a bunch of fresh chives with scissors, sprinkling the green flecks over mini pancakes topped with cream cheese. I walked over to her.

"Excuse me, could I borrow those for just a few minutes?"

"The chives?"

"The scissors."

"Oh, well of course. Just give me a second." She cut up the remaining chives then washed the scissors and handed them to me, curiosity on her face.

I gestured to my bedroom. "Just remembered something I forgot to do earlier. Have to, um... cut something." I scooted off before I sounded more ridiculous and the fact that earlier she had seen me half naked and in the midst of being strangled by rip-proof fabric meant she knew exactly what the scissors were for.

I was really bursting now, so I quickly closed the bathroom door – but didn't lock it in case an emergency rescue was necessary – then eased the dress up towards my hips. It didn't need to be all the way up, just enough that I could get at the support suit with the scissors to cut a strip either side to free things up a bit and be able to wriggle the knickers down enough to do the deed. Getting them back up again... well, I'd deal with that when the time came. If absolutely necessary, I could wait for backup to arrive in fifteen minutes.

I held on to the fabric and positioned the scissors on each side, before pressing down to snip the suit. Only it didn't snip. I tried again, but the scissors only slid sideways as though blunt, which they weren't because I'd distinctly heard the sharp snipping sound when the caterer used them.

Bloody, bloody hell.

I tried stabbing part of the fabric with a sharp corner of the scissors, but it only stretched the suit, not even unravelling a single thread of the triple-woven-rip-proof-piece-of-crap-weapon-of-mass-destruction. If I ever got this suit off, it could be rolled up to double as the heavy duty stretchy rope that William had wanted from the hardware store.

I tried and tried and tried to break through the fabric, but the material was obviously cut-proof as well, at least in terms of regular kitchen scissors. Maybe I needed a surgical scalpel. I even considered hollering out the bedroom window to my Lycra-clad neighbour to ask if I could borrow her garden clippers, but I needed to go to the toilet. Now. I put every ounce of strength I had into lifting the support suit to the minimum height necessary and after beads of sweat moistened my forehead and track marks appeared on my thighs from my fingernails, I did it.

I took as deep a breath as I could and reached my arms underneath to start attacking the support knickers and if it wasn't for my strong desire to go, I would have given up. Eventually they cooperated and I managed to create a small channel of freedom to comply with the anatomical requirements of the situation.

A minute later I met with relief, until I had to reverse the movements for the second time tonight, but at least I only had to go part of the way. To humour myself I tried the scissors again, which was a complete waste of time, although that didn't really matter because it meant I would be slightly closer to the elusive birthday cake/happy birthday singing/make a wish time of the evening.

Despite probably needing some dressings – or perhaps skin grafts – on my fingernail-induced wounds, I emerged relatively unscathed from the bathroom, discarding the pathetic excuse for scissors in the kitchen on the way back. Before I turned to walk back to the living room, aka, Party Hub, a large white cardboard box standing on the kitchen bench took my eye. The caterers were busy facing the other bench, so I sneaked behind them and gently lifted the lid on the box just a fraction.

My birthday cake!

I couldn't make it all out but it appeared to be a model of a water fountain, with twinkly decorations dangling from the top like sprays of water. One large candle protruded from the top and my eyes lit up as though candles themselves. If I could just light it, I could make a quick wish and this party, this life, would be just a memory. In minutes I could be waking up in my fresh organic cotton sheets, stretching my limber arms and sauntering to the bathroom to smile at my twenty-five-year-old face in the mirror...

"Mrs McSnelly!" The caterer I'd stolen the scissors from flicked the lid closed and I blinked and jumped back in surprise. "You go back and enjoy your party, you mustn't be in the kitchen. No more peeking, okay?"

I dipped my head in shame like a schoolgirl caught skipping school and with the help of her gentle yet firm hand on the small of my lower back I scurried back to the party where Elaine looked anxious.

"I was about to go in after you!"

"It's okay, I survived, but the damn thing is scissor-proof!"

"You tried cutting yourself out of it?" Elaine's ghostly eyes rounded and she looked quite eerie.

I nodded and she shook her head with a chuckle. "Oh, Kel, you poor thing! Do you think you'll get through the night?"

"Hopefully. But I'll just go easy on the food and drink. I can't be having to do that every hour or so." I wiped remnants of sweat from my forehead.

"Actually, I'm thinking I might have a similar problem, only I have too much material." She eyed her costume and lifted the layers. "How am I going to lift all of this? I don't even know if I'm going to fit in the bathroom."

I looked at my friend's concerned face and she looked at my sweaty face, and we burst out laughing. "We make a funny pair, you and I," she said, draping an arm around me as we walked towards some guests who were feigning fright at Elaine's costume.

An hour later I mentally kicked myself at not having the willpower to resist the delicious food and drinks on offer. You'd think I would have learned after my last trip to the bathroom, but somehow my subconscious – or my stomach – seemed to be in control, making me eat everything that was offered. Elaine asked if I was sure I had enough room in my stomach, to which I replied, "I'll make room," popping another mini cream-cheese pancake into my mouth. Big Night Caterers had done a fine job and if I remembered when I got home, I'd invest in their company. Not that I knew how one goes about investing, but I could find out.

I glanced around the room at my guests, all laughing, talking and eating, and noticed Ryan approaching Bungy Ben in his frog/snake outfit outside in The Galaxy. His mouth opened to speak, but another young man went up to them and joined the conversation, and Ryan's body stiffened at the intrusion. I was about to go out there in the hopes of luring the young man away for some reason I hadn't decided on yet, when Will's voice took over the room.

"Attention please, everyone," he said into a thin silver stand that was obviously a microphone. "I've taken the liberty of creating a little quiz in honour of this milestone in Kelli's life, so bear with me while I pass around a barcode for you all to scan into your e-pads. Then you can open the quiz answer sheet on your screen." Will walked around the room with a small card and multiple beeps ensued as people scanned the card into their e-pad. Even Mr and Mrs Caveman had e-pads, although their colour matched their fabric sashes.

Hang on... you can change the colour of your e-pad? I quickly opened my menu and clicked on 'settings', scrolling down until I found 'e-pad appearance'. Sure enough, a choice of colours was available. I clicked on 'red' and instantly my e-pad strap transitioned smoothly to a shiny red to match my dress. Nice!

I held out my e-pad when Will approached but he skipped me. "You don't need to do your own quiz, honey, you can just listen and enjoy."

"Fair enough," I said.

Will took his place again at the microphone and cleared his throat. "Okay, time to find out who knows Kelli the best! Anyone who scores one hundred per cent gets a special treat from the lucky dip," he said, pointing to one of the waiters who held up a round receptacle and shook it gently. "So, this is how it's going to work. I'll read each question aloud and you'll have a brief amount of time to choose an answer. I'll reveal the correct answers as we go along. I've programmed your answer sheets to automatically tally your scores at the end of the quiz, so there'll be no cheating." Will eyed Ryan.

"Hey, why are you looking at me?" Ryan defended. "Are you suggesting I don't know enough about my own mother?" he said with a tinge of sarcasm.

To be honest, he probably knew more about me than I did.

"Let's begin," Will said in his best game show voice. "Question one: What is Kelli's middle name?"

Ha! I took back what I said about Ryan knowing more about me than I do. This quiz would be a cinch!

Regina, aka, Marilyn Monroe sidled up to me. "So, what is it, hon?" she whispered.

"Hey, no cheating, Regina," Will scolded with a determined glare.

"Oh come on, it's what I do best," she replied, and I didn't know if she was being literal or cryptic with that comment.

I made a show of zipping my mouth shut to deter potential cheaters, as Will continued. "Okay, time's up. The answer is… Diana. Kelli Diana Crawford and now Kelli Diana McSnelly."

I flinched, but wasn't sure if that was because I still wasn't used to my hideous surname or because of my mother's name being a permanent part of my own.

"Oh darn it, I put down Diane instead of Diana, I knew I shouldn't have listened to you, sweetheart," my father-in-law Homer Simpson said, playfully nudging his wife in the ribs with his elbow.

"Question two: What was Kelli's career before starting KC Interiors?"

Ha! Another easy one. Shame I wasn't being tested, I really wanted a surprise from the lucky dip.

"And the answer is of course… she was a model."

I put my hands on my hips and flashed a pout, although inside I coiled at the phrase 'was a model'. I still am!

"Question three: Where did I propose to Kelli?"

Okay, I take that back about taking that back about Ryan knowing more about me than I did. I bet he knew this. Will had probably told our children a million times if it's important enough to be included in the legendary Quiz About Kelli.

Guests whispered and multiple eyebrows furrowed in concentration. The room looked bizarre with the holographic screens floating in front of everyone and I wondered how and where Will actually did propose. I bet it was a traditional down-on-one-knee at my favourite restaurant kind of proposal.

"Now those who were at our wedding should remember, as I mentioned it in my speech. I proposed to Kelli at a business conference I was speaking at when I was just twenty-six. She only accompanied me so she could go shopping while

I participated in the seminars, but agreed to sit in on my talk to see me in action. I think she was half asleep by the end of it when I clicked on the final slide of my PowerPoint presentation, which showed a photo of us and the words: *Kelli, will you marry me?* Apparently someone had to tap her on the shoulder and tell her to look at the screen, then she walked up on stage in front of three hundred delegates and said 'yes'. It was the best moment of my life, well, apart from our wedding and the day our kids were born." Will smiled and winked at me, and I felt a little gooey inside, and also a little guilty, as I knew Grant would be proposing to me when I got back.

"Okay, speaking of our children, question four: What did Kelli say after giving birth to Diora? a) I've had worse constipation than that, b) If you could bottle that pain it would be a fool proof contraceptive, or c) I need a martini?"

Laughter filled the room and even though I didn't remember saying any of those things, a rush of heat warmed my face and I was sure it now matched my dress and updated e-pad. I dipped my head and decided it was the martini answer, mostly because I could have done with one right at this moment.

This question got everyone talking and some of the women discussed what they had said after giving birth themselves. Elaine remarked that this was when she realised why her mother only had one child.

"Okay, settle down everyone. Ready for the answer?"

"No, I haven't finished yet," Marge Simpson said. "Give me a second."

"Okay... *one.*" He winked at his mother and shrugged when she shot him a *don't be cheeky with me, young man* look.

"The answer is b) If you could bottle that pain it would be a fool proof contraceptive." Will grinned.

You're kidding? Who knew I could come up with something

witty like that, huh? It must have hurt real bad, thank God I didn't really go through it.

"That's a classic, Kelli," one of Will's brothers said. I couldn't remember his name.

"Right-i-o, question five: What role did Kelli play in the parents and children's school production of *Snow White and the Seven Dwarfs?*"

Oh. Another one I didn't know. But I bet the answer was Snow White, no, the Evil Queen – yes, I bet that's right.

"I know that one!" Elaine piqued up, entering her answer into her e-pad screen. "We were backstage buddies."

"I know that one too," Diora said.

Will smiled and waited for everyone to enter their answer. "The answer is... Grumpy! Kelli played Grumpy, one of the seven dwarfs."

No way! How could that be? It wasn't fair! And I was far from dwarfed.

"I played the Evil Queen," Diora said, looking the complete opposite in her pink fairy costume.

Yes of course. She would have been perfect at that. Not that she was evil, but she could definitely take control of any given situation.

"I was Sleepy," Elaine said. "Which I played well because I was actually sleepy at the time." She laughed.

"Question six, another multiple choice: What affliction did Kelli endure after our family ski trip last year? a) broken ribs, b) gastroenteritis, or c) a broken fingernail?"

Skiing? I've never been skiing before in my life. Probably the broken fingernail, it's so annoying when that happens, especially when you've been growing them all to the same length and then you have to go and cut the rest to match the broken one. Or get acrylics and put up with the mask-mouthed nail technician going on about the injustice of health insurance companies not covering manicures, which kind of made sense when you thought about it. Nails were part of the human body after all, why should they be treated any differently to feet, or eyes, or even hair for that matter. Yes, hairdresser fees should be covered by health insurance too.

"They all sound unbearable to me," Regina said, curling her fingers to examine her own fingernails.

"Time's up. The answer is a) broken ribs. Poor Kelli bit off a little more than she could chew when she opted for the Daredevil ski challenge. She spent the next several weeks recovering and I tried to keep her from laughing, sneezing, or coughing, which considering she caught Ryan's cold a week later made for a very difficult situation!"

"Yeah, it was a tough time," I said, nodding and absorbing the looks of sympathy from my guests.

"Now something a little different... question seven: What did Kelli buy me for my fortieth birthday party?"

"C'mon, no multiple choice for that one?" someone called out.

"No, we're getting to the tough end of the quiz now."

"I know this one too!" Elaine busily typed up her answer.

What would I have bought my husband for his birthday? A watch? A subscription to *Business Monthly* magazine?

"A Man Spa salon pampering package, including a massage and facial!" Will revealed.

Yeah, that.

"I bet you enjoyed it, didn't you, man?" one of his police officer brothers said.

"How else could I look this good?" Will stroked his chin with his thumb and forefinger, then laughed. "If you must know, it was a very relaxing day." He smiled at me and I smiled back.

"Was it better than sex?" Elaine called out, and immediately her hand flew to her mouth. "Oops, I can't believe I just asked that, sorry! Must be the champagne talking." Her ghostly pallor brightened a little as some of the guests laughed.

"And lastly, question eight: What is Kelli's favourite movie?"

I've been redeemed. *Sex and The City* for sure. The first one, not the sequel.

"And the answer is of course, the Oscar winning movie, *Destined.*"

What?

"We saw it on our first anniversary and as the credits rolled, Kelli turned to me and said, 'That is the best movie I've ever seen'. I asked her last week and she still agrees."

Never even heard of it.

"Woohoo, I got all of them right!" Elaine stood and pumped the air with her fist, as did Diora. Well, Diora pumped the air but didn't stand, her rounded body perched permanently on a pod in the Bliss Garden. Three people I didn't recognise also 'woohoo-ed' and the waiter approached them with the lucky dip bowl. They each reached inside and plucked a mystery gift, but by the looks of it they were all chocolate, each with a unique name.

"I got Chocolate Passion," Elaine said, lifting her cellophane-wrapped chocolate truffle. "I'll take any passion I can get." She pulled off the wrapper and popped the chocolate into her mouth.

"Chocolate Dream for me," Diora said, while the other three winners got Chocolate Scandal, Chocolate Secret and Chocolate Love.

"Can't I get a lucky dip too? I only just missed out, seven out of eight," Ryan said.

"Me too," Kasey declared. "Close enough?"

"Nope, rules are rules. Congratulations to our five winners

and don't worry, we'll have chocolates and coffee later, as well as delicious cake."

Cake. I leaned forward and peered longingly towards the kitchen, the key to my doorway home residing in that cardboard box. Two out of eight, that's all I got in the Quiz About Kelli. That's a measly... um... *oh, I don't know, some measly percentage.* I was sure my e-pad had an inbuilt calculator but what was the point? I'd failed miserably in a quiz that was all about me. Elaine, a woman I knew nothing about, knew everything about me. Who was this woman I'd become?

Chapter 15
There's No Time Like the Present

"When the music changes so does the dance" – *Nigerian proverb*

"Oн, look! Kelli's doing the robot dance," one of Will's brothers said as he approached the makeshift dance floor in the living room-Party Hub.

"No I'm not," I interjected, but on looking down at my stiff torso and rigid arms I realised I *was* dancing more robotically than intended. Not that I'd planned to dance even remotely robotically. Will's brother – was it Steven? – sidled up next to me and matched my movements, holding his elbows at a ninety-degree angle and moving them up and down. Will joined in too, pulling off a rather brilliant robotic performance and I agreed that I was in fact doing the robot dance.

More guests participated, competing for the impromptu Robot Dancer of the Night award, which Will awarded to Cleopatra, the woman who'd asked me about some business proposal. Turned out she used to be a dance teacher, so no wonder she won, although if the caterers had participated I think they would have been in with a good chance.

After another fifteen minutes in the bathroom wrangling with my support suit, this time armed with Band-Aids to dress the fingernail wounds and body lotion to help the fabric slide more easily, I emerged to find Diora standing for a change, at the microphone.

"Listen up, everyone, it's time for the best part of the evening..."

"The cake?" I asked with a little too obvious enthusiasm.

"No, Mum, the presents!"

Bugger. Then again, I did like presents.

"So, Mum, if you'd like to take a seat over here." Diora gestured towards a stool near the present table. "You can begin opening the presents. Dad, you all set to take photos?"

I sat on the stool and Will stood nearby, e-pad at the ready with a little square shaped hologram hovering above it. As I picked up the first present, a small box with gold wrapping and a red bow, Will snapped a photo of me.

Seriously, what would a person in this day and age do without their e-pad?

"That's from me, Mum." Diora beamed.

I looked up at my daughter. "But you already bought me the facial earlier today. You didn't have to get me anything else." Then again, who was I to refuse? "Thanks, sweetie." I pulled at the red ribbon.

"Wait, don't forget to read the card," she said.

What card? I glanced at the sparkly gift and on the underside was a small barcode stuck to the paper. Oh, right! Hoping like hell it wasn't just the barcode from the wrapping paper, I subtly held it near my e-pad and with relief a beep sounded.

Do you want to open or save document? the screen asked.

I pressed 'open' and a beautiful birthday card came to life before my eyes. It showed a woman walking through a magical forest, staring at the twinkling stars in the sky. She pointed to one and it glowed, before bursting into a thousand tiny flickering embers of light, leaving behind the words: *May all your wishes come true on your birthday ~ your daughter, Diora.*

I smiled in delight and glanced again at my daughter, her face weary but happy. "I certainly hope they do. Thank you, darling." I pulled off the ribbon and lifted the gift from its wrapping. When I opened the box a shiny pendant winked at me, its smooth oval shape framing a red jewel in the centre.

"And I didn't even know you were wearing red tonight, how appropriate!" Diora said.

"It's perfect." I lifted the necklace from its case and held it up to the peering crowd. As it spun side to side on its chain, an inscription on the back caught my eye. I squinted and held it at arms-length to read it.

If I am this gem, then you are the precious metal, because without your strength and support I could not shine my light to the world. ~ Diora.

Oh my God. Was I *crying*? A gentle warmth radiated from within and caressed my body. My eyelids blinked over slippery eyes. "Diora, that's beautiful. I don't know what to say." I stood up and walked to her, my arms encasing her just like the necklace, although not all the way around because there was the issue of the restricted arm movement, compounded by Diora's large belly.

"Happy birthday, Mum," she whispered.

Composing myself, I resumed my position on the stool and picked up the next present.

"That's from me," Elaine said.

"Another one from you too? Wow, I'm totally spoilt." I smiled.

Inside a rectangular box was a plastic gift card with Wildfire

Women's Resort on the front. I squinted again at the writing on the back, which told me I was entitled to a two-night stay.

"I've got one too, so we can have a girl's weekend away!" Elaine beamed. "I was thinking sometime next month, but whatever works for you."

"Thank you, Elaine." For someone who seemed fairly budget conscious, this plus the facial from today must have been a stretch. A strange and unfamiliar sensation crept its way around my body, peering into nooks and crannies and believe me, I had developed quite a few of those. My heart softened like cotton wool. "I'm humbled by your generosity."

Her ghostly figure floated towards me and embraced me. "How are you coping with the suit?" she sneaked in before pulling away.

My parents-in-law weaved to the front of the crowd as I picked up their present. I tore away the Victorian floral paper and stared at the package. *Household Helper - Instant Vacuum.*

How could this be a vacuum cleaner, the box wasn't large enough. "Oh, thanks. I've been wanting one of these!" I forced my eyes wide to express excitement at such a gift.

"I thought you might, especially after last Christmas when you complained about your sore back from all the vacuuming," Marge Simpson said. "This will make things much easier for you." She turned the box over and pointed to the illustrated instructions. "You just install the devices in a corner of each room, make sure there's nothing small and valuable on the floor, press the red button, and voila! All dust from up to seven metres away is sucked into the device."

Now that's my kind of housework.

"But how does all the dust fit into such a small device?" Elaine asked, her forehead furrowed as she examined the box.

Homer Simpson waddled his ample belly towards the fascinated guests gathered around the Household Helper.

"What happens is, the dust is compressed to half its size and then dispersed into nanoparticles which the device then compresses again, causing a compound effect which reduces the molecular size tenfold." My father-in-law should have come dressed as Einstein.

"In other words, honey, it makes the dust smaller so you don't have to empty the device that often," Will added.

"I have to get one," Elaine stated.

"I got one a few months back," Regina said with a flick of her blond Marilyn wig. "A reward to myself for my business going above and beyond its income targets."

"Ah, so the matchmaking industry's still going bug guns, eh?" Will asked Regina.

"Totally. I think ConnectNow's success comes from the fact we also have a showroom, something the online-only dating websites can't compete with."

So that explained Regina's interest in all things romantic. She's a professional flirt! But a showroom for potential romantic partners? How did that work? I imagined walking into such a showroom and asking, 'Do you have any tall, dark, handsome doctors in stock at the moment?' to which the salesperson might say, 'Sorry, we're all out as they were on special last week. Can I put you down for a backorder and notify you when one becomes available?'

I swallowed my giggles and thanked Marge and Homer for the gift, then picked up a flat rectangular package wrapped in a luxurious silk scarf.

"The scarf is the real present, Kelli," Regina explained. "What's inside is more of a... how do I say it?... novelty gift, if you like. One cannot turn fifty without a little gimmick in honour of advancing age now, can they?" She winked and my stomach plummeted.

Oh man, what could it be? It wasn't going to be those

incontinence pads, was it? Or some kind of adult diaper? I reluctantly tugged at the package. Worse. A sense of déjà vu washed over me as cardboard packaging greeted my eyes, complete with a picture of a slim woman smiling in her beige underwear.

A SlimFX Magic Suit version 2.0, *New and Improved*, the label said. *Now with expandable release valve for ease of use!* In other words – *now with expandable release valve for getting in and out of the damn thing without requiring hospitalisation and emergency surgery.*

I faked a laugh. "Haha thanks, Regina. Just what I've always wanted!"

Elaine glanced my way with an expression that said 'How dare she give you something like that in front of everyone' and Ryan's mouth appeared about to explode with a lump of laughter. Despite the awkwardness of the situation, I wished Regina had given me this earlier so I could have saved myself the trouble of dealing with version 1.0.

"Anyway, not that you need one, Kelli, but they're actually pretty good. Gives you a nice smooth line under a fitted dress. I'm wearing the discreet strapless version now, can you tell?" Regina twirled and her Marilyn Monroe dress lifted and spun with her, and no, I couldn't tell. "Sorry, I just had to do that! Get into character, you know?" She winked again and it could have been a coincidence but Will's brother stepped slightly to the side, away from Regina.

I opened more presents, including a heat-sensing automatic temperature-adjusting blanket from Kasey and Max, along with a donation on my behalf to the Ants Have Feelings Too research foundation, and watched more amazing moving birthday cards, until only one thing remained on the present table. A white envelope.

It seemed strange that among all this technology, paper still actually existed. I slid my finger under the seal and pulled out a plastic card about the size of a book... if books still existed, I certainly hadn't seen any around the house.

"Oh, whoops, that was supposed to be for later," Will said. "Ah, might as well have it now, then." His face went slightly pink.

"What is it, Kel?" Elaine asked with curious eyes.

"It's a..." I began, my cheeks becoming hot.

Ryan came over and plucked the card from my hands. "C'mon, the suspense is killing us!" He read the card and grinned. "It's a couple's intimate photo shoot at Image of Desire studios."

"Woo-woo!" Regina said and a few cheers and whistles escaped the mouths of my guests, as Will held out his hands.

"Now calm down, everyone, it's just a makeover and photo shoot for married couples, nothing raunchy."

"Yeah right," Ryan exclaimed. "Have you seen the portfolio on the gift card? Look." He pressed a button on the card and a slideshow played, showing various couples wearing minimal clothing embracing in imaginative positions like strands of spaghetti clinging to a fork.

A makeover and photo shoot I could handle, but with Will? Doing... that? My stomach lurched as I attempted to steal the card back from Ryan, who was holding it up in the air for everyone to see, keeping it out of my grasp. "Give it to me, son, that's enough of your teasing," I said in a motherly voice and interestingly, it worked.

"Sorry, Mum. It's just funny, that's all." He handed me the card and I shoved it back in its envelope as Will mouthed a red-faced 'sorry' at me. I flicked my hand as though it was nothing and then reopened Diora's gift in an effort to distract myself – and everyone else – asking the nearest person to help me latch the necklace around my neck.

"There is another present, Mum," Ryan said in a more serious tone.

"Huh? But you already took me bungy jumping."

"You went bungy jumping?" Marge Simpson leapt from her seat, her beehive wig almost toppling forward.

"Didn't you know?" Homer asked. "I told you yesterday, remember, when you were baking that soufflé?"

"Darling, you should know by now to never talk to me when I'm baking, especially a soufflé, I won't remember a thing for the concentration it requires."

"Yes, she sure did," Ben said. "She was awesome!" Ryan glanced longingly towards Ben and smiled, before turning back to me.

"This is something extra special, I've been planning it for a while," Ryan said.

Oh dear God. Don't let it be skydiving, or hang gliding, or a one-way trip to Mount Everest. Please!

But Ryan simply walked over to the microphone along with Ben, who sat at a small drum set – how did I not notice a set of drums in my living room before? Another young guy picked up two guitars, handing one to Ryan, who held on to the stem of the microphone and looked in my direction. "Mum, this one's for you."

He strummed the guitar and a rhythmic melody filled the air, accompanied by Ben's slow and steady beat on the drums and the other guy's twang on his guitar. Guests gathered around, some swaying to the music with their loved one, while I stood in the centre, my eyes fixed on the sight before me and ears taking in the unexpected beauty of the music my son was creating.

Then he sang, his slow crooning tone perfect, merging with the music.

"The one whose gifts she shared,
     The one who always cared,
     Mum... she's the one."

They were just words, but the way he sang them with such emotion and conviction, it was as though they were pebbles dropping into a pool of joy, their impact spreading outwards in loving ripples.

"She never left my side,
     She taught me to express, not hide,
     Mum... she's the one."

Guests turned on the light on their e-pads and held them up in the air, waving and swaying them to the music like they were candles and I did the same, while a smile played on my lips.

"When times were so tough I thought I'd die,
     She held me till my tears were dry,
     Mum... she's the one...
     And as I get ready to leave the nest,
     I want you to know you've been the best,
     Mum... she's the one...
     Yes, Mum... you're the one."

His voice lifted high on the last note, raising a swirl of emotion to the roof and letting it float softly back down, filling the room as he drew the words out in one slow, last breath.

He bowed his head and stood still for a moment as applause lifted the energy of the room back up to the roof. My heart pulsing and filling with pride, I walked up to Ryan – my son – and slid my arms around his back as a lone tear slid down my face.

Chapter 16
Be Careful What You Wish For

"Why is a birthday cake the only food you can blow on and spit on and everybody rushes to get a piece?" – Bobby Kelton

Our embrace broke as a high-pitched tapping rang through the air. Will approached the microphone, tapping at a glass with a spoon and Ryan moved to the side to allow his father to take centre stage.

"If I could have everyone's attention, please. The time has come for me to say a few words about my darling wife, Kelli. I've taken the liberty of creating a little show for you, so pull up a pod and enjoy." He put down his glass and picked up a remote, like the one I used at the meeting and pointed it at a blank area of wall behind him. A screen grew to life, showing a picture of me along with a heading: *Fifty Years of Kelli McSnelly* – Oh joy.

A song I didn't recognise played and an image of myself as a rosy-cheeked baby appeared, much to my embarrassment. The image transitioned to another of me as a four-year-old, standing on top of the tree house Dad had built. Kasey was also in the picture, stuck on the bottom rung of the ladder, as she'd been too young. There were school photos, ranging from the younger years to the early teenage years and photos of me with my friends at a birthday party; my fifteenth from memory. Cringing, I wondered if I'd really thought floral dresses were cool?

This was my life – set to music. As if aware of the rapid shift in my life from age twenty-five, the song's tempo intensified and pictures I didn't recall faded in and out on the screen. Will and I at our engagement party and wedding, arms entwined with wine glasses in our hands. My heart raced as I discovered this life of mine one picture at a time, the gap between when I went to bed last night and this very moment gradually being filled. I tapped my foot to the music and also because I was anxious to see the next picture.

Oh my God. Was that my stomach? In the photo I was standing side-on, one hand placed over my swollen belly, ready to pop at any moment. The next picture showed me in the hospital holding a squashed up little human and smiling like I'd been given the best present of my life. I glanced over at Diora sitting on a pod in the Bliss Garden, her glossy eyes fixed on the screen, rubbing her belly and felt a warm pang of an emotion I'd never experienced before.

The photos continued... Diora as a tiara-wearing toddler, commanding the room with her toy microphone and another hospital photo, this time with baby Ryan whose hair must have had delayed growth because he was completely bald. Willing my eyes not to blink so as to not miss a moment, I glued them to the wall as photos of me with Will and the children graced the screen.

On Diora's first day of school I had red blotches under my eyes and a tissue in my hand, the other hand holding firmly onto Diora's. There was the four of us on holiday at a water park, my hands outstretched to catch Ryan at the bottom of the water slide. I laughed, along with all my guests at the photo of me and Diora at a festival with our faces painted like cats, and Will and I collapsed on the floor during a game of Twister.

There were several photos of me, Elaine and Diora dressed in our costumes for the production of *Snow White and the Seven Dwarfs*. My face was scrunched up to suit my Grumpy character. Not very becoming at all, but funny nonetheless and probably the trigger for the beginning of my crow's feet and forehead furrows – definitely the lip wrinkles.

More photos slid by, including me working at a large table, drawing designs onto paper and glancing up at the camera with a look of peace. Another where I was dressed in a suit and standing in front of a display table full of homewares from KC Interiors, and another right at the moment of opening a bottle of wine, my face turned away from the liquid spraying everywhere. Next was a picture of me with a group of about ten sitting on the beach at night, eating fish and chips, with the heading 'Kelli's 49th birthday'. A caption above my image said, 'This is the most memorable birthday ever,' and the one above Ryan said, 'You just wait till next year, Mum.' Boy, was he right or what?

And finally, a photo of our family on the skiing trip where I broke my ribs, followed by the video of my bungy jump from this morning, luckily without a close-up view of my screams for life. Strange, to see the jump from an outsider's point of view, when my memory felt so different to what it looked like on the screen. At the end of the video, the music ended with a photo of me as I was today, smiling and wrapped in a woolly jumper. Everyone cheered, raising their clapping hands in the air, some raising their tubes of champagne. I nodded my thanks at everyone and Will tapped his glass again.

"Wasn't that great? I'm so proud of Kelli," Will said, as the crowd quietened down to listen to the man of the house speak.

"When we first met, Kelli was a twelve-year-old towering beauty, while I was a pudgy kid with pimples. Somehow, the universe conspired to bring us together again years later and before I could pinch myself, Kelli had accepted my proposal and become my wife."

"That's my bro!" One of Will's brothers cheered and draped an arm around me, his beer breath filling my nostrils. "Ah, you've made my brother very happy, Kel."

"He's, er... made me very happy too," I replied.

Will blew me a kiss before continuing. "I must admit, when I was younger I was overwhelmed by her stunning beauty, but as I got to know her, I became more overwhelmed by her amazing creative talents, not to mention her inner drive and passion. Separately, we are quite different, but together, we fit. Like two opposing pieces of a puzzle, or a lock and a key, we're a perfect match." Will took a deep breath and his Superman chest puffed outwards. "Kelli, honey, you're the reason I get up every day, you're the reason I smile before I go to sleep every night and you're my inspiration to keep being the best I can be. You're the love of my life."

His voice faltered at the last few words and a slight trembling vibrated my lower lip as I placed an appreciative hand over my heart. He walked towards me and I met him in the middle, allowing myself to soften into his arms. Despite his costume I could feel his heart beating in sync with mine. We stood like that for a few moments until he pulled back.

"I forgot, I have another present for you!" Will scurried over to a corner table and lifted a lamp, under which another envelope was hiding. He took residence in front of the microphone again. "In honour of the life we've shared together and this momentous occasion, I wanted to treat Kelli and myself to a special birthday gift. Open it, honey." He thrust the envelope in my hand and I ripped it open. I couldn't care less if it was another intimate photo shoot, or a voucher for a couple's tantric yoga class, I was beyond feeling embarrassed. I simply buzzed with the excitement and joy of being in the moment.

Everyone stood by in silence as they awaited my response. I gasped on lifting the itinerary from the envelope, then leaned in towards the microphone.

"Wow, this is amazing." I looked at the faces fixed on me. "It's a four-week European holiday! Oh, Will, I've always wanted to go travelling!" I hugged him.

"I know you have and I know you gave up your plans of modelling internationally when we started a family and then the business, so I thought it was about time we ventured out of the safety of our own country, see the world!"

I jumped up and down, excitement bubbling through my veins. The guests cheered again, Elaine shouting, 'Take me with you!' and Diora saying, 'Come back safely, I'll need you to babysit', when one of the caterers approached, carrying the triple-layered model of a water fountain that was my birthday cake.

I hadn't noticed its pure brilliance before, the white, almost silvery frosting embracing each layer and the dangling sprays of edible silver baubles acting as water streaming from the fountain took my breath away. It was a masterpiece. Elaine moved towards it with her mouth gaping, clasping her chest. She was practically having a coronary just looking at it.

The caterer placed the cake on a small table nearby and gestured for me to sit in front of it. The lone candle flickered backwards and forwards, as though unsure which direction to go... and then my heart stopped.

My cake. The time had arrived. The moment I'd been waiting for sat in front of me with an open invitation to my old life. Yet I was that flame, rocking backwards and forwards between two worlds.

"Happy birthday to you,
    Happy birthday to you,
    Happy birthday dear Kelli,
    Happy birthday to you!"

Forty or so voices filled the room but all I could hear was the ticking of my mind.

Tick, tock, tick tock, past, future, past, future...

"Aren't you going to make a wish and blow out your candle?" Ryan asked.

I sat there, frozen, despite the flame tempting me with its inviting glow. I glanced around at all the people, my friends and family, urging me on, their love and support diffusing through every fibre of my being. Will... the words from his speech echoed in my mind and thoughts that I might feel the same way about him jumped around in confusion. At that moment, I was me and I was happy.

Could it be that good old William McSnelly had brought out the best in me? Rescued my heart from its Prada snakeskin enclosure and set it free? What about Diora and Ryan? If I went back and married Grant, they'd never exist. Their life would never happen. Diora's baby would never happen. All day I'd known what I wanted, but now, with the opportunity waiting, I couldn't decide. The life I'd planned or the life I'd glimpsed today?

I glanced around one last time, my friends and family clapping rhythmically and chanting, 'Kel-li, Kel-li, Kel-li...' and sucked in the deepest breath possible, air filling and expanding my lungs. The flame blurred under my focused glare and I blew out the air from my lungs as hard as I could. The scent of smoke and melted wax wafted in the air as I clamped my eyes shut.

Chapter 17
Rebirth

"Your work is to discover your world and then with all your heart give yourself to it." – Buddha

I KEPT my eyes closed as voices emerged around me, counting and clapping hands... one clap for each birthday. If they stopped at twenty-five it meant I was back home. I kept my eyes shut tight as the count passed eighteen. *Was this it*, I wondered as they reached twenty-five. Was I back? The counting continued. When I'd blown out the candles, I hadn't wished to go back and I hadn't wished to stay. I'd wished for the best possible life for me to unfold as it should. Taking another breath, my eyes inched open to a blur of smiling faces around me. Fifty!

"Happy birthday, Kelli!" The claps stopped their repetition and dispersed into a random cacophony. My eyes darted towards Will, snapping photos and to Ryan, thumping his lizard tail on the floor in rhythmic enthusiasm and Diora, seated on her pod in the Bliss Garden nearby, her smile radiating to space. I was home. Not home as I knew it, but home where my heart was.

"Speech, speech, speech, speech..." the crowd chorused, and Ryan lifted me to my feet towards the microphone, while my mind struggled to think of what to say.

I tapped the microphone to check it was working. "Thanks, everyone, thank you so much. Wow, where do I start? It's been an amazing day, I–"

"Uh-oh," Diora called. Ryan leapt towards her with a gasp and his hands flew to his face as the giant origami lotus under Diora's pod wilted from dampness. "My water broke!" An apologetic smile flashed across Diora's face.

"My lotus broke!" Ryan knelt down at the dying flower's side, then shot back up again. "Your water broke? Mum, Dad, her water broke! Where's Jason?"

Dumbledore flew to his wife's side. "Are you okay? Do you feel okay?"

She nodded, but rubbed her belly. "Well, I have been getting these twinges all day. Maybe they're not just Braxton Hicks after all."

My daughter was in labour! Talk about timing, my birthday speeches always seemed to get interrupted.

Will's frozen shock quickly melted and he shot into action. "Right, Jason – you and I will help Diora into your car. Kelli – you grab a towel and some water just in case. Oh, and scissors!"

"What do you need scissors for?" I asked, although the same could have been asked of me earlier.

"The umbilical cord."

"I don't think things will progress that fast, the prenatal classes told us it could be around twelve hours before the baby comes out," Jason said.

"Owww," Diora moaned. "I think I'm having a contraction." Jason rubbed her back and waited for it to pass while I grabbed the supplies. Although, it took me a while to find the towel since there weren't any in the bathroom. I couldn't exactly bring the whole body-dryer thing-a-ma-jig with me. I eventually found one tucked away in a linen cupboard in the hallway and returned to my daughter's side. The party guests hovered about trying to appear helpful.

"Mum, I want you to come with me. You've been through this, I need you with me," Diora's eyes pleaded.

"I'll go too," Will said. "I'll sit in the front while Jason drives and keep him calm. Honey, you can look after Diora in the back. Okay?"

"Okay." I think. I'd never seen anyone in labour before. I'd only seen those horror shows they made us watch in school – the ones that make you never want to have children.

"You guys go, I'll look after things here," Ryan said, ripping off his lizard mask and gesturing to the stunned caterers. "Could we get coffees and teas all round, please and make sure everyone gets a slice of cake. Mum, quick, you just need to make the first cut on the cake! It's bad luck to have someone else do it."

I looked towards the cake, then back at Diora and back at the cake again. "Okay then." I raced to the cake and a caterer handed me a large knife. As I pushed it through the firm yet yielding sponge, I made another wish. That Diora's birth would go smoothly, and that she and the baby would remain healthy. Satisfied with my intention, I turned to Ryan. "Save me a piece, will you?"

"I'll save you the biggest piece of all, Mum." He smiled and I hugged him briefly before saying a quick thanks to all the guests and returned to where Jason and Will helped Diora towards the front door. My daughter needed me and I wasn't going to leave her side.

"Do you need us to come too?" Marge called out after us as we walked down the front steps.

"Thanks, Beryl, but I think she'll be right with the three of us. We'll call you with any news," Jason said.

Beryl, so that's my mother-in-law's name. Beryl McSnelly. Poor woman.

"I reckon it'll be a boy!" Homer called out, his belly taking up more universal space than Diora's.

"No, Reg, it'll be a girl, I tell you," Beryl replied, before closing the door.

Reg McSnelly.

Diora stopped by the side of the car. "Oooh, my stomach's tightening. God, this is weird. Oww..." She leaned forwards onto the car and I rubbed her back while Jason started up the engine. Will opened the passenger side door and lay down a towel, placing the scissors into the pocket behind the driver's seat and the water bottle in the drink holder. Jason took a sip of coffee through the straw of his in-built coffee machine, before turning his head around.

"How's it going?"

"Can't... speak," Diora panted through her contraction.

"I think this one's just about done, then we'll get in," I said, as Diora's face relaxed again. "Okay, in we go." I helped her angle into the passenger seat and offered her a sip of water, which she pushed away.

"I don't want any," she said, a tear running down her face. "I'm scared, Mum. What if I can't handle the pain?"

"Oh, sweetie," Jason began. "Do you want me to come back there with you?"

"No! Just drive and get me to hospital. I need my mum," she blurted, and another tear escaped. "Sorry, hon, I'm just feeling a little overwhelmed."

Jason extended his hand behind the seat and rubbed her knee before returning it to the steering wheel and driving down the road.

"You'll be fine, I know you will," I said, placing her hand in mine – which was a mistake.

"Argh!" Diora gripped my hand tighter than the SlimFX Magic Suit gripped my torso. "Ooohh, oww, eoww!" A series of primal moans flooded the car and after a couple of minutes, subsided. "Oh, man, they're getting worse!"

"It's okay, sweetheart, it's natural, your body knows what to do." Fat chance my words were of any comfort. From all I knew – which was little – about childbirth, it hurt like hell. Worse than twenty broken bones all at once, I read somewhere. Forget about whether she could handle it, I didn't know if I could watch her try to handle it.

"Should I ask for an epidural?"

"Definitely," Will said.

"She should?" I asked.

"Honey, don't you remember how much easier it was for you the second time around when you had an epidural with Ryan?"

"Um, that's right," I replied and looked at Diora. "But you should do what feels right for you. Ask the nurses what they think."

Diora nodded and leaned back on the seat, closing her eyes, as if to conserve all her energy.

"Oh, what the hell?" Jason said, the car slowing down.

"What? What?" Diora's head shot up.

"It's just a slight build-up of traffic, that's all. Don't you worry, focus on yourself and I'll focus on getting us to the hospital." Diora didn't see Jason silently mouth a profanity.

The car came to a stand-still, car horns beeped and voices yelled "Oh, c'mon!" and "Hurry up losers!" Jason's fingers drummed impatiently on the steering wheel and the car spoke:

"This traffic incident was unexpected. Recalculating route..." And after a few minutes, "There is no alternate route suitable at this stage, go straight on. Estimated travel duration at current speed... three hours and thirty-seven minutes."

"No!" Diora exclaimed, just before her stomach hardened into a tight lump and sweat beaded on her forehead.

Jason thumped his fist on the steering wheel. "This isn't happening. No way!"

"Give it a few minutes, maybe it'll ease up. Might have just been a truck spilling its load," Will suggested.

"If we don't get to hospital my wife will be spilling *her* load!" he replied.

"Take a deep breath, mate. We'll get there, don't you worry. We can always call an ambulance if necessary, but I doubt it will be."

"Okay, okay, it's all going to be fine. Yep, all's good," Jason said, mostly to himself. "There'll probably be hours and hours to go yet anyway."

"Don't say that!" Diora cried.

"Oh, I don't mean hours and hours, honey, just that there'll be plenty of time to get to hospital."

"I need to puke." Diora leaned forwards, her cheeks bulging and a hand flew to her mouth.

"No, no, no! Damn, should've brought a bucket!" Jason turned to face us in the back seat, his eyes darting everywhere. "Try and hold it in. What can we use as a bucket?"

Diora had her own idea though and simply opened the car door and released her stomach contents onto the road. Thank God the car was idle or the cars behind would have needed high speed heavy duty windshield wipers. A kid about six in the car next to us saw the performance and his face scrunched up. An older kid about nine sitting next to him opened the window and said, "Awesome! There's a puking fairy next to us!"

Diora closed the door, wiped her mouth on the towel and opened the window. "I need fresh air." Her hand went to her belly and she circled it firmly as another contraction hit. "Yeow!

Argh, orgh, igh, ugh…" Diora went through all the vowels for a bit of auditory variety.

"Bloody hell." Jason revved his engine as though that alone would make the cars in front move, but it only annoyed the driver in front who stuck his hand out the window with his middle finger pointing to the heavens.

"Hey! My wife's having a baby, you moron!"

He mustn't have heard or cared, because he gave his finger another sharp prod to the sky.

"I'm going to see what's going on." Will opened his door and got out of the car.

"Will, what are you doing?" I pressed a button on my side of the car and the window slid down.

"Just taking a look." He stood on his toes and peered forwards, but that mustn't have been adequate because he climbed onto the front of the car and stood, the sculpted calves of his red Superman boots over his blue legs visible through the windshield.

"Hey, Mum, there's Superman!" The kid in the car next to us stuck his head out the window and pointed at Will.

"He's wearing a costume, he's not really Superman, you know," the older kid said to his brother.

"How do you know?" he replied. "I think he's here to save everyone from the traffic jam."

"Yeah right, as if!" The older kid crossed his arms.

Jason peered out the driver's side window. "Can you see anything?"

"Well, what do you know? I was right! A truck's spilt a pile of boxes and the contents have fallen out."

"Why now? Why now, of all times, huh?" Jason's forehead glossed with sweat and he took off his wizard's hat.

"I'm sure they'll get it cleared up soon," I said.

Will hopped off the car and came around to the driver's side. "I'm going to see if I can help speed things up."

"But, Will, isn't that dangerous? We're on a busy road!" I leaned over Diora as she moaned again.

"We're not in the middle lane so I'll just walk up the side of the road and besides, my costume's enough to stop traffic." He winked and took off at high speed.

Jason leaned his head back on the seat and mouthed another profanity. After a deep breath, he turned to face Diora. "How's my beautiful fairy going?"

"Don't feed me that crap," she replied. "I have a stomach the size of an airbag and... look, I have a streak of vomit on my dress, and as if that's not bad enough, we're stuck in this... Arghh! Not again! They're coming so... close to... gether." Diora gripped the edge of the seat with one hand and my hand with the other.

C'mon, Will, hurry up!

"It's okay, just breathe through it," Jason said.

"I can't! Oww, agh..."

"Breathe, hon, breathe. Remember, you told me if you got overwhelmed to remind you to focus on your breath, so that's what I'm doing."

Diora's grip on my hand eased as the contraction subsided. "Yeah, well I didn't know it would hurt this bad now, did I? Breathing isn't going to do a damn thing for this pain!" As if speaking exhausted her, she leaned back on the seat and closed her eyes again.

After more contractions and half the water bottle used up by Jason to rehydrate after his anxious sweats, Will's muscular figure emerged from the tangle of metal cars in front of us, his hands raised in a thumbs up sign.

The kid next to us snapped a photo and as Will got back in the car he fanned his face with his hands. "Phew, saving the world is sweaty work, especially in this suit. It needs air vents."

Tell me about it.

As the line-up of traffic began moving forwards, the kid yelled, "See, I knew Superman would fix the traffic jam!" His wide smile grew smaller as our car moved further along than his and I couldn't help matching his expression.

"What did you do?" I asked.

"I got their butts into gear with cleaning up the mess. Apparently they were waiting for some official clean-up team because of occupational health and safety reasons, while sitting around pretending to look useful. I said that was ridiculous and together we could have the road cleared in minutes."

"What did the truck spill that the buggers couldn't clean up themselves, radioactive missiles or something?" Diora managed, before the next contraction claimed its hold on her.

"Cans of hair spray, would you believe? A truckload of Mystique Extra Strong Hold Power Spray. The guys said their insurance wouldn't cover them for injury resulting from the cans bursting. Apparently there's enough pressure in those cans to do some decent damage when punctured and some of the bottles had dents in them."

I should have helped. Could have aimed one at my support suit to blast a hole through it.

"So, instead of holding up someone's hair they held up the traffic, hey?" Jason turned to Diora briefly, attempting a joke, but her focus was elsewhere. "So, ah... how'd you get them to agree to cleaning up, Superman?"

"Told them Lex Luther would be after them otherwise. Nah, I asked them if their insurance covered complications from having a baby born without medical assistance on the road they were holding up."

"Good one," Jason replied, his hands on the steering wheel and eyes back on the road.

"What? I'm not having this baby on the side of the road!" Diora exclaimed.

"Don't worry, hon, you won't be. We're on our way to the hospital, traffic's speeding up now," replied Jason.

"Arghh, these freaking wings!" Diora turned to look behind her shoulder and she tried to wrench the wings off her costume but only managed to extract a glittery corner which she threw out the window. "Knew I should have dressed as a watermelon."

"Here, let me see." I grasped at the wings where they attached to the dress but they wouldn't budge and I didn't want to hurt my daughter by pulling too hard. "When we get to hospital you can change into a gown. It won't be long."

Soon, we pulled into – or more accurately, swerved violently into – a parking space at the hospital delivery suite entrance. Jason and Will fetched Diora's designer luggage from the boot – one big suitcase and a smaller birthing equipment carry bag – while I helped her out of the car. She'd only manoeuvred part of the way out though, when another contraction hit, causing her to lose muscle strength and fall back into the car. Her strong grip on my hand made me topple forwards into the car, my body bending at the waist and bum sticking out of the door.

Split!

Was that my dress? I swivelled around to find Will and Jason's eyes on my behind.

"Oh dear," Will said. "I hope you've got a safety pin, or four, or five."

"Damn! How big a hole did it make?" I tried to angle my body to look at the split but once again the Death Suit prevented it – and why didn't *it* rip instead? – made worse by my hand attached permanently to Diora's. Diora's moaning reminded us that her situation was marginally worse than mine and the three of us helped her from the car once her contraction ended.

"Quick, inside before another one comes!" Jason urged, draping his wife's arm around his neck and the other one around Will's while I held on to her back as we scurried rather pathetically towards the entrance.

We entered through the automatic doors when Diora stopped suddenly in pain, the broken corner of her wing poking me in the eye.

"Ouch!" I instinctively flung my hands at my eye, but Diora lost her balance so I quickly returned my hands to her back, squinting my injured eye madly with the pain. "Holy hell!"

When Diora regained her ability to stand, I finally opened my eye to find hospital staff looking at us with a combination of shock and amusement on their faces. You'd think they'd never seen a woman in labour before. Then I realised it wasn't every day you saw Superman, Dumbledore, a pregnant fairy with a vomit-stained dress and broken wing, and a middle-aged wannabe model with a ripped dress and deformed eye walking through the doors of a hospital.

"Here you go, love," said a weary-looking woman as she rolled a wheelchair towards Diora. "Take a seat and let's get you into a room and out of this costume. Why don't you," she glanced at the three of us, "fill in the admission forms and wait over there while I examine... what's your name, love?"

"Diora."

"Diora. I'll let you know when you can come in. I take it one of you is the baby's father?"

Dumbledore's lengthy beard bobbed up and down as he nodded, and he went over to the reception desk while Will and I collapsed into some chairs nearby. For a brief moment I considered admitting myself so the SlimFX Magic Suit could be surgically removed but decided I'd had enough embarrassment for one day. Somehow, I'd get out of it, but I didn't want to think about it yet.

Fifteen minutes later, we walked into a delivery suite where Diora was hooked up to a monitor around her waist. "Why does she need that? Won't it hurt?" I asked.

"That's to monitor the contractions," the nurse said.

"Remember, you had one when the kids were being born?" Will said.

"Oh. It's all such a blur," I replied.

"Here comes another one... I need something to hold on to. Where's my fairy wand?" Diora asked.

"I think you left it back at the party. Here, take mine."

"I don't want yours, it looks like a stupid branch. Mine has a star. I want it, it makes me feel better, it... argh!" Diora accepted Dumbledore's wand and promptly snapped it in half, much to her husband's dismay. Once she finished sucking on a gas mouthpiece, Jason took the liberty of sucking some in for himself.

"Why don't I nip out and get you a coffee, Jase?" Will asked.

"No, but thanks. I think I've got enough sustenance from the party food and I don't need to be any more jittery than I already am."

"Are... all of you staying for the birth?" the nurse asked, her eyes moving from us to Diora.

"Diora said she needs me, so–"

"Actually, Mum, I think I'll be all right with just Jason. I was scared before, but I feel better now I'm in hospital," Diora said.

"And she's only a few centimetres dilated, so the baby probably won't be here till morning," the nurse added.

"She's right," Diora said. "You should go and get some sleep, you've had such a big day. When you wake up, you'll have a grandchild. That is, if he or she cooperates and doesn't decide to break a world record for the longest birth ever." She managed a tired smile and my hand instinctively cradled her face.

I glanced at Will and he nodded. "Okay, well if you're sure?" Diora nodded and Jason pulled up a stool next to the bed. "All right, but call me straight away if you change your mind, or if you need anything, okay?" I eyed the nurse as well as Jason. "C'mon, Superman, let's go."

Will took my hand and we walked down the corridor and out of the hospital doors.

"There's a taxi stand over there." I pointed around the corner, but Will had his eyes in the other direction. "What are you looking at?" I followed his gaze to the spectrum of city lights, flashing and merging into a colourful swirl as a Ferris wheel slowly turned.

"The fun fair is on near the harbour tonight. Fancy a detour before we head home? Like old times?" He shone a lopsided smile and held out his hand.

"Why the hell not?" I slipped my hand in his and we walked towards the lights.

Chapter 18
Fun and Games

"If the swing goes forward it will go backward too." – Sri Lankan proverb

WILL WAS right at home at the fun fair in his Superman costume, having already been asked for six photographs with tourists. "I've never had this much attention in my life," he said.

I chuckled, then pointed at the moving clown heads. "Oh look! I haven't had a go of them for years." I tightened the knot in the large scarf Will had bought me to wrap around my waist and hide the rip in my dress, which was nice of him to suggest as I'd completely forgotten about it.

What had gotten into me? Normally I'd be terrified of anyone seeing such a wardrobe malfunction, but somehow seeing Diora about to bring a new human being into the world put things in perspective.

The attendant at the clown game had me swipe my e-pad and I stood with my hand at the ready, waiting for the perfect moment to drop the ball through the clown's mouth and land in (hopefully) the number one position. Then I'd win a large fluffy teddy bear and could give it to Diora's baby. My hand hovering, I traced the clown's movement with my eye, before pushing the ball through its mouth. Damn! Number four instead.

"Here you go, madam," said the attendant, handing me my prize – a multi-coloured glitter tinsel wig. It was ridiculously bright and would totally draw attention to myself, but I was beyond caring. I placed the wig over my head, messing up my chignon and shook my head side to side, the tinsel strands shimmying around my face.

"What do you think?" I asked Will.

"It suits you," he replied, tousling my hair with his fingers.

"And here's your prize, sir," the attendant said after Will's clown delivered the ball to number three.

Will slid the googly eye sunglasses onto his face and the bloodshot eyeballs sprung up and down, looking the way my eyes felt during the bungy jump this morning. A laugh spluttered out of my mouth and Will set his e-pad to the camera function and turned the holographic screen around to face us, so we could see ourselves. "Ready? Smile!"

Click! A memory captured forever. Or would it be?

"Now, let's see if we can win one of those big bears for Baby Bellows." Will tugged on my hand and we walked over to the ring toss game.

"Step right up, win a prize, five turns for every game!" The attendant spoke in a traditional sideshow voice, attracting visitors to the game. "Toss a ring onto a lily pad and win!"

It looked pretty hard, considering the lily pads were floating on a bed of water. It'd be hard enough to get the ring to land on one that was still, but maybe Will had better aim than me. We'd soon find out.

Will handed me his googly eyes and pushed up his Superman sleeves, holding on to the ring and pinning a lily pad with a laser stare.

"Look, folks, this is a first. Superman attempts the ring toss! Will he succeed, or will he fail? Come and watch, folks!"

Talk about pressure! A crowd of onlookers gathered, mostly teenagers and older couples, as it was obviously too late at night for young children.

"Okay, here goes." Will gently threw the ring towards a lily pad, but it rebounded off the edge and landed with a slight plop in the water. Will clicked his fingers in disappointment. "Damn!"

"Four more turns, anything can happen, folks. Let's see if he can live up to his costume and be a Super Winner, huh?"

Geez. Even more pressure. Poor Will. Another toss. Another fail. Third time lucky? Nope. Plop.

"C'mon, man, you can do it," someone called from the crowd.

Yeah, maybe if everyone wasn't standing around watching him like a hawk. I bet Will wished he'd dressed as a ghost too. This time the ring touched the little stick poking up from the lily pad and, although it landed on the pad, it didn't capture the stick as per the rules.

"One turn left, folks. Can he do it?"

"Focus, Will, focus. Think as though your life depended on hitting the target," I urged. "Pretend that lily pad is something you really want and without it your life is not worth living. You can do it!" Okay, so it was just a game, but the unblinking eyes and silence of the still crowd had created suspense to rival Hitchcock.

Will took a deep breath and I could almost hear his heart beating through his plastic muscle-clad chest. He extended his arm out and back twice, lining up his target and then tossed the ring towards the bed of unsuspecting lily pads.

"We have a hit!" The attendant raised his fist in the air and the crowd cheered as the ring hula-hooped around the stick a few times before coming to a standstill.

I jumped up and down like a teenage groupie at a concert, clapping with more enthusiasm than was warranted. "You did it! Well done." I surprised myself by kissing Will on the cheek and his chest seemed to rise with pride.

He performed a subtle bow to thank the crowd and accepted a large coffee-brown coloured teddy bear wearing a cute tartan jacket and bow tie. Normally I'd never be one to call tartan cute – now that was a fabric that should just not exist at all – but tonight wasn't exactly normal, so tonight, it was cute.

Will handed me the teddy bear and I rubbed its silky soft fur on my cheeks as he took a photo. A few more people asked to pose with Superman, then we strolled around the fair, Will with his googly eyes and me in my glitter wig, only realising after a few minutes that our hands were entwined. It just felt so natural.

"Ooh, a fortune telling machine. Should we see what it has to say?" Will pointed to what looked like a large arcade game, with two big hypnotic eyes painted on the front and a screen with swirling psychedelic colours.

I went to tell him I'd already had a psychic reading today, but bit my lip. "Sure, I'm game, if you are?"

"Of course, I have nothing to fear, the future can only be bright with you by my side." He gave my shoulders a squeeze. Although leaning towards melodrama, his affection for me was quite endearing.

I eyed him curiously. "Will, what did you think of when you hit the target on the lily pad?"

"You, of course. I imagined you were on the lily pad needing to be rescued and it worked. It's the same in life, I think. You have a goal, you focus on it and take a step forward with confidence, trusting in a good outcome."

"True," I replied, a tingle of warmth spreading inside. "Okay, you first, Superman."

Will scanned his e-pad on the machine and it sparkled into action, the swirls on the screen spinning faster and faster and faster, until faint letters appeared, all jumbled up at first, then forming a sentence: *Your life will soon undergo a big transition. Ride the waves and keep moving forward.*

A card ejected from the machine and Will glanced at the fortune written on it. "Hmm... wonder what that's about?"

I shrugged. "Let's see what it says for me."

Again, the swirls spun fast and the words became visible: *Tomorrow is a brand new day, anything is possible.*

"That's not much of a prediction," Will commented. "Not very specific."

Before I could reply, the machine made a jingling noise and the swirls spun again. Then something else appeared on the screen: *Congratulations! You have been selected to receive a Bonus Fortune!* More swirly spinning, then: *Your heart holds the answer to all your questions.*

"How about that? It must have known it was your birthday or something," Will said. "Still, not overly specific."

"Actually, I think it's quite appropriate. It's telling me I can create my own future, if I listen to my heart." I plucked the two cards from the slot and held them to my chest.

"I think you're right." Will nodded. "Who knows, tomorrow if Mr Turrow accepts our proposal then this could be the big transition and this will mean that anything is possible for the future of our business."

"Could be," I replied, although I took these predictions as more personal in nature. "Ooh, ooh – let's get a show bag!" I tugged on Will's hand like a hyped-up child and led him to the show bag stand which appeared to be closing up for the night. "Can we grab a couple of bags before you close?" I asked the attendant whose eyes were half closed, his bottom lip hanging low like an overstretched hammock.

He plucked two bags from under the table without a word, as though too tired to speak. I scanned my e-pad, chose credit payment and he handed over the goods. Will and I wandered off, plucking surprise treasures from our bags. I unwrapped a lollipop and let the sticky sweetness glide along my tongue.

Will smiled. "You wouldn't think you're fifty," he said. "You've still got it, Kel."

"Got what?"

"You know, *it*."

"Oh, you mean, sex appeal?"

"No, your inner child." He looked at me, then laughed. "Of course I mean sex appeal!" He flung a show bag encumbered arm around my waist as we walked.

"If anything, I think you've gotten better with age," I told him.

"Really?" His eyes widened. "Hang on, does that mean you never thought the pudgy, pimply me at school was attractive?" He winked.

What could I say? I had never thought of him as attractive – ever. Until... now. "It's what's inside that counts, remember?" I said.

"Of course, all those bones, organs and lengths of intestines are really irresistible." He rubbed his stomach in circular motions and I gave him a friendly slap.

"I think someone's been drinking too much champagne," I said, knowing too well the four I'd had – or was it five – hadn't done me any favours.

"I only had two!" he defended. "But being here at the fair with you, wearing this costume, it does dredge up my own inner child. What about you? Are you feeling like your twenty-five-year-old self, wearing that dress?"

Far from it. "Um, let's just say I'm feeling more... me, right now, than I have for a while."

"We bring out the best in each other, I tell ya. What did I say at the party? We're like a lock and key, you and I." Will slid his tongue along his own lollipop.

"So which one am I, the lock or the key?"

Will's eyes searched the sky. "I think you'd be the key. A lock's more idle, more like a possibility. A key, well, that turns the lock and brings the possibilities into reality. Like you've done."

"I have?"

"Yep. Without you, I'd be a lock that hasn't been opened, still waiting for the right key."

The warm tingle I'd felt earlier returned. "You're good with words, Will. Although, I don't think you give yourself enough credit. Of course you'd be happy and successful without me."

"Successful maybe, but completely happy? I don't know... content, perhaps." He kissed my cheek, leaving a slight sticky sensation behind. "But I don't have to even think about the other possibility, because you're with me and I'm very happy."

I smiled. "Hey, do you want to go on the Ferris wheel?" I pointed to the large circle encroaching on the clear night sky.

"Sure, like old times." He smiled.

"Sorry, closing up for the night," the man said when we approached.

"C'mon, one last ride?" I pleaded.

The man looked at his e-pad and scrunched his weary face.

"It's my wife's birthday, you know," Will said. "The big Five-O."

"Is it? Well, happy birthday. My wife turned fifty two weeks ago." He looked at his e-pad again, not that the time would have magically changed or anything. "All right then, in you get. But only because it's your birthday." He ushered us into a carriage and pulled the protective bar in front of us. "I can only give you one cycle though, okay? Up and back down again, that's all."

"That's fine, thank you," I said.

The wheel began its slow ascent towards the sky, music playing softly in the background as Will and I gazed at the city skyline. "So beautiful, isn't it?"

"Yeah, hard to believe we're just tiny specks in this massive universe." Somehow, the universe had picked me to launch forward and see the future. Shocked and traumatised at first, a ripple of gratitude now rolled through me. "Will, I'm sorry if I ever teased you in school."

One corner of his mouth rose up. "Why are you bringing this up?"

"Dunno. Just didn't know if I ever said sorry, that's all."

"Come here." He pulled me close to his bulky chest. "You only went along with what your friends were doing. I know you didn't mean it and besides, marrying me was the best damn apology I could have ever received."

"I'm glad you don't hold any resentment towards me."

"Would I have married you if I did?"

"Guess not."

"Well there you go." He tucked a few strands of multi-coloured tinsel behind my ear and allowed his finger to graze my cheek, his thumb resting on my lower lip. "I love you, Kelli."

He tilted his head and leaned in close. In stark contrast to earlier that morning, I leaned towards him. His breath warmed my face as his lips neared mine and, as my lips parted slightly, a sudden clunk jolted our carriage.

"What's happening?" I peered over the edge.

"I don't know." Will peered over the other side.

Stuck. At the top of the Ferris wheel, wobbling in mid-air. Why did these things always happen to me?

"Hellooo?" I yelled down to the man in charge, hoping he

hadn't gone home for the night and left us here to dangle till morning.

A tiny figure of a man was holding something. "Everything's all right," he spoke through the loudspeaker. "Just a little glitch, happened earlier this evening too. Nothing to be alarmed about."

"A little glitch? What if we can't get down?" I asked Will, my hands flying to my cheeks. "What if we have to climb down ourselves, or get an emergency helicopter to airlift us to safety? Oh God!" I imagined having to climb up a rope towards a hovering helicopter, handicapped by my inability to raise my arms above my head and then my tinsel wig getting caught in the propellers, chopping it to glittery smithereens.

"Don't worry, I'm sure the wheel will get moving in no time," Will assured. "If not," he puffed out his chest, "I can summon my inner man of steel and fly us down."

I looked at my husband's smiling face and relaxed back in the seat. I was probably overreacting and Will always seemed able to resolve a dire situation – costume or no costume.

"Let's make the most of waiting," he said and I thought he was going to lean in and continue where we left off but instead, he opened the show bag and rummaged inside for more treasures. "Oh cool, a whistle." He blew on the plastic toy and a whiny high-pitched whistle sang through the sky. "Oops, didn't know it'd be that loud!"

"At least we can whistle like mad if they forget about us all the way up here." I giggled.

Will continued searching through his bag. "Oh, remember these?" He pulled out a long stick of wrapped candy. "Super Stretchy Surprise. Did you get one in your bag?"

Will's inner child took over his inner man of steel and it was very cute. "Yeah, a blueberry one. What flavour did you get?" I said, holding mine up.

"Lemon. Wanna trade?"

I nodded and we swapped our candy sticks, ripping them open and taking a bite, only with Super Stretchy Surprise's one bite goes a long way. I gripped the end of the stick in my teeth and managed to pull the stretchy candy all the way out to arms-length, before it snapped and sprung back to my mouth in a delicious curl of sugar.

"Mine stretched further," Will said.

"Yeah right, mine stretched further."

"Did not."

"Did too."

We collapsed in laughter at the bizarre nature of our situation as the carriage clunked and moved again.

"I'm bringing you back down now," the man called through the loudspeaker.

"Oh," Will complained. "Just when I was starting to enjoy myself."

Ten minutes later we slid into the back seat of a taxi, Will having to pre-scan his e-pad in order to be accepted into the vehicle and a protective screen separated us from the driver. To speak to him, we had to press an intercom button. Will gave him our address in Bellbird Drive and the taxi merged with the traffic.

"I wonder how Diora's going? Should I call Jason?" I asked.

"I'm sure she's doing fine. They'll call if they need us."

"You're right." Leaning my head against the back of the seat, I stared out the window at the blur of buildings and lights rushing past. Warm skin brushed against my hand as Will covered my hand with his. His fingers delved between mine, his fingertips curling underneath to touch my palms. I curled mine to match and our hands lay on top of my right thigh sending pulses of heat up my arm. I glanced down at his strong manly hand, strangely mesmerised by the veins bulging beneath his skin. As his thumb stroked the back of my hand, the pulses of heat became tidal waves of passion and if it wasn't for the taxi driver in the front seat, I think I would have kissed him then and there. My heart beat quickened and a subtle tingling bubbled up inside as my eyes turned to meet his and an 'I know what you're thinking' smile played on his lips.

The slow melody of a saxophone accompanied by velvety crooning oozed from the front of the taxi. The driver pressing a button which sent the volume up a notch and the rhythm swayed in and out, back and forth, in time with the movement of our chests with each breath. Will's hand unfurled and pushed gently down on mine, his thumb now stroking my thigh causing the tingling bubbles inside me to pop like fireworks.

"Here we are," said the driver, his gruff tone piercing the anticipation in the back seat. He instructed Will to scan his e-pad again, which removed his hand from my thigh, leaving behind a remnant of warmth which gradually cooled.

We thanked the driver and my heels clicked as we walked the steps to the front door which Will unlocked with his e-pad. Apart from a soft light in the kitchen, darkness greeted us as we entered, but not so dark as to miss the two figures sprawled on the couch in the living room. Bungy Ben was cosily squashed into the corner of the armrest where one arm lay, the other arm cradling the back of the couch. Ryan lay on his back, his head resting on Ben's shoulder and his chest rose slowly up and down as his mouth hung lazily open.

"I think those two have finally revealed their feelings for each other," Will whispered as we tiptoed into the kitchen and Will placed his googly sunglasses on the bench while I placed the teddy bear and glitter wig onto a chair.

Smiling proudly at my son's courage, my smile widened on seeing the two cling-wrapped plates containing slices of cake adorned with edible silver baubles on the kitchen bench. On top was a Post-it note:

Hope you had a memorable birthday, Mum. Enjoy the cake! ~ Ryan.

Will picked up one of two small forks that had been left on the bench and peeled the cling wrap from one of the plates. "Can you fit in a bite or two?" he asked.

"Sure, I can make room for a bit more sugar. Just one bite though, I think I'll save the rest till tomorrow." I couldn't believe my appetite was still strong after the horde of food I'd eaten today, but my appetite for something unrelated to food was even stronger.

Will dug the fork into the pointy edge of the triangular slice, lifting away a morsel and bringing it to my mouth. Vanilla cream frosting and velvety sponge kissed my tastebuds, the fork cooling my lips as it slid out of my mouth.

"Oh wow, this is divine," I sighed. I picked up the other fork and cut away a piece for Will, delivering it to his eager mouth and letting his lips wrap around the fork.

"I see what you mean," he said. "Delicious."

"Maybe I could fit in a tiny bit more." I pinched my thumb and forefinger together in the air and let the corner of my mouth rise upwards. "I could even just eat the icing alone, it's heavenly."

Instead of digging the fork back in the cake, Will swiped his finger against the top of the cake, frosting clinging to his skin. My lips parted as he brought his finger to my mouth and I enveloped it eagerly, pulling the vanilla cream off his fingertip and leaving behind a glossy trail. Licking my lips, I followed his lead again, swiping a lick of frosting from the cake and delivering it to Will's warm, hungry mouth. He grasped my hand as he devoured the cream and tilted his head towards the bedroom.

He switched off the kitchen light as we walked past and kicked the bedroom door closed behind us as he pulled me close to his body and ran his finger across my cheek as he'd done on the Ferris wheel. Our breathing quickened in sync with each other and he leaned his mouth towards my ear.

"Don't go anywhere," he whispered. "I'm just going to get out of this costume and have the quickest shower in the history of mankind. Be right back." He teased me with an expectant smile and let his hands trail down each of my arms before he trailed off to the en suite.

Tingles shot along my nerves and I glanced around the room, spying a large red candle on the dresser. I scurried over and picked up the lighter lying next to it, pointing the flame towards the wick. A yellow glow sprung from the candle and the flame flickered, casting a pinky-red arc across the wall. I kicked off my shoes and fluffed the pillows on the bed, before laying down and assuming the sexiest position I could muster, considering the disadvantage brought on by my underwear, which hopefully Will had some bright idea about how to remove, or else our romantic encounter would turn into a wrestling match.

I bent my elbow and propped my hand behind my head and slightly bent one leg so that it dipped over the other to accentuate the hourglass shape of the female form. The muffled sound of running water from the bathroom soothed my senses and I basked in the bliss of the moment. The anticipation, the excitement, the... knowing.

Knowing that the perfect end to this day was only moments

away. Knowing that the man in the next room loved me more than life itself. Knowing that... Oh my God. Knowing that... I loved him too. *I love him.* A sharp burst of realisation shot through me and the hair on the back of my neck bristled. *I love Will.*

The truth dispersed throughout my body, filling it with the most amazing, unimaginable sensation I'd ever experienced, as though this was what life was all about. Immediately I knew, without hesitation, that Will was my soulmate and this was the life I was truly destined for.

My thoughts turned to Diora, who right at this moment was enduring immense pain to bring new life into this world and Ryan, who through courage took a risk in the hope of finding love, and Will, the magician in this magical future of ours I was so lucky to have glimpsed.

A smile oozed from my lips at the thought of the three most important people in the world to me and as love filled my heart, peace filled my body, and my muscles turned into warm soothing liquid, melting into the bed with each breath. My eyelids flopped down, unable to remain open and my body became a weightless sensation of pure joy as I surrendered completely to the welcoming darkness behind my eyes.

Chapter 19
Happy Birthday

"Birthdays are good for you. Statistics show that the people who have the most live the longest." – Father Larry Lorenzoni

My eyelids eased away from the tangled embrace of my eyelashes and I squinted at a small spear of light coming through the edge of the curtains. I must have dozed off. "Will?" I called, but only silence replied.

I rubbed my eyes and flung my legs over the side of the bed, the balls of my feet cushioned by the soft carpet. I pushed up to standing, my body overtaken with post-sleep fogginess. I slid the en suite door open and switched on the light, still rubbing my eyes as I headed straight for the sink. Cool water awakened my face as I bent over the sink, then I stood back up and met my reflection in the mirror.

I was about to wipe some sleep from my left eye when a jolt of shock coursed rapidly from my toes to my scalp and I gasped, flinging my hands to my mouth. The wrinkles I'd met earlier had disappeared. The crow's feet I'd despised were nowhere to be found. Instead of laughter lines, forehead furrows and the dreaded lip wrinkles lay smooth, unblemished skin. *I'm back! I'm twenty-five again!*

I stood and stared at my face, examining every feature, making sure there were no remnants of fifty-year-old Kelli. I lifted my nightgown and let my hand grace my flat stomach, then cupped my firm breasts that were back in their correct geographical location above the equator and twirled my varicose-vein-free ankles in easy, creak-free circular movements.

Ha! My old young self had definitely returned! I lifted my wrist to check my e-pad, but no e-pad was there. Of course, they hadn't been invented yet. I dashed back into the bedroom and plucked my phone from its charger to check the date. Yep – definitely my birthday! I swished open the curtains and daylight flooded the room and, as I blinked my eyes to adjust to the light, I remembered. Diora!

She should have had the baby by now, only how could she, when my return to the past signalled the return to a life she was not yet a part of? I didn't even get to meet my grandchild! I didn't even know if it was a boy or a girl!

Ryan! I wanted to thank him for taking care of the guests after we left the party due to the unexpected waters-breaking incident, and ask him how Ben reacted on sharing his feelings for him, even though their cosy presence on my couch implied he responded just as Ryan would have hoped.

And Will! He might have come out of the shower wondering where the hell I'd disappeared to. Except... he wouldn't have because if I was back in the past, he was too. He was probably getting out of bed like on any other Friday morning, shaving the small growth of hair on his face and putting on a pinstriped shirt with a plain tie, sliding a pen or two into his shirt pocket, ready for work.

I missed them already. How could I have become so connected to them in only one day? I ached to see them again, but knew there was only one way that would happen. I had to make things right. I had to change the course of my life before destiny slipped through my fingers into the ether of lost possibilities.

I pinched the screen on my phone and then shook my head at my stupidity. No holographic phones here yet. I made a quick phone call to the restaurant my party was to be held in, then pressed the screen for a new message option to appear, adding multiple numbers from my contacts before typing a text message:

> Hi guys, change of plans. Have cancelled restaurant for tonight, feel like something different. Meet at 8pm on North Beach for fish & chips ~ K

Selena replied instantly. Selena!

> Okay then, but why? Oh, and happy birthday hon ;)

I replied back:

> I already told you why. Feel like something different. And thanks xo

Soon after, Kasey replied too:

> Oh right, change plans at the last minute to suit yourself, typical!

Bugger, Kasey was still mad at me. A few seconds later another text from Kasey came through:

I replied back telling her thanks and that I was sorry and couldn't wait to see her tonight. I thought my other friends would reply too but the phone stayed silent. I guess I would just see them all tonight.

I slid my hands across my flat stomach again. *Oh, how I've missed you!* Then I sighed in relief at not having to try and get out of the support underwear. I'd been saved! I'd never buy one of those in the future – ever, not even version 2.0 with the expandable release valve, uh-uh.

I opened the web browser on my phone and summoned the Foogle, I mean, Google page and typed in a search, and on finding the website I was after made a phone call.

"Hi, I'd like to book in with your best personal trainer," I said into the phone. Five minutes later I was scheduled in to see Roxanne at 9am Monday.

Now, for something more important... I opened my contacts page and pressed C in the surname list. As I was about to select Malcolm Crawford, a text message came in:

Warmth crept through my eyes and I blinked away tears. Dad was still here and there was no way I'd be going through this day without seeing him to set things right with him and Kasey.

Dad replied:

> If it's important, then I'll be there for sure. See
> you then.

I sent the same request to Kasey, not mentioning the fact that Dad would be there. I knew she would have just found out he wasn't her real father. She said she'd come but probably couldn't get there till 12.15 pm, which was fine with me as I wanted to see Dad alone first.

I looked at my text messages again and noticed one from Grant that I'd missed:

> Happy birthday gorgeous, dying to give you
> your present, wanna meet earlier today? How
> about 10am in the park, at our usual spot? ~
> G xoxo

Crap. The proposal. He wants to propose to me in... I glanced at the time on my phone... one hour and fifteen minutes. I typed a reply:

> Actually, that would be good because we need
> to talk.

After showering and putting on a floaty purple winged top over slim black pants and wedge heels – no curved coral hems for me today – I strode down to the park. I paused for a moment, spotting Grant sitting on the bench opposite the fountain, his leg tapping up and down. Black sunglasses covered his eyes and his hair looked tidily messy, the sight triggering a slight yearning for him again. Swallowing the lump that had wedged in my throat, I pushed on, reminding myself of what I was doing and trying to keep the fifty-year-old image of him hand-in-hand with what's-her-name at the front of my mind.

"Hey, gorgeous," he said, standing to kiss me on the lips which I accepted but subtly pulled away from before it lingered and before I changed my mind and threw my arms around him, telling him how much I missed him. "The big twenty-five today, huh?"

"Yeah, guess so," I replied, finding it extremely difficult to maintain eye contact.

"Look, Grant... I–"

"Here." He held out a small, wrapped present. "This is for you."

Oh, man. The ring. "Grant–"

"Open it," he urged, smiling.

Oh well, better get it over with and then break the bad news.

I tugged at the curly ribbon and slid my finger under the folded corner of the wrapping paper, pulling out a velvet box. My heart raced as I remembered how much I'd longed for this day and now here I was, dreading it. Because I knew I wouldn't be saying yes and I didn't want to bruise his ego. Not that his fifty-year-old ego had seemed bruised.

I glanced up at Grant whose eyes eagerly awaited me to open the box. I gulped on the lump in my throat but like a cork in water it bobbed back up. Drawing a light breath in through my nose I slowly lifted the lid, catching a glimpse of something shiny until the full beauty of Grant's gift captured my attention. A perfect circle of silver tied like a piece of string in a mock knot, with a lone diamond on the end, sparkling under the morning sunlight.

I stifled a laugh of relief. It was a bracelet! A very beautiful, original DSJ designed bracelet, which would have cost a lot, especially considering the size of the diamond.

"Do you like it?" Grant asked, eyes wide.

Those weren't the words I'd expected to hear. "I love it, I really do, but–"

"Put it on," he said.

"Grant." I closed the lid on the box. "I really appreciate your gift, but before we go any further I need to talk to you."

His eyebrows drew together curiously. "Okay then, what is it?"

"What would you say if I told you I was planning a career change?"

His eyebrows drew so close together they almost collided. "What sort of career change could you possibly be interested in? And why?"

"Well, when I was younger, I used to spend a lot of time drawing and designing things, and I was thinking I'd like to take it more seriously now. You know – do up some proper designs, make a portfolio of beautiful homewares and look into options for manufacturing them. I have a feeling it'd make a great business."

Grant shook his head in confusion. "So let me get this straight, you want to give up on a lucrative modelling career for... homewares?"

"I'd still do some modelling jobs to make ends meet, but once the business turned a profit, I'd consider letting the modelling slide. I can't do it forever anyway," I explained.

"I don't understand, why pursue a little hobby like that when you can make money from," he gestured his hands down the length of my body, "this?" He shook his head. "It's ridiculous."

I stood, his words jolting me like the paper being ripped by Mum all over again. "Because it's something I love to do, it's what I'm most passionate about!" I raised my voice and a few people walking by stared in our direction, but I didn't care. "I enjoy modelling, but to be honest, sometimes it bores me. I need to use the creativity inside me, do something with my hands and create things." I moved my hands about with enthusiasm.

"Don't you get it? You are the creation. The photographers, like me, show you in your best light and the graphic designers and artists enhance the picture to create a piece of art. Most women would kill to look like you and have your job!" Grant stood too, redness rising up his neck. "We're a team, you and I, and if you go off and do something else, it won't be the same, it won't feel right."

"It'll feel right to me," I replied.

"And what about me?"

"Why should my career choices affect you?"

"My career takes me all over the place and I plan on it taking me overseas on a regular basis, as should yours if you stick to your plans of gracing the catwalks. But if you're serious about starting a business, you'll need to stay put and that just won't work for us."

"Then maybe we should do something about that," I said quietly, sitting on the bench. "Grant, I've been thinking a lot about my life and what I thought I wanted, I don't think I want anymore. Sure, I'll keep modelling for a while, but it's not my passion. I also think I'd like to have a family one day too."

Grant collapsed on the seat next to me. "What? Are you serious? I thought you never wanted children!"

"Well, let's just say I've been persuaded," I said, looking him in the eye. "I didn't want to become a mother for fear of dredging up memories of my own mother, but I don't resent her anymore. I know what a privilege it is to bring a child into this world and have a family. It's what I want."

"How do you know?"

"I just know."

Grant kept shaking his head. "This isn't just a hormonal

outburst is it? Some temporary insanity thing? I've read that can happen to some women, you know."

Oh my God, he was infuriating me! "Absolutely not, how dare you even consider that!" I stood again. "This is real. This is me, this is what I want. If you don't want to be a part of who I am, I guess we shouldn't be together." I ran my fingers through my hair and looked up at the sky.

"Unless there's any hope of knocking some sense into you, then no, I guess we shouldn't be together."

"Believe me, I have more sense now than I ever did."

"So this is it then, you're breaking up with me, on your birthday?" Grant asked, still sitting on the seat, his eyes peering up at mine.

"That's exactly what I'm doing," I replied with a straight tone. I went to walk away but then turned back. "I'm sorry, Grant. I didn't mean for things to end like this, but I have to do what's right for me." I placed the bracelet box into his hands. "As beautiful as this is, I think you should save it for someone else. Someone special, who's traveling the same journey as you are." I closed his fingers over the box and looked him one last time in the eye. "Bye, Grant."

My shoes clicked as I walked away, my eyes firmly fixed on the path in front of me.

At five past twelve I looked up from my table at Parkside Cafe to see my dad walking towards me with a large present wrapped in pink, the sight of him completely smashing the bizarre memory of seeing his grave only yesterday. I stood, wrapping my arms around him without a word.

"Whoa, you'd think we hadn't seen each other for years. Is

everything all right?" He pulled back and held on to my shoulders.

"Everything's perfect. I'm so glad to see you, that's all." I blinked away the threat of tears that hung by a thread from the edge of my eyes.

"I'm glad to see you too," he said, smiling. "Happy birthday." He handed me the gift and I sat down to unwrap it.

I held up the vase after pulling it from its box. "Oh, I love it. Thanks, Dad!" It was shaped like a splash of water rising upwards in a spiral, clear glass marbled by a hint of magenta swirling from the bottom to the top. The vase! The one I'd seen on the gift table at my fiftieth birthday party! So I didn't design it – Dad gave it to me, which held even more importance. "I'll treasure it forever."

"I'm glad you like it."

I smiled then stiffened as Kasey came to a standstill near the entrance, having just noticed Dad sitting at the table with me. She turned to walk away.

"Kasey, wait!" My chair screeched as I pushed it out from under the table and ran towards her. "I know about you and Dad. I know you've just found out the truth."

"He told you, huh?"

I ignored the question. "Look, I invited Dad so we can all talk about this. You two need to get all your doubts and fears out in the open, otherwise you'll regret it later. Trust me."

"Oh, I don't know. It's probably not the right time. It's your birthday. We shouldn't be discussing something like this today. Besides, I have to get back to the university soon." She looked longingly at the exit.

I grasped her hand. "C'mon, have some lunch, talk to Dad. Tell him what a great father he's been to you."

She drew a deep breath and nodded. "Fair enough."

"Kasey, hi." Dad stood and gestured for her to take a seat.

"What a nice surprise." His words belied the uncertainty in his voice. I'd taken a risk bringing them both together when the emotions were still raw, but if they didn't make time to talk now, they never would.

"Let's order, shall we?" I suggested, signalling a waiter before the discussion began. We exchanged small talk for a while and ate our meals, and finally Dad said, "I think Kelli wants us to discuss our situation, right, Kel?"

I nodded. "I couldn't bear the thought of seeing you two lose the great father-daughter relationship you've had. I thought it would be good to get everything out in the open now, before it's left too long."

Kasey squirmed and Dad cleared his throat. "Well," Dad turned to Kasey. "How are you feeling after finding out the truth?"

"How am I feeling?" she responded. "How do you think? I've just been told my dad isn't really my dad, and the person responsible for this secret isn't alive for me to confront her about it. I'm angry at Mum, and I'm angry at you for not telling me until now, and I'm angry at, oh I don't know, I'm just angry that I've been taken for a ride. This spoils everything I thought was real in my life, it's all been a lie!" Kasey's eyes welled up with tears and her face reddened. Dad placed his hand over Kasey's on the table but she sharply withdrew it.

"It hasn't been a lie. Our relationship, the times we shared, Kasey, they were real. Nothing's changed."

"Are you kidding? Everything's changed! My mother's dead and my real father might as well be since I haven't even met him."

"Look, we can talk about the possibility of finding him sometime, if that's what you want, but for now, we need to talk about us." Dad pulled her hand back onto the table. "Kase, I was angry at your mother too, maybe I still am a little bit, but more for hurting you than me. I'm still the father you've always known, even though we have different DNA."

"It just feels weird, you know? I feel like the odd one out, not that that's new to me, but this confirms it. I'm not a Crawford."

"In my eyes you are," Dad said, as my head swivelled right and left from my father to my sister as their conversation continued. Dad lowered his head. "That is, if you still want me in your life? The way you reacted I thought... maybe you didn't want anything to do with me anymore."

"What? Of course I do, I mean, I just need some time to process everything and... hang on – you thought I wouldn't want anything to do with you?"

Dad shrugged.

"But I thought the opposite. I thought you wouldn't want to continue this paternal facade now that the truth was exposed. I thought you'd be glad to see the back of the daughter who will always remind you of your wife's infidelity." Kasey swiped her eyes with the back of her hand.

"Kasey, no. I may not be your biological father, but I raised you. Even though we don't share genes, I'm one hundred per cent sure you've carried on my propensity for hard work, for persisting with something until you're satisfied, for never giving up. When I see you the only thing I'm reminded of is the amazing young woman you've become, nothing else. As far as I'm concerned, you'll always be my daughter." Dad's voice faltered on the last word and he cleared his throat.

Kasey's bottom lip trembled. "I don't want to lose you, Dad. I still want you to be my father." Her eyes pleaded and my own bottom lip trembled too, as Dad shuffled his chair closer to Kasey and enveloped her in his arms.

"I'll always be here. I'll always be your father," he said, stroking her hair as her head rested on his chest. "Let's make that a given, huh? I'm sure there'll be more emotions to deal with, but as they come up, we'll deal with them together, okay?"

Kasey nodded, more tears flowing down her face, until eventually she sat up again and wiped her eyes with the tissue I handed her. "I'm sorry, Kelli, it's supposed to be a happy day for you and here we are crying," Kasey said.

"Oh, it is a happy day, sis, it really is," I replied, a smile widening on my face. "This is the best birthday present I could have received. Well, besides the vase, Dad." I winked.

Dad smiled and Kasey said, "Oh, I didn't have your birthday present with me, but I'll bring it tonight. You really want to have a party on the beach instead?" she asked.

"Yep. Oh, and could you bring some wood and branches from your backyard, I want to make a small campfire."

Kasey's eyes brightened. She practically lived outdoors when she wasn't holed up in the university laboratory or lecture halls. "Consider it done. I'll bring some newspaper for kindling too, and matches. Hey, do you want me to drive us both there?"

"That'd be great, thanks."

"So anyway, what's new with you, sweetheart?" Dad asked.

Actually, I just returned from the future where I was married with grown children and ran a successful company and didn't look one bit like a model anymore.

"What's new? Oh, not much... except that, I'm going to get back into my creative pursuits. Start drawing and designing again."

Dad sat up straight in his seat. "Really? I'm so glad to hear that, you always had a knack for all things artistic. It was such as shame to let your talent go to waste after–"

"After Mum literally ripped my confidence to shreds?" I interjected. "It's okay, I've forgiven her now. I know she didn't mean to hurt me. I'm really excited about what I could do with my skills. I'm actually planning on setting up a business eventually, once I've worked on a decent portfolio and done a course or two."

Dad's face beamed. "If you need to run anything by me, I'm here. I'd like nothing more than to see you follow your dreams."

"Thanks, Dad."

"And hey, maybe you and I could go into business together, huh?" Kasey laughed. "Although I'd have to be a silent partner because unless you're designing lab equipment, I'd be hopeless." She winked, not knowing she'd be playing a very important role in the realisation of my dream.

"Who knows? You never know what might happen around the corner." I winked back and noticed Dad staring at his hands. "What's wrong, Dad?"

He flicked his hand in the air. "Ah, nothing. It's just... I wish I'd been able to help your mother more. I should have got more help for her. If only she hadn't shot you down like that. I'll never forget your face after that dreadful day."

I held my palms in front of Dad. "Stop, Dad. Don't go there. You did everything you could, it wasn't your fault."

"But if I'd taken her to a different psychiatrist, got a second opinion, maybe she would have had a better chance."

"No, Dad, you can't waste time or energy wondering what might have been, you can only change what's in front of you right now. You did your best and Mum made her own choices in life. Her happiness wasn't your responsibility." I grasped his arm with my hand and he brought his other hand up and patted mine.

"You're right." He nodded. "What's important is what we choose to do now."

"Dad, promise me we'll never let life get in the way of our family? Promise me you'll never go away, that you'll always stay close?"

"I promise. I'm not going anywhere," he replied, his eyes unblinking and fixed on mine.

Only the future would tell me if that was true and although he would eventually leave us of course, at the end of his life, I hoped and wished that that day would not come for a very, very long time.

After wandering around admiring the delights of the city, basking in the pleasure of not needing to be anywhere right now and just walking where my feet took me, I remembered something. I dashed back to my apartment, flipped open my laptop and typed FastForwardExperiences.com into my web browser.

The webpage cannot be displayed. Damn. It didn't exist yet. Oh, I wanted to submit my experience! Unless... I searched for domain name registration and then typed the web address into the 'search for a domain' field. *This domain is available! Click here to register this domain.*

So, the person who made the website in the future hadn't registered it yet. I should just wait and check on it every now and again. Unless... What if it's meant to be me? What if I was the one who was supposed to have made the website?

Tentatively I clicked on the registration link. I'd never registered a website domain before, I didn't even know how it all worked, or how to make a website, but heaps of people had them so it couldn't be that hard, could it?

But what if someone else was destined to make the website and me registering it would stuff things up for them somehow? I thought about the experiences I'd read on the site, especially the one about Polly who seemed permanently stuck in her fast forward, and a pang of sympathy ran through me. One way or another, this website needed to be born. If someone was to contact me down the track and say they had thought of creating this website, then I would simply let them take it over.

Yes. That sounded like a plan. Okay, here we go. I typed in my details and gave up my credit card number, something I was quite used to doing and the website tried to get me to purchase other domains as well.

Would you like to add the following to your order?
fastforwardexperiences.net
myfastforwardexperiences.com
fastforwardexperiencesnetwork.com

Um, no, thank you very much. One would be enough and I wasn't just talking about websites. As valuable and life-changing an experience it was, I couldn't bear to go through another shock like that. I just wanted to get on with living my life and creating the future that was right for me.

A minute or two later I was the proud owner of a domain name. As for the website itself, I'd figure that out later, at least for now I'd got the ball rolling.

Oh damn! While I was in the future why didn't I think to check on Foogle for other important things that had occurred between my twenty-fifth and fiftieth birthdays? Like, winning lotto numbers, fashion trends, Oscar winners – apart from Selena – and whether anyone else had been to the moon. Maybe there was a hotel on the moon. Or a prison. Oh, I can't believe I didn't check! Oh well, too late now.

I went to close the laptop but hesitated. There was one more thing I wanted to do. I opened Facebook and searched for a profile. As expected, there was only one William McSnelly. I clicked on his profile and giggled at his picture. I'd become used to seeing him as a fifty-year-old man yet here he was, a twenty-five-year-old with a soft, sexy smile on his face, gentle eyes, cropped brown hair – much better than the wavy disaster he'd had in high school – and a simple blue shirt. Unassuming, but from what I'd discovered, completely, totally and utterly irresistible.

I hovered the cursor over 'add friend', then moved it away. This wasn't the way to go about reconnecting with him. I knew exactly how I would do it, but today was about my birthday, my friends and my family. Will could wait a little longer. I was saving the best for last.

"Right, I've got the wood, newspaper and matches for the campfire, anything else we need?"

"Hello to you too, Kasey." I chuckled as I opened the door of my apartment to my sister.

"Oops, sorry. Hi, and happy birthday... again. Now, what about a picnic rug?"

"Oh yes, hang on." I dashed to the linen cupboard and withdrew my non-tartan rug, which I had to order online. Did you know how difficult it was to find a non-tartan picnic rug?

"Okay, let's go," I said.

"Wait, let me give you your birthday present now." Kasey smiled as she handed me the large slim package she had tucked under her arm.

"Okay, thanks! Here, let's swap." I handed her the picnic rug and accepted the gift. I placed the package on the dining table and tore off the paper, realising how cool it was that I'd got to experience two birthdays. Shame I wasn't able to bring back the gifts I'd received from the future, I'd have to wait another twenty-five years to get my hands on that magical vacuum cleaner!

"Oh, Kasey," I said, eyeing the artist's quality sketchbook, drawing pencils, empty portfolio and a selection of inspiring home magazines. "This is perfect." A shimmer of anticipation rose up inside and appreciation for my sister who knew what mattered to me. "Thank you so much, I can't wait to get started with all this!"

"And I can't wait to see what you come up with."

"Thanks," I said again, wrapping my arms around her and pecking her cheek.

"So, let's get this party started!"

Fifteen minutes later, we were spreading out the picnic rug by Kasey's awesome campfire on North Beach. I looked up to find Selena approaching and flung my arms around her.

"It's so good to see you!" I almost apologised for missing her call yesterday during the meeting but bit my tongue.

She smiled curiously. "I only saw you last night, but I'll accept your compliment anyway." She greeted Kasey then handed me a small gift.

I unwrapped it and held the garnet teardrop earrings up to my ears. "They're beautiful," I exclaimed. "Thanks, Selena, I'll put them on now." I took my silver hoops off and replaced them with my new earrings. Selena snapped a photo with her phone while I flashed my best model pose.

Then Selena sidled up close to me. "So, when's Grant getting here, are you ready for his proposal?" She nudged me in the ribs.

"Ah, actually, he's not coming."

"What?" Selena and Kasey said in unison.

"We broke up."

"What?" they said again, mouths gaping.

"Are you okay? What happened?" Selena asked.

"I'm fine, it was my decision. It's a long story, but it's for the best," I replied.

"But I thought he was going to propose. Did he propose?" Selena asked.

"No, he didn't. When you saw him walk out of DSJ, it was because he'd bought me a bracelet. It was beautiful, but I gave it back to him."

"Oh my God, I'm so sorry. I was sure he must have bought an engagement ring!" Selena covered her mouth.

"It doesn't matter, I would have assumed the same."

"How did he react?" Kasey asked.

"Well, things got a little heated, but to be honest, I think he was more upset by my decision to change career than my decision to end the relationship."

"What? What's happened to your modelling contract?" I thought I might have to call an ambulance for Selena soon if she didn't stop gasping.

"I've still got it, but I'm going to start working on a design business. Homewares that bring more beauty to people's living environments."

"Really? I didn't know you worked on art in your spare time."

"I don't. Well, I used to, years ago and it's time I got back into it," I said.

"Oh, Kel, so much is changing, are you sure everything's all right?" Selena asked.

I nodded. "Absolutely."

"Then in that case, promise me you'll design some kind of multi-purpose jewellery holder that attaches to the wall so I can free up space in my bedroom?"

"What a great idea!" I got out my phone.

'What are you doing?" she asked.

"Adding it to my ideas list. I already have an idea for an automatic decorative tissue dispenser."

Kasey and Selena laughed and agreed to test the prototype once it was manufactured.

I threw another stick on the fire and noticed Kasey gulping as she looked behind me. I turned to see Max Sheldon walking towards us, his loose white shirt hanging half out of his jeans and unbuttoned at the top revealing chiselled pecs. He was gorgeous, but funnily enough, we'd never had any spark between us. I saw him as a friend, or a brother and in the future, no doubt he'd become my brother-in-law. I held back a knowing chuckle at Kasey's nerves. If only she knew.

"Max is here, oh my God," she whispered, wringing her hands and clearing her throat.

"Happy birthday, beautiful," he said, kissing both of my cheeks and handing me a huge bunch of exotic flowers, along with a bottle of Moét.

"Thanks, Max, the flowers are gorgeous and I'm sure we can make use of this." I held up the bottle and winked.

He smiled, but his eyes held an edge of sadness. "I don't think we've officially met. You're Kelli's sister?" He held out a hand to Kasey.

"I'm Kasey. Nice to meet you, Max," she replied, shaking his hand and offering her best smile. I could practically hear her heart pounding in her chest and worried it might leap right out and knock Max to the ground.

Max kissed both of Kasey's cheeks, then did the same to Selena, but his usual charming demeanour seemed subdued as his eyes kept falling to the ground.

"Are you all right, Max?" Selena had noticed too. Kasey hadn't, she was still beaming from her face having made contact with an underwear model's lips.

"Yeah, fine. It's nothing." He shooed a hand towards us.

"It must be something," I said.

"Ah, don't worry. It's your birthday, time to celebrate." He rubbed his hands together and glanced around.

Okay, now I was worried. Max had never shown any emotion except happiness and complete confidence, but his eyes lacked their usual sparkle and his body appeared tense with apprehension. "Max, it's okay, if something's on your mind, you can share it with us."

He wandered over to the campfire and warmed his hands, then sat down on the picnic rug which Kasey had ensured was close enough to the fire but not too close as to be a fire hazard. Sensing an important revelation was imminent, I sat next to him as Selena and Kasey joined us.

"I have to go to hospital on Monday," he said. "I've been diagnosed with skin cancer. Melanoma."

Holy crap. Stunned faces stared at Max and he tossed a stray stick onto the fire.

"Max, oh my God." My hand covered my mouth, then rested on top of his forearm.

"Do you need us to come with you?" Selena asked and Kasey nodded, her radiant glow replaced with fierce concern.

"Thanks, but I'll be fine. I'm having surgery and they'll check if any of my lymph nodes are affected. Most likely I'll need radiotherapy or chemotherapy, or both." He ran a hand over his short hair. "Ah well, at least I won't have much hair to lose, eh?" He attempted a laugh, but the mood remained sombre.

"If you don't mind my asking, where is the actual melanoma?" Kasey asked and I shot her a "Kasey!" glance.

Max slipped off his left shoe and lifted his foot, exposing a small black lump on the underside, between his toes. "Can you believe it? Too much time lying on my back in the midday sun. Who thinks to put sunscreen on the soles of their feet, huh?"

Gosh. I never did. But I'd start, even if it did make my shoes all squelchy.

"It started to get itchy and that's when I noticed it. I thought I had something stuck to my foot, but it wouldn't come off, so I went to the doctor."

"Max, I'm so sorry. If there's anything I can do..."

"Thanks, Kel. I'll take it one day at a time, but I'm sure I'll be all right." He stared at the flickering fire. "I have to be."

"You will." Kasey placed her hand on his other arm and he sent her a gentle smile.

"Anyway," Max said. "Enough of this, I'll have plenty of time to think about it later, for now I just want to enjoy the night. So, is anyone else coming to the party?"

I glanced at my watch. My other friends were either late or not coming. I felt a slight pang of disappointment but then dismissed it. The only friends that really mattered to me were right here. It would be a small party, so what? Last night's adventure was enough excitement to last another twenty-five years anyway. "Um, looks like it might just be us."

"Okay, let's get some fish and chips, hey? Probably be the last time for a while I'll get to indulge," Max said, standing. "I'll duck across the road and get it. My shout."

"I'll go with you," Kasey said and they wandered up the hill and over the road, as Selena and I shared a concerned glance.

"I can't believe it," Selena said. "Max always seemed so... so... perfect. Like he was invincible."

"Yeah, I know."

Selena crossed her arms and chewed on her bottom lip. "Kelli, what if he doesn't make it? What if the treatment doesn't work?"

I slid an arm around her shoulder. "Hey, worrying won't do any good. I have a strong feeling he's going to get through this just fine." It finally made sense, what Kasey had mentioned in the future about her husband being involved in a skin cancer campaign. He wasn't a scientist, he was an ambassador. "Who knows, maybe something positive will come of this. With him being in the public eye, he might be able to encourage young people to better protect themselves in the sun."

"You're right. Wow, Kelli, you're so positive today with everything that's happened. It feels like..."

"Like what?"

"Like you've, I dunno, matured a few years overnight or something."

If she only knew the half of it. "Are you saying I was *immature* before?" I spiced my words with sarcasm.

"Haha, no," she replied. "Actually..." She brought a curved finger to her lips, squinting her eyes as though in deep thought, before laughing.

"Hey, you!" I gave her a friendly slap on the arm, then blew a raspberry in her direction. "Is that immature enough for you?"

"I can do better." Selena inhaled sharply and released a raspberry of epic proportions, her fringe flying up from her forehead before slapping back against it.

I burst out laughing, tears streaming down my face. "You know, if you really want to get serious, a burping competition would be even more immature."

Selena tried and failed to summon a burp. "If I was a guy I could do it. What is it with men? They can summon a burp at a moment's notice!"

"I know, it's crazy. I think they must store them up or something, keep them in a reservoir in their Adam's apple until required."

"Oh, Kel, you crack me up." Selena doubled over with giggles.

I pulled my friend close. "Selena, promise me we'll always stay close?"

"Of course."

"I mean, *really* promise me. When your career takes you around the world and little old me is left behind, let's not lose contact with each other. In fact, let's make a pact."

"A pact?"

I stood in front of her and held on to her shoulders. "Yeah. Let's make a pact that no matter where life takes us, we won't let a year go by without seeing each other."

Selena nodded. "Okay."

"Promise?"

"I promise." She crossed her heart with her finger. "Even though right now we hardly go a day without seeing each other, I promise to see you at least once every year."

"Good." I smiled. "And if you ever get a personal assistant, make sure you tell her to always put my calls through to you, without needing any special pass code or anything."

Selena tilted her head and cocked an eyebrow. "O-kaaay."

"Oh, and when you're a famous Hollywood starlet, don't succumb to the pressures of cosmetic surgery, okay?"

"Surgery?"

"Yeah, you know we will get wrinkles at some stage. But promise me you'll let nature take its course? You'll be much happier for it."

"If it's that important to you, then okay. But, c'mon, a little Botox never hurt anyone, I'd consider at least getting that."

I put my palm out in front of her. "No. None, you hear me?"

"Okay, okay," she said. "And hang on a minute, what makes you think I'm going to be a Hollywood starlet?" She placed her hands on her hips, angling her chin towards me.

Oops. "Um, I don't know, I was just getting carried away. But you would make a great actress."

Selena laughed. "It's funny you say that, because I've actually been thinking of taking acting classes. I was going to ask you tonight what you thought about it, but then Max brought up the whole cancer thing and it didn't seem important."

"I think it is important. If it's something you think you'd enjoy doing, then go for it, I say."

"You know what? I think I will." She gave her chin a sharp nod and smiled. "Thanks, Kel, I knew you'd be supportive. It looks like we'll both be branching out in the career department."

"It looks that way."

"Speaking of branching out, look at Kasey. Her confidence has soared all of a sudden."

I turned in the direction of Max and Kasey, armed with bags of food, standing in an embrace on the side of the road.

"Looks like she's made a new friend," Selena said. "And Max is going to need all the friends he can get."

He's going to get a lot more than that from Kasey. Wow, she must have been there – I mean, was going to be there – for him, throughout his whole cancer treatment. *Good on you, Kasey.*

"Kasey was just telling me about her innovative new research," Max said as they returned. "Fascinating stuff. This girl's gonna go far, I can tell."

Kasey glowed so brightly she was practically luminescent. "Oh, we'll see. Research is a slow process. I'm probably just paving the way for the next generation of researchers to carry things on."

"I wouldn't be so sure, you never know, you could find a cure for the common cold or something," Max suggested.

I covered my mouth as a laugh caught in my voice box.

"What?" Kasey asked, glaring at me. "You think I couldn't? Well, let me tell you that it's entirely possible. You just wait and see. One day, sis, one day."

"Oh, sure. Whatever you say," I teased. I'd let her have her victorious moment in the future, but it was so much fun to humour her now. No harm, it would make her feel more satisfied when she actually did find the cure, being able to prove me wrong.

"So, let's eat," Max said, opening a plastic bag and ripping the paper on a wad of hot chips and battered fish.

Greasy food at its finest. I wondered if the calories I'd consumed yesterday still counted today, but reasoned they wouldn't, so I happily tucked into a huge piece of fish and a handful of chips.

"Who wants a glass of this fine Moët, served in the most elegant of plastic cups?" Selena asked, taking the liberty of opening my birthday gift and pouring herself a generous serving.

"Me," we all said at the same time. Selena poured us each a glass, er, cup and we sat and talked and laughed, until the sound of someone crying turned our attention towards the shore.

A young woman about my age with frizzy blond hair had her face buried in her hands, tears dropping into the ocean as gentle waves swirled at her feet.

"Hey, are you all right?" I called out.

"I'm fine," she cried back, releasing another burst of tears.

I stood, brushing sand from the backs of my thighs and walked up to her. "It doesn't look like you're fine." I gave her a concerned glance. She looked up at me, then towards our intimate gathering.

"Oh sorry, I didn't mean to disturb you and your friends."

"It doesn't matter. Can I help?" I didn't know why I was so concerned about a complete stranger, I'd normally just examine my fingernails and pretend I hadn't seen anything.

"My boyfriend, he dumped me!" She revved the engine on her tears, unable to articulate any distinguishable words after that.

"Hey, it'll be okay." I rubbed her arm and seemingly

surprised by my random act of kindness, she pressed pause on her tears.

"It's so unfair, I did everything to please him, changed my life to accommodate his needs and this is how he repays me?" Her eyes pleaded understanding. "Why do I suck at relationships so much?"

"I'm sure it had nothing to do with you, it was probably just him. Didn't realise how good he had it." I hoped my words offered some sort of reassurance.

"Too right, he didn't." She sniffed back tears and nodded. "But I worry I'll never meet anyone decent in my life. I mean, I'm twenty-eight now, almost thirty for God's sake. I thought I'd be married with kids by now. What if I'm destined to be alone forever?"

"Oh, I seriously doubt that. There's plenty of time to meet the right man. He'll probably turn up when you least expect it."

"It's just that, I thought this guy was the one, you know? I really felt we belonged together, but apparently not, according to him." She raised her arm and let it slap against her thigh.

"You know, I had a guy I thought was the one too, but sometimes the one you think is right for you, isn't. You just have to believe there's someone better out there, waiting for you."

My mind flashed to Will, first in his Facebook profile picture, then in his business suit, then in his Superman outfit. A smile graced my lips at the vision of his lopsided grin and cheeky sense of humour and I couldn't wait to see him again. But I'd have to.

"I guess you're right. Time heals, so they say," the woman replied.

I glanced at my sister and friends, digging into the mountain of food. "Hey, do you want to come and join us? There's plenty of food left." I gestured towards the campfire and the woman assessed the situation with her eyes.

"Okay then, why not? Thanks." She managed a small smile and we walked over.

"I'm Kelli, by the way," I said, offering my hand.

"Nice to meet you Kelli, I'm Elaine."

I stopped dead in my tracks, hoping my jaw hadn't physically dropped to the sandy ground below.

"Are you okay?" Elaine asked and I looked deep into her eyes, flickers of recognition speeding along the memory highway in my brain.

"Um... yes. Sure. It's, ah, just that I knew someone called Elaine once."

"Oh, well I hope the name doesn't bring back any bad memories for you. Don't you hate it when you meet someone who has the same name as the kid who pulled your hair in science class at school, or the bully who tipped your lunch box over in the playground? Even though they have nothing to do with them, you still feel uncomfortable."

"You've got nothing to worry about, the Elaine I knew was very nice. In fact, you remind me a lot of her."

Even though our only light was the campfire, the moon and a distant streetlight, Elaine's flushed face was clearly visible. "Aw, geez. You hardly know me, but thanks!"

I flashed a smile and led her towards the fire, introducing her to Kasey, Max and Selena. She asked Max why he looked so familiar and he simply shrugged and said they'd probably passed each other in the street or something, even though I knew very well it was because she'd most likely glimpsed his gorgeous physique in a giant ad on the back of a bus. She'd find out soon enough.

As we ate and talked, I looked up at the sky, the same sky I'd looked at while on the Ferris wheel with Will and thanked the universe for this synchronistic turn of events. Elaine was now in my life and we could get to know each other properly, from the beginning. I would make damn sure that she followed her dreams of opening a cake business, or a restaurant and that she wouldn't sacrifice her own identity for the sake of her marriage. All I could do was try, but the rest would be up to her.

After we finished off the dinner, Selena got to her feet. "Oh, I forgot. I brought something for you." She scurried off to her car parked nearby and returned holding a lantern with a candle inside. "Happy birthday to you, happy birthday to you, c'mon everyone! Happy birthday, dear Kelli," everyone joined in, "Happy birthday to you! Hip hip, hooray! Hip hip, hooray!"

I blew my breath towards the candle, twice actually, because the first one didn't work, as I had to get the right angle to blow inside the lantern and finally the flame was replaced with a sinewy trail of smoke floating up to the sky. "Thank you, Selena."

"I didn't know it was your birthday, happy birthday!" Elaine said.

"Hey, you didn't make a wish," Max protested.

"Didn't need to," I replied with a smile.

"Well I wish that you'd all get up to shake your thang," Selena proclaimed, pulling me to my feet, then putting her iPhone on full volume, a dance track blaring from the tiny device.

We wiggled and swayed in time to the music, and Max, Kasey and Elaine joined in. As a techno track took over, an urge inside me took over and my arms bent at right angles, moving stiffly up and down, while my body jerked here, there and everywhere.

"You're doing the robot dance?" Kasey asked, laughing.

"Yep. I've been practising. What do you think?" I mustered up the sensation of the SlimFX Magic Suit stuck like cling wrap around my body and put it to good use.

"Two can play at that game." Max summoned his inner

robot and gave me a run for my money and the others tried to outdo us, but Max was a clear winner. I hoped he'd keep this memory with him to help him through the tough times ahead.

Worried I might get spasms from tensing my muscles for so long, I relaxed back into normal dancing. Selena wiggled up next to me and whispered in my ear.

"So, I guess you're not going on your weekend away with Grant tomorrow night after all."

I shook my head. "Nope. I have more important plans, actually."

Chapter 20
Reunion

"The end of separation is meeting again." – Turkish proverb

I STEPPED into my red shimmery dress and fed my arms under the straps, smiling at the rewarding buzz of the zipper as it slid up my back with ease. I'd wanted to wear this to my birthday dinner last night, but since it became a casual fun fest on the beach instead of a flashy soiree at a gourmet restaurant, it hadn't exactly been appropriate. It was very appropriate tonight however, for the occasion of my high school reunion.

I slid my feet into matching red shoes and put the earrings on that Selena gave me. One last push of the bobby pins secured my chignon and I pressed my lips together in front of the mirror, then grabbed my evening bag and headed for the car.

I arrived at the venue and clicked my heels up the steps, entering through an open door into the foyer. A voluptuous woman I didn't recognise was handing out name tags. "I know you, you're Kelli Crawford, right?"

Crap. I had no idea who she was. I'd only been out of high school eight years, surely that wasn't long enough to forget a face? Unless she was someone my teenage snobbish self had ignored. I cringed at the memory of who I used to be. "Yes, hi, how've you been?"

She must have sensed my confusion because she quickly revealed her identity. "Don't worry, you've no need to recognise me, I didn't go to the school. I married Cody Baxter, did you know him?"

Yep. He was one of Will's arch enemies and instigator of the whole Kick Me Post-it note craze. "Yeah, I did. Well, I'm very happy for you both," I replied. Poor woman. "How did you know who I was?"

"Your photo on the cover of *Beauté* magazine last month."

"Oh, right. Thanks," I said, wondering if she noticed that the cover shot had been photo-shopped to death. My jaw line had been sliced and chiselled to the point where if I really looked like that, I wouldn't have room inside my mouth for a set of teeth.

I pressed my sticky name tag onto the right side of my chest, up high enough near my shoulder to prevent the usual chest-staring from guys with the excuse they were just trying to read my name tag. I almost considered slapping it on my forehead, then they might at least look me in the eyes.

I wandered into the balloon-filled function room, my eyes searching for one person only, finding everyone but him. What if he wasn't coming?

I'd never thought of that until now. It would make sense, I mean he wasn't the most popular guy in school, far from it, so why would he want to revisit the past? But Will did say I was wearing this dress the night we met up again, so it either had to be tonight, or I'd have to wear this dress every night until I found him.

I weaved my way through the crowd, stopping here and there to greet people I recognised, until my eyes travelled to the far corner of the room. Near a table of drinks stood a guy with his back to me wearing a light grey shirt over black pants and cropped brown hair. His head tipped back as he downed a drink and then he turned around.

It was him. It was my Will. Well, he wasn't mine yet, but that was just a technicality, it would only be a matter of time. Or not. Who said it was important to take things slow, anyway?

My eyes fixed on the target, I waltzed over and stopped in front of him. "Hi, Will." A smile sliced across my face and his eyebrows rose.

"Kelli? Hi, how are you?" He tucked his hands into his pockets.

"I'm great, you?"

"I'm great too."

"That's great."

"Yeah, it is great."

Oh c'mon, Kelli! Two nights ago you were practically ripping him out of his Superman costume and now you can't even hold a decent conversation? I opened my mouth to ask him a question, when a guy came up and slapped Will on the back. Why did guys always hit each other to show their affection? No nice soft hugs, they just whacked and nudged and slapped each other silly.

"If it isn't the one and only McSmelly! Didn't think I'd see you here tonight."

"Cody." Will acknowledged him with a brief nod.

"And look at you, Kelli Crawford – still as stunning as ever. Trapped at the drink table with McSmelly, are you? Don't worry," he winked, "just pretend there's a call you need to take and make a run for it. He'll be none the wiser." Cody chuckled and grabbed a drink from the table, swigging it down his throat in one gulp.

"Actually, I'm talking to Will here, so if you don't mind?" I cocked my head to the side, gesturing for him to get the hell away from us.

"Huh." His eyes widened and he crossed his arms. "Well, I know when I'm not wanted. Which isn't often, by the way." He winked and nudged Will sharply in the ribs. "I think I'll go and see my lovely wife. After I've danced with my old flame, that is." He shot a glance towards the gorgeous Lucy Montgomery and swaggered in her direction.

"Idiot," I said.

"Yeah, some people never grow up," Will remarked.

"Ah, Will?" I grasped his shoulder and turned his body around.

"Oh, don't tell me, not again."

"Yep, 'fraid so." I plucked a Post-it note with *Kick Me* written on it from his back.

Will shook his head and sighed. Then he glanced at me. "Thanks for that."

"No problem," I said. "So, what do you do these days?"

"I'm in business," he replied, taking his hands out of his pockets. "Actually, I'm an employee, but I *help* businesses. I'm a consultant to various corporations on management skills, start-up planning and techniques for boosting efficiency and productivity." He nodded with pride. "I'd like to eventually run my own business, but for now I'm getting as much experience as possible."

"Sounds like an important job to me. I might need your services one day," I said, adding a subtle glint to my eye.

"Really? But I thought you were involved in modelling."

"I am, but I won't be forever. I'm thinking of starting up a homewares design company." I smiled, the more I told people about this the more excitement surged within. "Except, I know nothing about business, I'm only good for the creative side, so I'll need advice on all the other aspects of owning and running a business."

"Then I'm your man," he said, and his face flushed to match my dress, no doubt realising the possible double meaning of his words.

"I'm sure you are," I replied softly. "Do you have a business card?"

Will's eyes lit up, his fingers diving into his shirt pocket. "Sure do. Didn't think I'd need these tonight, so I'm glad I brought them."

He handed me his card, which had the same photo that was on his Facebook profile and included his office address, phone number and email address. "Thanks," I said, unclipping my evening bag and dropping the card inside, then closing the bag with a pop.

"Well, I wish you all the best with your idea, it sounds great to me. I remember you were always good with art at school."

"You do?" He did?

"Yeah, remember that mural all the students had to contribute to on the brick wall outside the library? You painted that little worm reading a book and he had these big googly eyes." Will's fingers circled around his own eyes and I withheld a giggle at the memory of our night at the fun fair with his novelty sunglasses.

"Ah yes, the bookworm." I nodded, then struck with an idea, I opened my bag and retrieved my phone.

"You're not doing the 'I've got to take this call' thing that Cody suggested, are you?"

"Huh? Oh no, of course not! Sorry, I'm jotting down an idea for a product. Since deciding to start this business I've been getting ideas at the most inconvenient times and if I don't note them down I'm scared I'll forget!" I jabbed at the keyboard on my phone. "Done."

"It's okay, I understand. So what's the idea?"

Wow, he really was interested in what I had to say and he hadn't even looked at my chest. His eyes fixed on mine. Unlike Cody whose eyes had done the usual 'Going Down' elevator trip, getting stuck on the way back up at the seventh floor instead of tenth where my eyes were.

I leaned forward, enthusiasm overtaking my body. "Well, when you mentioned the bookworm, I got this image in my mind of a bookcase, but one that's shaped like a worm, kind of long and curvy and you attach it to the wall and it has individual slots for each book, so it kind of looks like a domino effect, with the books following the curve of the design. Make sense?" Sensing a lack of oxygen from my verbal dump, I drew in a deep breath.

"Sounds fantastic! You could simply call it The Bookworm."

"I could. Oh, and it would look great attached to a wall beside a staircase, it could slant upwards along with the stairs."

"Well, I'd buy one, definitely," Will said with a smile.

I smiled back and tucked a non-existent strand of hair behind my ear. "So, are you married? Have any kids?"

"Nope. Not at this stage, but I'd like to."

"Me too."

"You would?" His eyebrows rose. "I didn't pick you as the marriage and kids type. Guess I was wrong."

"There's a lot about me that would surprise you, Will."

"Yeah? Like what?" he asked, tilting his head slightly.

"Um..." I looked at the crumpled Post-it note in my hand and smiled. "Do you have a pen?"

"Do I ever," Will replied, his fingers diving into his shirt pocket again. "Red, blue, or black?"

"Surprise me." I smiled.

He handed me a red pen. "To match your dress."

I leaned on the drinks table and placed a cross through the *c* and the *k* at the end of the work *Kick*, replacing them with *ss*. Then I stuck the Post-it note that now read, *Kiss Me*, on the left side of my chest, slightly lower in position than my name tag and waited patiently for Will's reaction.

His eyes practically popped from their sockets, resembling the bookworm I'd painted in the school mural. "Are you serious?"

"I've never been more serious in all my life."

He stood frozen to the spot for a moment, then laughed. "Ha ha, nice try. This is some kind of joke, right? I bet Cody put you up to it and any minute he'll pop out of the woodwork with a camera and yell, 'Ha! Gotcha!', and then he'll–"

I lurched forwards and pressed my lips urgently to his, my hands sliding behind his neck and down across his jaw line. When I finally pulled back, he was frozen in another position; lips protruding, eyes in blissful shock, his body about ready to slide to the floor like a lump of rapidly melting ice.

"Holy moly," he whispered.

I chuckled, then drew him in for another kiss, realising that after the whole adventure that was my fiftieth birthday, Will and I had not kissed. Not once. He'd tried of course, but never struck gold and when I finally wanted to kiss him, he went off to have a shower and left me laying on the bed a tingling pile of desire until I was launched back in time. I was glad though. This was meant to be our first kiss. Not in the future, but here, at the beginning, where it all started.

We smiled at each other as we came up for air and I gestured to the dance floor. "You don't like robot dancing by any chance, do you?"

Will grabbed my shoulders. "Do I ever! I'm like The King of robot dancing!" He led me towards the dance floor. "And that's not just because it's the only style of dance I know." He winked, his eyes telling me it most certainly was.

A crowd gathered in a circle around us, clapping and cheering, except for Cody who stood on the sidelines shaking his head in utter disbelief. When the song ended and slow music took over, he pulled me close to him. "You've got me under your spell, Kelli Crawford," he whispered.

"Then let's make some magic," I replied, leaning my head towards his and relishing the soft, warm touch of his lips again.

As we swayed in time to the music, he brought his lips to my ear and whispered, "Never in a million years would I have dreamed that Kelli Crawford would waltz into my school reunion and ravish me."

"It just goes to show, you never know what the future has in store for you," I replied, even though I was privy to some of it.

"That's right," he said. "Do you ever wish you could jump ahead in time and see what your future's going to be like?"

"Well, it could be... interesting, but nah, I'd rather stay exactly where I am and let life lead the way."

"Yeah, me too. Life is for living, is it not? If you're too focused on the future you forget to have fun in the moment." Will pulled back, putting a stop to our slow dance. "Speaking of fun, the annual fun fair's on in the city all month. Being Saturday night it should be open till late." His eyes twinkled. "What do you say we skip this joint and go have some real fun?"

A smile crawled onto my lips and I clasped my hand in his, eyeing the exit. "Hell, yeah!"

Chapter 21
Twenty-Five Years Later

"Mothers and daughters are closest, when daughters become mothers."
– Author Unknown

"WAKE UP, KELLI, WAKE UP!" I inched my eyes open to find Will shaking me gently. "Guess what? We're grandparents! Diora had a baby girl!"

I shot up to a sitting position. "Oh my God! A granddaughter? Oh, I'm so happy!" I flung my legs over the side of the bed and stood quickly, resting my hand on the bedside table momentarily to regain my balance. "How's the baby, is she okay? Is Diora okay?"

"They're both fine, although apparently Jason's wand has been snapped to bits," he chuckled.

"What's her name?" I asked, eagerly rummaging through my wardrobe and pulling out a random pair of pants and a shirt.

"They wouldn't say, said they wanted to introduce her to us properly," Will replied.

"Oh, okay." I imagined the baby holding out her tiny hand and saying 'Nice to officially meet you, Grandma', and then shook the absurdity from my mind. "I can't wait to see her!"

"Me neither, but you better come and have breakfast first, don't want you collapsing with low blood sugar at the hospital," Will said. "Although, you couldn't get a more convenient place, if that were to happen."

I whipped him playfully with my trousers before stepping into them and wiggling them up and over my hips. "I'll just get ready first, see you in the kitchen soon."

Will wandered out, pinching his e-pad and pulling the virtual strand to his ear. "Hi, Mum, it's me. She had a baby girl... I know!... yep... okay, so..." his voice trailed off.

I flicked on the light in the bathroom and splashed water on my face. Squirting a blob of moisturiser onto my hands I massaged it into my cheeks, circling the laughter lines that had deepened after many a fun night watching comedy movies with Will. Then I let the lotion glide over my forehead, seeping into the furrows that had developed from hours and hours of concentration hunched over my designing desk. I dabbed my ring finger in the jar of eye cream and patted the lines framing my eyes which had cried at the birth of my two children, then pressed lip gloss into the lips that had kissed many a sore knee after a fall at the park, and lips that had poured forth my love for Will onto lips of his own. As the moisturiser sunk into my thirsty skin, I rubbed lotion on the arms that had rocked babies to sleep and embraced my husband. I lifted my shirt to nourish the loose but resilient skin on my abdomen that had long ago stretched with the promise of new life, and adjusted the straps on my bra, supporting the breasts that had fed my two children.

My body was a living reminder of my wonderful life. It had done amazing, beautiful things and there was no way in the world I'd prefer to look like a twenty-something perfect beauty with a body untouched by life. Of course, I still valued my appearance, but as I dusted my face with mineral foundation I knew that if I chose not to bother anymore, it wouldn't make any difference. My family would still be here, my friends would still love me and my business would still be the award-winning empire that it was.

I flicked the light off as I strode confidently from the bathroom and entered the kitchen where Ryan and Ben were sitting at the counter stuffing their mouths with cake. "You call that breakfast?" I asked.

Ryan shrugged, his cheeks bulging. "It's got protein, carbohydrates and a little... okay, *a lot* of fat, but it's still a balanced meal, right?" He flashed a hopeful smile and Ben nodded.

"Definitely. And it's sooo good!" Ben shoved another mouthful towards his parted lips.

"Yeah, Elaine outdid herself with this one, didn't she?" I pressed my finger into the frosting on Ryan's piece of cake and licked it from my finger.

"Hey!" He slapped my wrist. "But yeah, this is the best one she's done so far. I thought the lotus cake she made for my twenty-first was something, but now she's raised the bar." He lifted his hand to show a level above head-height.

"And didn't she and Peter look great last night?" Will asked, placing a plate of yolkless eggs and steamed spinach in front of me.

"They did indeed. A very cute, albeit, spooky couple." I swallowed a piece of egg, remembering Elaine's floaty ghost costume and her husband's skeleton outfit. Apparently he had to wear some kind of support band underneath to hide his beer belly, Elaine revealed, and we had a quiet chuckle about it while he'd been busy chatting to Will in the Bliss Garden last night.

'So, do you feel fifty, Mum? Now that the excitement from the party has worn off?" Ryan asked.

Not as much as the first time. It had been much easier to gradually climb the ladder of age, as opposed to having it rudely shoved in front of me like an overpowering perfumed cardboard strip from a department store sales person. "I don't know, I just feel... like me." I smiled and wolfed down the rest of my breakfast, before standing and taking it to the instant dishwasher chute. "Oh, I'll have to call Dad. Tell him he's a great grandfather," I said, raising my finger like a light bulb in the air.

"No need. Already called him. He's going to meet us there," my always efficient, totally organised husband said, then his e-pad rang. "William McSnelly speaking," he said. "Yes, hello Mr Turrow."

Ooh! Mr Turrow! I hope he's –

"You are? Well that's fantastic, we're very pleased to have you as one of our valued clients." Will flashed a winning smile at me.

Yes! Good thing I'd had twenty-five years to perfect my presentation, he practically felt like an old friend by the time he turned up at head office yesterday.

Will told Mr Turrow what the next steps would be, scheduled a video meeting for Monday, then ended the call, his arms scooping me up in the air with excitement. "KC Interiors is going global, baby!"

"Woohoo!" I exclaimed, as Ryan and Ben clapped their congratulations.

"Now," he said, placing my feet back on the floor. "Are you ready to meet your grandchild?"

"Am I ready?" I replied. "I've been waiting for this day my whole life."

Fifteen minutes later we were driving through the city. "Oh, bugger! I forgot to get flowers for Diora. Will, honey, can you pull into the shopping centre so I can get a nice bunch from Franco the Florist?" I turned my head towards Will who was driving, with Ryan and Ben in the backseat, a large teddy bear in a tartan jacket wedged between them.

"The hospital has a flower shop, we can just get some there," he replied, his eyes on the road.

"Will, our daughter has just had her first child and you want to express our love for her with a shoddy bunch of carnations?" I said, a hand on my hip. "Franco will make up a beautiful piece of art for our darling daughter. I'm not prepared to go second best on this."

Will laughed in defeat and pulled into the shopping centre car park, which was packed full. "There are no spots left, I'll have to hover over here while you duck in and get them, okay?"

"Yep," I said, getting out of the car.

"But don't take too long," he called out after me.

I waved my understanding and scooted into the refreshing cool of the centre. I did want to get a quality bunch of flowers, that was no lie, but there was something else I wanted to do – and no, I wasn't about to run off and have a Better Than Sex facial if that's what you're thinking. I made my way to the New Age shop and entered, spying Liliana and Rosie in the booths. The one person waiting in line was ushered towards one of the other psychics and I took her place, resurrecting the queue.

I alternated impatiently from one foot to the other, until Liliana glanced with curious eyes in my direction. She excused herself from her client and walked out from behind the booth towards me. "Do I know you, dear?"

"Um... maybe," I replied. "But I wanted to give you some of these." I handed her a pile of business cards for FastForwardExperiences.com and on reading them her eyes bulged up at me.

"I've seen this website before, it's fascinating! Is this actually your site?" she asked, and I nodded. "Oh wow, thank you. What a wonderful thing it is that you're doing, spreading the awareness of this phenomenon." She held tightly onto the cards. "Wait, does this mean that you've experienced a... fast forward?" She leaned close to me in an attempt to keep our conversation private.

I chewed on my bottom lip.

"You have, haven't you? I can tell!"

Yep, one should never attempt to hide something from a gifted psychic. I nodded.

"Is your experience listed on the site?" she asked.

"Yes, it is."

"Wait, don't tell me! Give me a minute..." She closed her eyes, then opened them, flashing a cheeky grin. "Did you use the alias 'Grumpy', by any chance?"

I nodded, as an unstoppable smile crashed onto my face.

"Your story is amazing!" Liliana exclaimed, grasping both of my hands in hers. "But how did you know to give these cards to me? Did we actually meet... in your fast forward?"

I shrugged playfully. "Let me ask you a question, Liliana," I said boldly. "How was your daughter's engagement party last night?"

"Ah!" Liliana grasped my hands even tighter. "We did meet!"

I nodded again. "You were the one who told me about the website, but when I finally returned to the past, it didn't exist yet, so I made it myself," I explained. "You also passed on a very important message from my mother, so thank you."

Liliana held a hand to her heart, then lifted it to her forehead. "Oh wow, this is totally amazing! How bizarre that you and I met in an alternate life and now here we are, meeting again in real life," Liliana said. "Would you like to sit down for a chat, dear?" She gestured towards the booth where her client was impatiently fiddling with a piece of paper.

"I'd love to, but I can't. My husband's waiting in the car. We're off to see our firstborn grandchild."

"Ooh, how exciting. Well I won't hold you up, dear. But listen, here's my card." She plucked one from a light sash that hung diagonally across her body and handed it to me. "I also do private readings, so if you ever need one, give me a call."

"Thanks, Liliana, I will." I took the card and put it in my back pocket, then waved as I walked out the door and dashed to Franco's where he whipped up a colourful, elegant arrangement and even gave me a ten per cent discount as a congratulations gift.

On my way back to the car, I walked past a lingerie store and doubled back as something caught my eye. I shook my head and laughed at the thing that had the potential to make the female race an endangered species – the one and only SlimFX Magic Suit version 2.0. I was still laughing to myself when my e-pad beeped.

> You have a new high priority email message.
> Press to view.

Oh my God. It was a submission form from the Fast Forward Experiences website. My eyes read through the submission as quickly as humanly possible and a weight lifted off my shoulders. It was from 'Polly', the politician turned journalist who'd been hanging about indefinitely in the future. She'd finally returned back to age forty, after her years of research uncovered the evidence required to expose a big secret

– a trail of corruption in her political circle which she was then able to go back in time to report before it got out of control. She wouldn't say what the implications would have been otherwise, just that they would have been huge.

I closed the message and smiled, glad this woman had finally found her way home, as I had. Life was as it should be again and even though my marriage was built on good communication, my fast forward experience was something that didn't need to be revealed to Will. It was better that way. It was and would remain, my little secret.

As I slid back in the car to cries of 'What took you so long?' and 'Geez, about time!' my e-pad jingled again. This time with an incoming call.

"Hi, Selena!"

"Hey, hon, happy birthday for yesterday! Sorry you couldn't reach me," she said. "But I wanted to let you know I'm definitely able to fly in next weekend for a visit."

"Oh great, I look forward to seeing you," I replied.

"So, any ideas what we should do to make the most of the weekend?"

A smile made its way to my lips and I said, "Selena, have you ever thought about bungy jumping?"

Ten minutes later we walked through the hospital doors, this time as normal-looking human beings with no stained clothing or injured body parts. We followed the directions to the maternity ward and I peeked through the door to room five.

"Mum!" Diora called out with a smile as big as the room. "You're here! You just missed Kasey and Max, though, they left a few minutes ago."

I walked in to find Will's parents, Beryl and Reg, standing next to the bed and my dad handing Diora a glass of water. Jason sat next to his wife on the edge of the bed and a tiny mound of skin protruded from the firmly wrapped blanket in Diora's arms.

"Oh my God," I whispered as I tiptoed towards my daughter and kissed her on the forehead, placing the flowers on the bed, their beauty paling in comparison to the angelic face of my granddaughter. Her little hands wriggled about the sides of her face and I held my finger to one of them. Transparent fingertips with paper-thin fingernails grasped at my finger and held on with a strength that transcended age.

"Mum, Dad," Diora said. "I'd like you to meet Aurora."

A hand flew to my heart and I glanced at Will who had a sliver of a tear running down his cheek. Even Ryan, half his body obscured by the giant tartan-clad teddy bear, had shiny eyes.

"Our little Aurora," I said. "She's absolutely beautiful!"

"She was born at dawn," Jason said. "Which is what her name means. She's our little Sunrise Goddess." He caressed his daughter's cheek as he spoke.

Diora looked up at me with loving eyes. "And her middle name's Kelli."

Right, that was the last straw. I couldn't hold it in any more. My face scrunched itself up and warmth rushed to my eyes, spilling tears down my cheeks.

"Do you want to hold her?" Diora stood and positioned Aurora in my arms, and I placed a gentle hand behind the baby's head.

I swayed gently from side to side and Aurora's tiny eyelids slid open, revealing midnight blue eyes that seemed to be a universe of their own. I stared deep into them and silently thanked the amazing power that was responsible for allowing me to see the truth of what my life was all about. I'd been given a gift twenty-five years ago and it was still giving right to this day.

As I traced her faint eyebrows with my finger, I realised that my eyes were like hers – wide open and eager, ready to soak up new sights, new discoveries and new experiences. Aurora's life was just beginning and even though I was fifty, it felt like mine was too. As far as I was concerned, the magic of my life was only just starting to reveal its true beauty.

THE END

Also by Juliet Madison

The Tarrin's Bay Series

The January Wish

February or Forever

Miracle in March

April's Glow

Memories of May

Home for June

Acknowledgements

I'd like to thank Kate Cuthbert for first giving me my start as an author and believing in my writing, and to Juanita Kees for your editing expertise with this book.

BIG thanks to my wonderful critique partner, friend and talented author, Alli Sinclair, for giving such valuable feedback on this book and demanding I write more chapters as quickly as possible. Your encouragement really helped me power through that first draft! Thanks also for our fun online chats (who said writing was a solitary occupation?).

Thanks to my beta readers for this story; Efthalia, Rebecca, Natasha, Kerrie, and Monique, and to Diane Curran for critiquing the opening chapters and for your ongoing support and friendship.

Thanks to Stephanie Olivieri and Sami Lee for advising me on the intricacies of bungy jumping since I was way too chicken to try it for myself! And a HUGE thank you to RWA – Romance Writers of Australia – for helping me develop my craft and introducing me to many wonderful writers and new friends. I also appreciate my online writing friends from around the world – thanks for being there and helping with research.

I can't thank my parents enough for their support and encouragement in following my dreams. Dad, thanks for instilling in me a love of books, and Mum, thanks for your wise words and for reading everything I write. A special mention also to my cousin, Jennie, for being one of my first readers when I was starting out and encouraging me to 'keep writing'!

A special thank you to my firstborn son, Jayden, for being the caring and creative person that you are and for your wacky sense of humour (as I write this, you suggested I make mention of your charm, intelligence and witty personality – so there you go, I mentioned it!). Thanks for listening to me rave on about my latest plot developments and sorry for all the dinners that were late when you were growing up because I 'just had to finish this scene'.

Huge thanks to Betsy Reavley and the Bloodhound Books team for believing in my writing and republishing this novel! And lastly, thanks to YOU, the reader for choosing this book. Enjoy!

About the Author

Juliet Madison is a bestselling and award-nominated author of books with humour, heart, and serendipity. Writing both fiction and self-help, she is also an artist and colouring book illustrator, and an intuitive life coach who loves creating online courses for writers and those wanting to live an empowered life.

With her background as a naturopath and a dancer, Juliet is passionate about living a healthy and positive life. She likes to combine her love of words, art, and self-empowerment to create books that entertain and inspire readers to find the magic in everyday life.

Juliet lives on the picturesque south coast of NSW, Australia, where she spends as much time as possible dreaming up new stories, following her passions, being with her family, and as little time as possible doing housework.

You can find out more about Juliet, her books, and her courses at http://www.julietmadison.com and connect with her on social media at Facebook http://www.facebook.com/julietmadisonauthor and Instagram http://www.instagram.com/julietmadisonauthorartist

A note from the publisher

Thank you for reading this book. If you enjoyed it please do consider leaving a review on Amazon to help others find it too.

We hate typos. All of our books have been rigorously edited and proofread, but sometimes mistakes do slip through. If you have spotted a typo, please do let us know and we can get it amended within hours.

info@bloodhoundbooks.com